WEALTH MANAGEMENT

Also by the author:

The Day After World War III: The U.S. Government's Plans for Surviving a Nuclear War

Small Fortunes: Two Guys in Pursuit of the American Dream

WEALTH MANAGEMENT

A NOVEL

EDWARD ZUCKERMAN

An Arcade CrimeWise Book

Arcade Publishing books may be purchased in bulk at special discounts for sales promotion, corporate gifts, fund-raising, or educational purposes. Special editions can also be created to specifications. For details, contact the Special Sales Department, Arcade Publishing, 307 West 36th Street, 11th Floor, New York, NY 10018 or arcade@skyhorsepublishing.com.

Arcade Publishing® and Arcade CrimeWise® are registered trademarks of Skyhorse Publishing, Inc.®, a Delaware corporation.

Visit our website at www.arcadepub.com.

10 9 8 7 6 5 4 3 2 1

Library of Congress Cataloging-in-Publication Data is available on file.

Cover design by Erin Seaward-Hiatt

ISBN: 978-1-956763-05-8
Ebook ISBN: 978-1-956763-11-9

Printed in the United States of America

For Mike Rosenbaum, who never got around to writing his

And, of course, for Margot and Molly Jane

PROLOGUE (2017)

BASHIR

It sounded like a lawn mower, but Bashir didn't know that, because he had never seen a lawn mower or, for that matter, a lawn. Nevertheless, by a second or two, he heard it first. He stopped and looked up, shielding his eyes from the fierce midday sun, while the others continued running in and out of the small brick building, smiling in a manic way, carrying the sacks of cash. American dollars. Crusader money, but highly valued, even in the Caliphate. Even more now that they were in retreat.

It must have been brought to the bank office in this regional trading center from the vaults of Mosul, before Mosul fell, for safekeeping. And then what? Simply forgotten? Well, not by everybody. Now Mosul, along with most of the Caliphate, was back in the hands of the *Rafidha,* but someone knew, and orders reached their commander, and last night Bashir and the others were dispatched from their camp to the north. Bashir's brothers were dead, and his father had disowned him, and his wife had disappeared one night, sneaking across the desert with the baby, but Bashir was still loyal, fighting for god. And if he wasn't, if he ever stopped, what would he go back to? He had nothing behind him, only the promise of paradise ahead.

They were in three Toyota pickups. A dozen men with AK-47s and a heavy machine gun mounted on the bed of one of the trucks, the other beds left empty to leave room for the money.

The bank manager had not been cooperative. Now he lay next to a mound of goat droppings by the side of the road, blood still running from the gash in his throat, turning the sand black.

It was Hazim, tossing a sack into the bed of the lead pickup, who heard the sound next. He had been in the struggle longer, and he knew what the sound was, and he shouted to the others, and those who heard him ran to the trucks, their hands full or empty, and leapt into the cabs or onto the beds on top of the sacks. Hazim started the engine of his vehicle and put it in gear and stomped on the gas, spraying gravel as the truck surged forward, but it got no farther than two meters before a Hellfire missile from the Predator drone struck, just where the windshield met the hood, and the Toyota and Hazim exploded in a fierce hot ball of flame and metal and dirt. Now everyone was at the remaining trucks, some in the cabs, some on the beds, some hanging on to door handles, running or being dragged. Bashir was sprawled in a truck bed on bags of dollars when the second Toyota exploded. He couldn't see who was driving the one he was riding on, but whoever it was accelerated violently, swerving off the road onto packed dirt, heading for a concrete bridge over a dry riverbed to hide beneath. The truck bounced through a gully and Bashir tumbled sideways. He grabbed a side panel to avoid falling out and looked back, toward the bank, where he saw someone who might have been Nasruddin, their team leader, the most devout, who monitored the others' prayers, sprawled on the ground, not moving, his clothes on fire. He saw scattered metal junk that had once been Toyotas. He saw ragged sleeves on arms detached from bodies.

And, looking up, he saw flocks of hundred-dollar bills, burning and spinning, more than he could count, pirouetting in the crystal desert air.

PART ONE

PHILATELISTS

Lot 74 opened at two hundred Swiss francs, a screen displaying the equivalents in dollars, euros, pounds sterling, and yuan, these beneath a giant blown-up photo of the lot. Which was a postage stamp, an old postage stamp, just like the seventy-three lots that had preceded it and the 212 that were to follow. This one, dated 1893, was from the Niger Coast Protectorate and bore a picture of Queen Victoria, looking solemn and remote and wearing white lacy headgear that looked sort of bridal, although Rafe was sure that wasn't the intention, that it was more likely some sort of crown equivalent. Rafe wondered what indigenous residents of the Niger Coast Protectorate in 1893 would have made of that image, of the old white woman (their queen? their empress?) who was "protecting" them from what, France? Assuming the locals had ever seen these stamps of their British overlords. Did they ever make their way from villages and fields to a post office? (Were there post offices on the Niger Coast, wherever that was, exactly, in 1893?) To whom would they mail a letter?

Rafe's mind returned to the twenty-first century, the one he lived in, which was odd enough. He looked around the room again—a grand reception hall in a hotel on the Quai du Mont-Blanc, blond wood walls and crystal chandeliers. Probably the site of many weddings, elegant Swiss marrying elegant Swiss. Today the room was filled with folding chairs mostly occupied by men whose own weddings were far in the past, if they were married, and, if they weren't, well at least they had their stamp collections to keep them company. Rafe guessed he was the youngest person in the room by forty years. He wondered if he would take up stamp collecting when he was seventy. He didn't think so.

The Niger Coast stamp sold for three hundred Swiss francs and Rafe didn't care. Neither, apparently, did the overweight man with the ambitious combover sitting three rows in front of Rafe, who had a good view of the man at an oblique angle, which he'd accomplished by some minor chair shuffling. The man had not raised his paddle to bid. He had bid so far on just three lots—an old Chinese stamp picturing a writhing dragon, a ragged specimen from British Guiana that looked like it would shred if you breathed on it, and a scorched stamped envelope that had been on the Hindenburg when it exploded. The only thing these lots had in common was their prices. High. In his copy of the glossy illustrated auction catalogue, Rafe circled every lot the man had won and noted his winning bids—18,000 Swiss francs, 68,000, 22,000.

Now here came an old American stamp with a picture of an early automobile in the center. It was, per the catalogue, an "invert"—the automobile had been printed upside down relative to the stamp's frame. Presale estimate: 70,000 francs. Just the kind of thing the man might bid on for his unlikely crashed zeppelin-Chinese-British Guyanese stamp collection. And the man did, and he won it bang on the nose—70,000 francs.

Rafe bid on the next lot. He was at a stamp auction after all, it wouldn't look right if he didn't occasionally bid on a stamp. It was something from the Kingdom of Hawaii, on an envelope, with an estimate of eight thousand francs. Like the Niger Coast Protectorate issue, it featured a queen, this one called Kaleleonalani. Her look was as glum as Victoria's. Is this what royalty did to people? Uneasy lies the head?

The lot opened at 3,500 francs, well below its estimate. Rafe bid the next increment—4,000. Then waited for someone to bid 4,500, at which point he could gracefully bow out.

No one did.

The auctioneer, over sixty but aging nicely with a grand head of hair and a peppy blue suit, looked around, surprised, or feigning surprise.

"Personne?" *Nobody*? Apparently not. "C'est très bon marché." *So cheap*. Still nothing. *Shit*, thought Rafe.

The auctioneer began his countdown: *Quatre mille, une fois . . . quatre mille, deux fois . . .*

The auctioneer's hammer hovered over its pad. What would the auction house do if he failed to pay? Rafe didn't want to find out. He had registered with his real name.

And then, thank god, *Quatre-cinq*. The bid came in a faint voice from behind Rafe. An old man in an ancient blazer leaning forward onto a walker. Maybe he'd just woken up. Rafe wanted to kiss him. The auctioneer looked at Rafe. Did monsieur wish to raise his bid? Monsieur pretended to consider. Monsieur concluded his deliberation and shook his head. Queen Kaleleonalani sold for 4,500. The man with the walker nodded, satisfied. The overweight man with the combover, apparently done for the day, stood up and headed for the door.

Rafe waited ten seconds, then stood and followed him out.

HARVARD CLUB

Catherine was still getting used to the Genevan don't walk signals. Back in the States, when Don't Walk started flashing, you could still start across the street without a thought. You had plenty of time. You could finish applying your lipstick. You could crawl. But here in Geneva, even though this was relatively easygoing Suisse Romande, not German-speaking Switzerland (which is more German than Germany), the don't walk signals didn't take any shit. If you were in the street when they flashed, you ran. If you were on the curb, you stayed on the curb. Or risked being run down when the signal stopped flashing and cross traffic got a green, which would happen in about two seconds.

Which Catherine figured was long enough. She'd been on the diving team at Cornell not that many years before. She was still in good shape. She didn't like to stand and wait. And she needed a drink. So as she reached the curb and the don't-walk started flashing, she ran.

*

Rafe and Majid looked toward the sound of the honking. "Is that Catherine?" said Rafe. They had a clear view of the street from where they were standing, the terrace of a hotel bar adorned with a sign welcoming members of the Harvard Business School Club of Switzerland, a well-dressed mob of ambition and prosperity grabbing shrimp and paté from passing servers. "Who else?" said Majid. He hadn't seen Rafe since Cambridge, where they'd been friends or, at least, friendly acquaintances. Rafe Sassaman was a casually privileged American, or that's how he had appeared to Majid. Harvard was awash with casually privileged Americans, but Rafe's casualness seemed less of a mask over insecurity and competitiveness than that of most of their classmates. Also, Rafe had seemed interested in the fact that Majid was from Dubai, although not enough to stay in touch after they graduated. But then today, here he was, popping up in Geneva, giving Majid an enthusiastic greeting, offering to buy him a drink and then even remembering to ask whether Majid still didn't partake. Now Rafe swirled a bourbon on the rocks and Majid held a Sprite, an homage to the Muslim observances he mostly didn't observe.

"She's here?" Rafe asked.

"Yes," said Majid. "At a private bank. Didn't you know?" *Didn't he? That would be good.*

They both watched as Catherine leapfrogged a braking Citroën.

"No," Rafe said. "I didn't."

Ah, thought Majid. "Ah," he said, sipping his Sprite. "So you haven't been in touch? I would have thought . . . I mean, back in Cambridge, you and she . . ."

Had been fucking like rabbits.

"She holds a grudge," Rafe said.

"*She* does? Shouldn't her *fiancé* have been the one with a grudge?"

"Oh. Right. Him."

"What was his name?" Majid said.

Rafe shrugged. "Chester? Hector?"

"Rafe?"

*

And there she was. Catherine, maneuvering through the crowded bar, looking at him, surprised, but not to the exclusion of keeping an eye out for a waiter with a tray of drinks.

"Catherine. Yes. Hi. Wow. Long time." Rafe took her in. It had been five years. The only change he saw was a lessening of a softness in her face she'd had when she was twenty-four. Now sharper lines, a more elegant beauty.

"Yeah. Wow." Her wow in a lower tone than his. "What are you *doing* here?"

Where to begin? Rafe thought. The answer: *Don't.*

"Right now, being cross-examined by Majid. He's out of control, never could hold his Sprite."

"He's still funny," Majid said. Rafe had always been a joker. The smartest clown at Harvard Business School. Admittedly not a place with a lot of competition for the title.

Catherine furrowed her brow, which could have meant concern, or skepticism, or that the sun was in her eyes. It was setting over France, just across the border.

"That was always a matter of opinion," she said. "*You* thought he was funny, Majid."

She still scanned the room for a waiter. "What are you doing here?" she said again.

"Business," Rafe said. "I've got a little startup wealth management firm. I'm prospecting . . ."

He paused for a moment, seeing Catherine looking at him, waiting for him to go on. *Her eyes.* Sometimes they hadn't made it from the doorway to the bed. When was the last time he had sex on the floor? Jesus.

". . . for prospects," he finished. Not exactly brilliant, he had to admit.

"Wealth management? So you'll be competing with Majid?"

"I think there's room for more than one wealth management firm in Switzerland."

"At the moment," said Majid, "there are six hundred eighteen." Reminding them that he was still there. Catherine and Rafe turned to him. "That's how many are registered. With FINMA," he said.

Rafe turned back to Catherine. "Always did know his facts. Teacher's pet."

"Hey," Majid said, mock offended. "High honors." Catherine was still looking at Rafe.

"What's your firm called? Where's it set up?" she asked.

"I just got here a couple of weeks ago. It's early days. In flux." Weak, Rafe thought. But at least better than "prospecting for prospects." His story needed work. "Hey, let me get you a drink. Vodka martini, up, twist?"

*

They watched Rafe move away through the crowd. "He's new in Europe," Majid said. "He'll ask for a martini and get straight vermouth."

"Fifty-fifty," Catherine said.

Majid looked at her, trying to read her. Never easy.

"What you said . . . about him competing with me . . ."

"In *business*," she said. "He . . . Cambridge is ancient history." And her arm moved, lightly brushing Majid's hand, possibly on purpose, as they both watched Rafe heading to the bar.

ITALY

Majid stared at his computer screen, willing it to change what it displayed.

It didn't change.

What he saw shouldn't be, it couldn't be.

It still didn't change.

"You're overreacting," said Ron.

Ronald Haywood Harrison Mayfield, second cousin to the earl of something, about 500th in line to the British throne, was Majid's partner in Sterling Wealth Management, which had been established eighteen months before in a small but tastefully appointed office on the Quai des Bergues, near where the Rhône flowed into the lake. The two had met on a flight from Heathrow to Dubai, Majid flying there to visit his family, Ron going ostensibly to attend a tennis tournament but actually to take a break from his. Majid felt his career was moving too slowly on the bond desk of a Wall Street firm; Ron was looking for something to do that wasn't in England. Geneva suited them both, Majid for its abundance of people with money, Ron for its comfortable distance from Sussex.

The office furnishings had been purchased by Ron, who had brought capital into the firm from his relatives in England (who had not been grief-stricken to see him move away). He had a degree in business studies from the University of London but generally deferred to Majid's financial expertise, which made life easier for both of them. Majid might have brought capital from his relatives in the Emirates but asking them would only have given them another chance to ask why he didn't return home for good. With his Harvard MBA, he might have worked in the central bank or the sovereign wealth fund, and "work" could have meant actual work or anything he wanted. His brother had a position in the state tourism authority to which he diligently devoted about six hours a week, unless he needed those hours to tend to his stable of racing falcons.

Majid didn't look up from the screen. He only shook his head.

"You're *not* overreacting?" said Ron. He had a round face with puffy cheeks. Sometimes he looked twelve.

"Tomorrow's Friday," Majid said.

Ron looked hard at the screen. Did it say there somewhere that tomorrow *wasn't* Friday? No, it said that the German prime minister had come out in opposition to the Italian bailout, which meant the European Central Bank would follow suit, which meant things looked grim for Italy.

"So?" said Ron.

"MIB options expire at 9:05 a.m."

"MIB? The Italian index?"

Majid nodded.

Ron's cheeks deflated. He said, tone flat, "You bought calls?"

Majid nodded. Buying calls was a bet that the index would go up. They would be a total loss if the index went down.

"How much did you bet?"

Majid didn't answer.

Ron corrected himself. "How much did *we* bet?" Tone no longer flat.

"The bailout was happening." Majid said. "It was the only logical move. Our returns are under two percent. People could do as well investing in Beanie Babies. We need to show results. We need to get on the map."

"On the map," said Ron. "Bloody marvelous. How . . . much . . . did . . . we . . . bet?"

Majid didn't answer. Which was worse than answering.

"Unhedged?" said Ron.

Majid nodded.

"For fuck's sake," said Ron. "We're called a fucking *hedge* fund!"

"I didn't want to limit our upside."

"Brilliant," said Ron. "Fucking brilliant." He rubbed his nose with his right hand and slumped into a chair. "So, tomorrow morning, at 9:05?"

Majid finally turned and looked at him. "We're fucked."

"So . . . if any of our clients should want to redeem . . ."

"We need more capital."

"Under the circumstances," Ron said firmly, as firmly as he ever said anything, "I'm not inclined to go back to my uncles."

"I know," said Majid. "I'm working on it."

PLESKI

The glassed-in room at the Holborn Bank was called "the fishbowl," a name that had two explanations. One was the obvious one that its glass walls made it transparent, so that anyone in the adjacent reception area could see in. The other was that it was where the bank's "relationship managers" met current and potential clients—the fish.

Catherine was meeting there with a not particularly pleasant fish named Stanley Pleski. He was in his early fifties and pudgy, with a futile combover and suits that should have fit better, considering what he paid for them. Catherine thought he was repulsive, but he had ten million dollars invested with Holborn, under Catherine's guidance. He was her fish. Today he was pulling on the line.

Half of his investment with Holborn, five million dollars, he had put, on the bank's advice, on *Catherine's* advice, into low-priced shares of a company called Kemper Media that owned a chain of struggling newspapers in the midwestern United States. It had seemed like a good idea at the time. The bank's analysts had predicted, and Catherine had proceeded to advise Pleski, that Kemper Media was ripe for a takeover (to be followed by dismemberment), and in fact a takeover bid had come, from a media conglomerate called Plenum, the consummation of which would yield Pleski a handsome profit. But the deal had not been consummated, at least not yet, and it should have been.

"The offer expires next week," Pleski said, which of course Catherine knew, and he knew she knew, which Catherine restrained herself from pointing out. "Plenum will renew it," she said, "if it comes to that. They know the delay is a temporary situation." She was sitting across a polished mahogany table from Pleski. The chairs were rich and comfortable. Her dress was pale blue, which was said to be a calming color.

Pleski was not calmed. "Temporary? You sure? You want to tell that to my five million dollars sitting in the stock of a dead company walking?"

Which Catherine chose to take as a rhetorical question. "Kemper Media is family-controlled," she said. "Selling a company like that, it's always an emotional issue."

"How about the emotion of joy?" said Pleski. "All they have to do is say yes to Plenum's offer and that entire family walks away rich."

Dealing with a client like Pleski in a situation like this was part of Catherine's job, at which she wanted to do well. When the skies were blue, and markets were moving in the right direction, it was easy. But sometimes prices moved the wrong way. Sometimes predictions were wrong. Sometimes there were wars, crop failures, pandemics, or outbreaks of spectacular human stupidity. That was reality, but clients didn't expect reality. They expected wizardry. But Catherine had to stay nonconfrontational no matter what. She had to be soothing and persuasive. She could even try honesty.

"The family knows that," Catherine said. "They want to get rich. They're tired of the struggle to keep their grandfather's newspapers alive. They'd rather be floating on yachts sipping Mai Tais. There's only one member who's holding things up."

Pleski waited.

"One of the grandsons, Kevin," Catherine said. "He wants to keep the company and run it himself. He thinks he can turn it around."

Pleski leaned forward in his chair and scoffed. "Turn around *newspapers*?"

Good point. Catherine had considered calling the kid herself and telling him he was delusional. But she hadn't thought that would be productive.

"Whatever his plan is," she said, "he's going to pitch it to the rest of the family at the next board meeting."

"Which is when?"

"A week from today."

"And how's it looking? Are mom and dad going to give little Kevin the company to play with?"

"I don't believe so. That wouldn't be the smart decision."

"No shit," said Pleski. "Next week? You hear anything, any time, you let me know." He checked his watch, picked up his briefcase.

"I think we're going to be all right," Catherine said.

"Damn better be. This play was *your* pitch." He stood up, turned, and headed for the glass door in the glass wall.

RUE DE HESSE

The Holborn Bank's Geneva office is on the Rue de Hesse, just west of the steep cobblestone streets of the old city, in a neighborhood where row after row of stolid granite buildings bear discreet brass nameplates: ROTHSCHILD BANK, ASSET ADVISORS, INVESTMENT CONSULTANTS, PRIVATE BANKING. Parked down the block from the entrance to the Holborn Bank was a black BMW with an Uber placard in its window. The driver was a thirty-eight-year-old man in jeans and a polo shirt. He was not large but he was a lot stronger than he looked. His name was Frank. The man in the back seat was dressed in a dark suit and a colorful (but not too colorful) tie, like a thousand other men in the neighborhood. He looked like a banker who had just gotten into his Uber.

But the Uber wasn't going anywhere. And it wasn't an Uber. And the man in the back was Rafe.

He and Frank were watching the door to the Holborn Bank. It opened, and Stanley Pleski appeared.

"That's him," Rafe said.

"Your pal from the stamp auction. You going to get together later and swap stamps? Three of my green ones for two of your red ones?"

"I don't think that's how they do it. They usually—" Rafe stopped. In the doorway to the bank, Catherine had appeared beside Pleski.

"They usually what?" said Frank.

Catherine and Pleski exchanged some words.

"What?" said Rafe.

"You were about to enlighten me about stamp collecting. The suspense is killing me."

"I know her," said Rafe.

"Who? The blonde?"

Rafe nodded.

"Lucky you," said Frank.

Catherine turned back into the building, and Pleski came down the sidewalk with a waddling gait. Rafe and Frank looked straight ahead, keeping him in their peripheral vision. Pleski looked at his phone as he came near, his briefcase bumping against his left thigh.

Frank, back on the job, took it in. "Case looks heavy. He carry cash?"

Rafe nodded. "Sometimes."

"How much?"

"Millions. Sometimes."

Pleski was even with them now, not twenty feet away, talking into his phone, taking no note of the fake Uber.

"We could just grab him," Frank said. "Get this over with."

"No," said Rafe. "Not yet."

TEXTS

Majid gazed at Catherine's martini like a hungry cowboy looking at a plate of sushi.

Catherine took a sip. Saw him looking. Asked, "Did you ever drink?"

"Not really. I experimented as a teenager back home."

"Where drinking is illegal."

"Illegal but legal, one of the charms of Dubai." He took a sip of iced tea. "Anyway, my stomach objected more than my faith."

"Well," said Catherine, "cheers."

They were on the terrace of the bar of the Fairmont Hotel. Over Majid's shoulder, Catherine could see sailboats coursing on the lake while *mouettes*, the bright yellow water taxis, cut between them. The sun was making a rainbow in the spray from the Jet d'Eau. Haze obscured the lower slopes of the mountains in the distance, but the white snowy shoulders of Mont Blanc were visible above it. The beauty of this place still amazed her.

"How was *your* day?" Majid asked.

"Well," said Catherine, "there is definitely going to be a second martini." (*This play was* your *pitch.*) "I'm waiting for a deal to close. A 'sure thing.' You know how that goes."

"Yeah," said Majid, "I've heard." (*How . . . much . . . did . . . we . . . bet?*)

They'd been sleeping together for three months now, but Catherine could deduce nothing from Majid's tone. He held himself together as well as she did. That was probably why she liked him. She never had to worry about wallowing in his emotions.

"And your day?" she said.

"I've had better," he said. Like, for example, the day the immigration officer at JFK had pulled him out of the line because of his Arab name and Arab face and Arab passport and locked him in a room for five hours while unseen hands disassembled his suitcase and sliced open the stitching of a two-thousand-dollar Canali suit. Even that day was better than this one.

He smiled and put his hand on hers. "Let's make it better later. What if I come to your place tonight?"

"Sure." She smiled back. This had been happening more often now. From once a week to twice a week, which felt about right. He was a considerate lover, thorough but not overstepping bounds, physical or emotional. He was in it for sex and company, and so was she. It didn't hurt that he was handsome. Tawny skin, firm jaw, penetrating eyes. She had no false modesty about her own looks; why should she settle for less in a man? The thought made her think of Stanley Pleski's fat pasty face, the ultimate contrast. And that made her raise a hand to signal a waiter for that second martini, just as her phone dinged with a text. She looked down. It was from Rafe. *When can I see you?*

"Word on your deal?" asked Majid.

"Hmm?"

"Your deal? The one you're waiting to close?"

Oh, right, that. She didn't hesitate. "No," she said. "It's nothing." She looked again at the message from Rafe. And Majid's phone went *ding*.

He looked at it. And smiled.

"Good news?" said Catherine.

"It is," he said. "I'll celebrate vicariously. Have that other drink."

CATHERINE

Twelve hours later, the predawn sun still behind the mountains, Catherine stood on the three-meter board at the Piscine des Vernets, south of the city center, on the bank of the Arve. Other early risers were swimming laps at the indoor pool. The adjacent bar area, filled in the evenings with people who were about to swim or had finished swimming or who just liked the pickup scene at the bar, was deserted. Catherine tested the board with a bounce. Getting ready to dive, there was nothing else in her mind. No Pleski. No Rafe—she hadn't even answered his text. And not Majid. He'd come over late, they'd had sex, he'd left while she was sleeping. It was perfectly satisfactory.

She bounced on the board again. And again. Not enough play. She stepped off and turned the wheel that adjusted the fulcrum. Remounted and bounced again. And now it was right. She stepped back into starting position and took a breath, then moved. Three forward steps, quick but smooth, then jumped straight up, high. She landed on the board and rode it down, her weight and momentum pushing until the board stopped, and then the rebound vaulted her up into empty air.

Diving had been her sport since she was ten. A sport without a team. And no racing side-by-side against a competitor. Everything up to her alone, under her control, for better or for worse. No gyrating markets, no clients, no men, except her father, always there, always supportive (always him, not her brittle, unpredictable mother). And even he was not on her mind when she was alone on the board, then alone in the air. "Oh," someone once said to her, "just you alone, like a golfer staring at a ball."

"Yes," she'd said. "But no."

Up in the air, the board below her, she tucked and flipped into a somersault, once, twice, three times. Flying. Using muscles most people didn't know they have. Then coming out of her tuck and bringing her hands together to slice into the pool, her pointed toes pulling the water above her downward. And the dive still not over. Most people didn't understand that. Submerged, she somersaulted again, then rode the air bubbles her entrance had created back to the surface, her body above them, dispersing them to minimize the size of their eruption.

The finale of a perfect dive.

No splash.

STAVRO

Passengers arriving at the Geneva airport have their choice of which country to walk out to—Switzerland or France. Stanley Pleski was waiting for someone on the Swiss side. Behind the usual scrum of limo drivers holding signs, he sat on a bench next to a kiosk selling low-end Swiss watches at inflated prices. He was holding the day's *Tribune de Genève*, open to his favorite section. His French was practically nonexistent but he had no difficulty understanding the ads. "*Jolie française, tous fantasmes, fellation, 69.*" What a country, he thought. You throw a cigar butt on the sidewalk and the cops are all over you, but hookers are legal.

A flight from Chicago had landed a few minutes before, and passengers were starting to exit the arrivals area. A man in a suit was greeted by his wife and toddler daughter holding a pink balloon. An athletic young couple, headed for the mountains, exited with backpacks and trekking poles. A short man wearing jeans and a leather jacket, carrying a small duffel bag over his shoulder, appeared and walked toward the watch kiosk. He took a seat on the bench next to Pleski, laying his bag on the floor between them. He pulled out a handkerchief and blew his nose. Put the handkerchief back in his pocket. Rubbed his right eye. Scratched his chest. Coughed. Then got up and walked away. Without the bag.

Pleski watched him go. Then he folded his newspaper and stood up and picked up the bag.

Rafe, twenty feet away, sipped a coffee, watching. He nodded to Frank, who was looking at magazines at a stand on the other side of Pleski's bench, and Frank took off following the short man in jeans. Pleski walked out of the terminal, heading toward the taxi stand. Rafe followed Pleski out.

Neither Rafe nor Frank paid any attention to another newly-arrived passenger, a tall Albanian man in a tan leather jacket, who had just come in on a flight from Doha. The Albanian pulled out his cell phone and dialed a number.

"This is Stavro," he said. "I'm here."

"Excellent," said Majid. "I look forward to meeting you."

RULES

It started with the Jews and ended with some Muslims.

In the 1990s, Swiss banks were sued by survivors of Jewish Holocaust victims who claimed, with just cause, that they had been denied access, by Swiss bank secrecy laws and customs (not to mention greed and anti-Semitism), to money in accounts opened by relatives who'd subsequently been murdered by the Nazis. Legal action, public opinion, and pressure from the United States government prevailed. Settlements were made, accounts were unlocked, and a hole was knocked in Swiss bank secrecy.

Then, after 9/11, the United States government, trying to track and eliminate terrorist Islamist financing (not to mention Mafia money laundering and old-fashioned red-blooded American tax evasion) led an assault on what remained of that secrecy and succeeded in imposing a requirement that banks and other financial institutions determine that all monies submitted for deposit be vouched for, accounted for, clean and legitimate in all regards.

In other words, kosher.

"It's called KYC," said Majid.

"Kentucky Fried Chicken?" said Stavro. He was taller than Majid, clean-shaven, with an unchanging stern expression that made it hard for Majid to believe that his visitor had just made a joke. But what else could it be? The man couldn't be stupid. But, then, money didn't always come with brains attached. So Majid took a middle ground—a slight smile and an explanation:

"K. *Y.* C. Know Your Client."

"Yes," said Stavro, not smiling back. "I didn't think you were discussing Colonel Sanders. But this is just as preposterous." He was looking at a questionnaire Majid had handed him. "You need to see my *electric* bill?"

"To establish your residence," said Majid. "Any utility bill will do. You said your current home is in Bosnia?"

"Yes," said Stavro. "It is. And I do have electric lights. But I would think that this is the only piece of paper that matters." He reached into an inside jacket pocket and pulled out a white envelope and extracted a check payable to Sterling Wealth Management. He handed it to Majid.

"I trust that meets your minimum investment," he said.

Majid held the check lightly. A slip of paper that would solve his immediate problem, give him time to recover from his Italian disaster.

"It does," he said, keeping his voice calm, no big deal here. Then added, dutifully, "But I am required to ask about the source of funds."

"These are American rules?" Stavro's brows raised. "Since when do the borders of the United States extend to the Alps?"

Majid shrugged sympathetically. "The pressure they exerted on Switzerland was intense."

"Not that it's a problem," Stavro said, although his expression showed otherwise. "These are proceeds from the sale of a partnership share. My family made a successful investment in a company providing computer services in the developing world. Our partners bought us out. We grew tired of worrying if Ugandan cement manufacturers could pay their bills."

"I see," said Majid. He gently laid the check down on his desk. "And your partners, the ones who bought you out, can you identify them and the name of their bank?" He gestured toward the form in front of his visitor, where all this was supposed to be inscribed.

"Actually, I'd rather not. They are private people. And they may have issues with the tax authorities in their country."

Majid nodded, understanding. "Of course," he said. "And the source of the funds *you* originally invested in the computer services company?"

"Many and various," Stavro said. "It would be burdensome to gather documentation."

He leaned over and lifted the check off Majid's desk.

"I'm not asking to see *your* bona fides," he said. "You come recommended, but there are other wealth management firms in Switzerland."

Six hundred eighteen, Majid thought. Or nineteen, if Rafe is up and running.

He nodded again, understanding again, understanding so much he felt he must be verging on omniscience. "'Many and various,'" he repeated. As if that answered every question.

He gestured again to the form on the desk. "Just fill it in as best you can. And welcome to Sterling."

KEVIN

The Meatpacking District was definitely getting old, but it was still better than hauling over to Brooklyn to drink bitter-tasting craft beer with a bunch of overpaid coders pretending to be poets. Anyway, Dawn probably thought Crown Heights was next to Portugal, too far to go.

But she was easy to be with and had a hot body, and Kevin liked her.

They walked out of the club on Little West Twelfth Street, Dawn trailing and consulting a text. "Cherie and Derek are at Cielo," she said. The street smelled of car exhaust and garbage.

He didn't want to stay out late. He had a 9 a.m. phone date with a friend from Princeton who was a numbers whiz at Goldman and was going to go over his figures.

"I said we'd meet them," Dawn said.

The meeting with his family was coming up soon. Kevin thought his Aunt Charlotte, at least, would side with him. She'd always been more sentimental than mercenary; she'd cried when they'd shut the paper in Toledo.

"How about the beer garden?" he said, pointing toward The Standard, nearby. "I could use some air."

His great-grandfather had started the business with one small daily in Kalamazoo. Kevin had worked at that same paper the summer after his freshman year, chasing sirens and covering city council meetings, and he'd loved it. The new owners would shut it down five minutes after their deal closed.

"I don't like beer," Dawn said, "and I don't eat pretzels."

His father had broken in at the Kansas City paper when it was still set with hot type, the composing room filled with linotype operators at keyboards, creating letters one at a time from buckets of molten lead, remnants of the Middle Ages in the twentieth century that linotype operators, if they still existed, would be happy to pour onto the heads of Wall Street takeover artists scaling the ramparts.

"They probably have gluten-free," Kevin said.

"Ha ha," Dawn said.

The papers still had loyal readers, and they had tradition and history, and if they died, he knew damn well no cloud news service was going to cover Kalamazoo City Hall. He was sure there was a path to survival: digital initiatives; combining business operations; selling and leasing back their real estate. Whatever it took to keep alive a company he wanted to spend his life in and the country needed, one that created an informed citizenry, which was hokey as hell but true, especially now.

"I promised Cherie," Dawn said.

"Okay," he said. "One drink." And then he'd go home, with or without her, to get ready for tomorrow.

He stepped into the street to look for a cab.

He didn't notice the white panel van idling down the block.

He did not see it start to move in his direction.

RON

Majid liked the cool weather. It was different from the cool back home, where the only cool was air conditioning that made you feel like meat in a freezer every time you entered a building. He was walking with his partner, Ron, over the Mont Blanc Bridge, wind whipping the Swiss and Genevan flags flying from its sides. Ron was from England so cool was his natural element. He had an endless array of jackets and coats, seemingly one for each one-degree variation in temperature. Today's was a quilted blazer. Burberry.

"So," Ron said, "this fellow Stavro just strolls in from God's green acre with a massive check?"

"He said we came highly recommended," said Majid.

"By whom?"

"He mentioned my cousin in Dubai."

"Don't you have a thousand cousins in Dubai?" Ron asked, then flinched as a speeding bicycle swerved around them. For some reason bicyclists used the bridge's pedestrian path as a thoroughfare. It was annoying and dangerous. It seemed so un-Swiss.

"No," said Majid, "not a thousand." He sometimes thought Ron thought his father lived in a desert tent with a harem. In fact, his parents lived in a two-bedroom villa on land given to them by the government, a perk of Emirati citizenship, and his mother had gone into the marriage with an understanding with his father that he would never take another wife. (On the other hand, there was his grandfather, who was in his eighties and had three wives and many children, including a three-year-old son, Majid's youngest uncle. Majid *did* have a lot of cousins.)

"I saw the paperwork," said Ron, looking suspiciously at an oncoming bicycle. "His underlying source of funds was 'various.' *Various?*"

"He did list some specifics."

"'Insurance proceeds'? 'Casino winnings'?"

They were approaching the river's south bank, where tourists with small children, some squalling, were waiting in line for the Ferris wheel in the English Garden. Majid saw Ron wince at the sound. He'd seen his partner walk out of a restaurant if there were children present.

"It saves our asses," Majid said. "Gives us breathing room."

Ron sighed, a kind of breathing. "Sure. If you can sell this fellow on the virtues of cash and short-term paper."

"He said he'll trust our judgment."

"God help him."

"He just had one request," Majid said. "He wants to short a company called Sahel Hydrocarbon."

"Never heard of it. Why?"

"He's worked in Africa. That's where it's active. He says he has doubts about its fundamentals."

"Africa? Me too. What does this company do?"

In the line for the Ferris wheel, a child holding its mother's hand started to shriek.

"Oil," said Majid. "One tricky thing. Our client doesn't want to be identifiable as the short seller."

"Why not?"

"He says he knows some of the principals in the company. He doesn't want to offend anyone."

"Well, that's very considerate of him."

"In fact, he doesn't want the trade traced to any single short seller."

"Really?" Another bike was coming up fast. Ron stepped aside. "Does he want to disappear in a cloud of mist? Shall we buy him an invisibility cloak?"

"He didn't say. He just made it clear that he values discretion. I can break the trade into smaller pieces. Use anonymous LLCs, maybe some off the shelf. Borrow the shares from different brokers."

"Lot of trouble," said Ron.

The shrieking child was still at it.

"Or," said Majid, "we can give him his money back and shut down the firm. You can go home to Sussex and work with your family."

Ron's siblings were in Sussex. They had packs of brats. Ron's father would expect him at the weekly Sunday dinners.

"Subterfuge!" Ron said. "What fun!"

LUNCH

Just lunch, Rafe had said.

Right. It had been a lunch in Cambridge, too. Catherine remembered. A late lunch, which became a drink. And another and . . .

They never got to dinner.

That had been stupid. Hot but stupid. She had been engaged, for God's sake. But reeling from what just happened to her honest, dutiful father—arrested! facing prison!—and she was questioning everything. Why do the prudent thing (which she had always done)? Why do the right thing (which she had always done)? Why do anything? And if a man who was sexy and smart and funny and sitting across from her with a killer smile and brushing her hand as he reaches for his glass and just that brush makes her *feel* something and they have a drink and then another and he is definitely coming on but not obnoxiously so and the feeling grows and it grows then why the hell not? She wasn't *married*. Not yet.

"So," said Rafe, "whatever happened with Hector?"

"*Victor*," Catherine said.

They were at an outdoor table at the Café du Centre on the Place du Molard. Around the corner, on the Rue du Rhône, Russian oligarchs and Arab oil princes and their wives in furs or burqas were buying hundred-thousand-dollar watches and twenty-thousand-dollar handbags, tossing them into shopping baskets like cantaloupes. In some of the stores there, you could find a plain cotton shirt for less than a thousand dollars. If you looked hard enough.

"Victor," said Rafe.

"I called off the engagement," Catherine said. "I realized it wasn't right. Obviously." Victor was a lawyer in Houston now. He had a wife and a baby. He sent Catherine Christmas cards. The baby looked like Victor. Unfortunately, it was a girl.

"Oh," said Rafe. "I didn't know."

"No," said Catherine. "You were gone by then."

"You kind of told me to go, if I remember correctly."

"You didn't need much encouragement to follow what's-her-name to California."

"School was over. I didn't feel like hanging around Cambridge for your wedding, to which, by the way, I wasn't invited."

Fair enough. Catherine recalled she hadn't gone out of her way to let him know the wedding was cancelled. His absence made her life easier, easier to plow ahead, to do what she had to do, undistracted. To stand by her father. To launch a career. A prosperous career.

A waiter came to take their orders. Mushroom risotto for her, a seafood platter for him. The sun was bright and the air smelled fresh and clean and there were people all around, seated at other tables or strolling through the square or standing in line outside the ice cream parlor. Catherine had picked the spot for this lunch, a very public place. Interesting, she thought—*as if she'd been afraid he would try to kidnap her?*

Rafe had said something.

"What?" she said.

"Nothing. Just reminiscing about Professor Nitzberg."

She remembered. "Capitalism and the State. The token socialist. Why did we even take that course?"

"I don't know why *you* took it," said Rafe. "I know why I took it. I took it because you took it." He sipped his wine. The Swiss white was excellent. You couldn't get it outside Switzerland, because it was never exported, because the Swiss, no fools, drank it all. He put down his glass and leaned forward. "It's really good to see you again. I didn't know you were here. I don't know why we haven't been in touch. I—"

"I'm seeing Majid now," she said. Cutting this off.

"Majid? Oh." He took another sip of wine. "I didn't know you two even liked each other back in Cambridge."

"I was engaged, and I was seeing you. My plate was kind of full."

Rafe nodded. Couldn't argue with that.

"Majid and I met again when I moved here."

"Oh." He paused. "At that Harvard Club party, you and he didn't seem too, you know, very . . ."

"What exactly do you think we might have been doing in front of two hundred people?"

"Well," he said. "Majid. I always liked Majid."

"That's nice. But I wasn't actually asking for your endorsement."

Then I fucking withdraw it.

Her phone rang. She glanced at the Caller ID. "Work," she said and answered. "Really?" she said into the phone. "When? Oh my God . . ." She sighed. "I guess that means the deal will go through but . . . I'll call him." She clicked off.

"You have a deal going through?" Rafe said. "Congratulations. I should make you pay for lunch."

"It's . . . complicated. It's been pending. A corporate takeover."

"So the executives cash out and a bunch of employees get made redundant."

She picked up her phone. "I have to call the client."

"Bosses win, workers get fired. Corporate takeover 101."

"Thank you, Karl Marx. I thought you took Comrade Nitzberg's course because of me." She was punching a number on her cell.

"I did occasionally listen to the teacher. I mean, as long as I was there."

"Hello," she said into the phone, turning away. "It's Catherine Cole. I have some good news. The deal is going through. Well, actually, it's kind of awful. The grandson is out of the picture. He died. An auto accident." She listened. "Yes. Okay. I'll see you tomorrow." She ended the call.

"Somebody died?" Rafe said.

She nodded. "He was involved in the deal. Sort of."

"The deal that is now going through." Rafe looked at her. "So the news was good, or the news was awful?"

"Both," she said.

Rafe sipped his wine. "Well, speaking of clients, I'm starting a fund that could be a good match for some of yours. Long-short, low beta, a real quant shop. You do put some of your clients' money into outside funds, don't you?"

She looked at him, surprised. "I didn't realize this was a business lunch."

"Both," he said.

OYSTERS

When the tide went out, the women of the village went to the creek to find oysters on the mangrove roots. They climbed into their dugout canoes and paddled to where the creek opened to the sea. It was hot, but by the ocean there was a breeze, and this was where the oysters were plentiful. Halima and Fatima pulled short knives from their belts and used them to cut the oysters off the mangroves. Coura used a machete.

"Where's your knife?" Halima asked. "A knife is better." The work was slower with knives than with machetes, but hacking with machetes could destroy the roots, which would mean fewer oysters next season. The Oyster Women's Association had taught them that.

"I lost it," Coura said.

That was a lie, but it was typical of Coura. Taking the easier way. Halima knew there was no point in pressing the issue. A woman like Coura took no responsibility. She didn't even rinse her oysters before she steamed them. Halima believed in doing things the right way even when it didn't profit her. She couldn't charge more for her oysters than Coura charged for hers. The market wouldn't bear it, except for the occasional customer who'd bought from Coura in the past and was tired of spitting out grit.

"Look at that," said Fatima. Halima and Coura turned to see what Fatima was pointing at with her knife. Out in the open water there was a big ship. They often saw ships going to and from the city, but this one wasn't a ferry, and it wasn't a tanker, and it wasn't even moving to or from the port. It was stationary, a few hundred meters out. The most notable thing: a long tube, yellow and firm, was slowly extending from its stern.

"It's looking for a girlfriend," said Fatima, and she started to laugh.

The long yellow tube—it was a pipe, although the women didn't know that—dipped down from the ship and entered the water.

"It's loving the sea," said Fatima, who was never without a boyfriend even when she had a husband.

Coura laughed, too. "Maybe it will make more little fish, or more oysters."

"Or baby ships," said Fatima. "Little baby ships." She and Coura were laughing harder. But not Halima. There was too much to do. After a quick glance at the phallic pipe, which was interesting but could bring her no profit, she went back to slicing oysters from the mangroves and tossing them into her blue plastic tub. Even working fast, there would barely be time to steam them and shuck them and set up her stand by the side of the road to sell before it got dark and the customers were gone.

SENSITIVE

Rafe drove up the hill toward the massive white columns of the Palais des Nations, where the League of Nations had cratered and the United Nations now did God knows what. He turned left at the forty-foot sculpture of a chair with one of its legs blown off, a symbolic protest against land mines. Next to the crippled chair, women in white head scarves had erected signs protesting a genocide of Tamils in Sri Lanka, a situation about which Rafe knew nothing. He turned left again at the International Tennis Club and headed up a drive to the first barrier, where a Swiss policeman approached and demanded, obligingly in English, "ID." Rafe reached into an inside jacket pocket and pulled out a laminated card and showed it. The policeman waved him on to the next barrier, where private guards allowed him to pass the concrete bollards. And then, after US Marines had one more look at his credential, Rafe was inside a wide seven-story building festooned with solar panels—the Permanent Mission of the United States of America to the United Nations and Other International Organizations in Geneva.

In the lobby he passed by the photos of the four ambassadors in residence (one to the United Nations-Geneva, three to other international organizations) and stowed his phone in a locker. The ambassadors' offices were upstairs, but Rafe took an elevator down. He exited to a concrete corridor that led to a steel door. He looked into the retinal scanner and waited for a green light. Then he pushed the door open and he walked through it and the door closed.

There were five people in the SCIF (pronounced "skiff," which made him think of the small boat he had gotten seasick in when his grandfather thought he should learn how to fish). It was a Sensitive Compartmented Information Facility, constructed in accordance with Intelligence Community Directive 705—walls, floor, and ceiling made of eight-inch concrete with five-eighths-inch steel reinforcing rods spaced every six inches, horizontally and vertically, and soundproofed to Sound Transmission Class 50, so that "very loud sounds within the SCIF, such as loud singing, brass music, or a radio at full volume, can be heard with the human ear faintly or not at all outside of the SCIF."

There were no brass bands in the room, though Rafe thought that might have made for a nice change. There were five individuals, all SCI cleared: Rafe, his colleague Frank, the local FBI legat who hoped this wouldn't take long because he wanted to drive over to France and play nine holes before the sun went down, the Diplomatic Security RSO who wanted to know everything about everything all the time, and Helen Sykes, the CIA chief of station, who was fifty years old and the toughest guy in the room. There were bottles of water on the conference table.

After cursory nods and greetings, it was Rafe's show. He had visual aids, because everyone liked visual aids.

"Stanley Pleski," he began.

On a screen behind him, there appeared a photo. A logo in a corner of the photo read: *U.S. Treasury Department—Office of Terrorism and Financial Intelligence.* Rafe's agency.

The photo was of Stanley Pleski exiting the Holborn Bank.

"Born Detroit, nineteen sixty-six," Rafe said. "Graduated Wayne State University School of Law, nineteen ninety-two. Disbarred, nineteen ninety-nine. When he was practicing law, some of his clients were members of the Chaldean mob—"

"The *Chaldean* mob?" asked the DS man.

Rafe stopped and explained, "It's a thing in Detroit."

"Where is Chaldea?" the DS man asked. The State Department's

Diplomatic Security Service had agents in every American embassy; he'd never heard of anyone assigned to Chaldea.

"Why don't we do geography lessons later?" said Helen Sykes. She was wearing a maroon blazer and black pants and had her hair in a short ponytail that might have looked girlish but somehow looked fierce.

Rafe resumed. "Pleski got involved in money laundering, setting up shell accounts and running bags of cash through the tunnel to Windsor for the Chaldeans . . . who I believe," he said, looking at the DS man, "originated in ancient Babylonia." The DS man nodded his thanks.

"The Chaldeans told their friends, and Pleski acquired new clients—first Mexicans, then Colombians, now Russians."

"Why does the Russian mob need a two-bit hustler from Detroit?" asked the FBI man.

"Because nobody suspects a two-bit hustler from Detroit?" said Frank.

"Except Treasury," said Helen Sykes, turning to Rafe. "How did *you* become aware? Did somebody make a mistake on their tax return?"

Was that grudging admiration or an insult? Everybody knew it was tax returns that brought down Al Capone. Even so, Sykes had made it pretty clear that, as an experienced CIA professional, she had less than total respect for Treasury agents as spies.

"No," said Rafe. "Financial intelligence." And then laid it out, clicking through images on the screen as he went. Photos of invoices, letters of credit, bank wire transfers, shipping crates, and a pretty full-color shot of a Belgian fried chicken restaurant.

"Our people in India became aware of a company called Gujarat Gems. It buys diamonds from Zimbabwe and sells them to a dealer in Brussels. Millions of dollars' worth. The Belgian dealer, who is actually a Russian named Shushkov, pays Gujarat with money allegedly earned from his interest in the Poulet Dansant fast food chain . . ."

Ever helpful, he paused and looked at the DS man. "Dancing Chicken."

"For God's sake," said Helen Sykes.

"Gujarat deposits its profits in an Indian bank. All legal, all kosher—except for one minor detail. There are no diamonds. The purchase invoices are fake. Nothing is sent from Zimbabwe to India. But, for show, packages are sent from India to Brussels." Rafe clicked to another picture: an open crate filled with broken tea cups.

"The only thing that *is* real is the money from Brussels, which is proceeds from heroin sales and human trafficking. It gets wired from the account in the Indian bank, these alleged profits from nonexistent diamonds, to the Holborn Bank here in Geneva, where Pleski directs the account."

"So you know everything," said Helen Sykes. "Shut him down."

"Too soon," said Rafe. "This got us to Pleski, but Pleski handles money from other sources, and we don't know who they are and we want to find out, so we can wrap him up and everybody he works for. One delivery came in yesterday, by courier."

He clicked and surveillance video played on the screen—Pleski entering the airport, Pleski sitting on the bench by the watch kiosk, the man with the duffel bag sitting down next to him, the man leaving the duffel bag, Pleski picking up the duffel bag.

"Who was the courier?" asked the DS man.

"His ticket said Leo Perelli," said Frank, who was a man of few words but was good at finding things out. "After he dropped the bag, he had four drinks at the airport bar, then got back on a flight to JFK."

"How much was in that bag?" asked the FBI legat.

"A million?" Frank shrugged. "Two million? More? The courier flew first class."

"And it went to the Holborn Bank?" asked Helen Sykes.

"Not yet," said Rafe. "It will be washed first. Pleski goes to stamp auctions, art auctions, buys things, gets loans with the things as collateral, defaults on the loans, lets the lenders keep the things and he keeps the cash, now certified as coming from a legit financial institution. Or he goes to casinos, buys chips, bets nothing, cashes the chips and, presto—he has gambling winnings, or that's what they are if anybody asks."

"And then," said Helen Sykes, "it goes to the Holborn Bank."

"Yes."

"Where, I believe, Mister Pleski's account is handled by a friend of yours."

Now she clicked a button to take control of the screen. (At which point Rafe's clicker stopped working. How did she do that?) On the screen, in response to Sykes's click, a photo of a woman appeared. Catherine. Her passport photo but attractive nonetheless.

Rafe shot a look at Frank, who looked back at him blankly, acknowledging nothing.

"Well," said Rafe. "I'm glad to see the CIA is on top of things."

"We try," said Sykes.

"Impressive. Can you tell me what card I'm thinking of? How many fingers I'm holding up behind my back?"

"Can you tell me why you saw fit not to mention your friend's involvement?"

"Yes," said Rafe. "I can."

The DS man, even the FBI man, perked up, the briefing getting interesting at last.

"She's a trader who handles a few clients," said Rafe. "She doesn't open accounts. It was never her job to check Pleski's bona fides."

"Are you aware of her father's background?" asked Sykes.

Was she? They did work fast around here.

"Yes."

"His *criminal* background?"

"Miss Cole had nothing to do with that. She didn't work where he worked. She was in grade school when he started there."

"So she had no idea her father was helping to swindle investors?"

"He was a minor player, a functionary, it was the guy he worked for . . ."

"And now she has no idea she's handling dirty money? Is anyone else beginning to see a pattern there? Is willful blindness genetic?"

"There's no reason to think she's aware. Or that anyone at the bank is. Pleski's money is layered before it gets there. He can show papers of origin."

"Including for the money in the duffel bag?"

"That money will make multiple stops before it gets there, as I'm pretty sure I just said. A casino, real estate, an art auction followed by an insurance loss or a loan default . . ."

"Uh-huh," said Helen Sykes. "And while it's touring Switzerland, what are you planning to do next?"

"Bring the mountain to Mohammed," Rafe said. "And my acquaintance with Miss Cole can help. I'm opening a hedge fund that might appeal to someone like Pleski. Long-short, low beta. A real quant shop." The DS man looked at him, questioning—*quant shop*?—but Rafe let it slide.

FUCK

"Fuck," she said, and she pulled the sheet up over her head.

Catherine was naked. "Fuck," she said again.

"Yes," said Rafe, "that's what we did."

He said it in the least sarcastic way possible. He was smiling and content, albeit still breathing heavily. It had been very, very good. Like back in Cambridge. Catherine had given every sign of enjoying it, too. It was hard to believe she could actually be upset. This had to be some kind of automatic reaction, a meaningless programmed response from ancient Puritan genes. She had always seemed to fight the pleasure. Which always seemed to make it more pleasurable.

She got out of the bed and pulled on her panties and stood facing him. She wasn't shy about her breasts.

"We can't start this again," she said.

"Why not?" He reached toward her. "And, by the way, I believe we already did." She took a step back.

"You're not even engaged this time," he said.

"It's too much," she said. "I need to focus on my work, on my career."

"So I, what, distract you? I'm all for work. I'm trying to do some myself. But not twenty-four hours a day."

"I don't want to talk about this now. I have to go." She was looking for the rest of her clothes.

"This thing with Majid . . . *he* doesn't distract you?"

"He doesn't cross-examine me when I make a simple statement." Her bra was in the sheets somewhere.

"No," said Rafe. "He doesn't. Distract you."

"I need to go home. I have to be at the office early."

Rafe got out of the bed but made no move to find his clothes. "Okay," he said. "Let's talk about work."

"What about it?" He'd been lying on her bra. She grabbed it.

"Have you thought about putting some of your clients into my fund?"

"Now?" she said. She looked at him. Not muscular but no flab. Trim stomach. Like Majid. But not like Majid. More relaxed. More abandoned. He was semi-erect. It wouldn't take much.

"I'll make you a deal. Toss me a client and I promise not to have sex with you. Unless you want me to."

"Rafe . . ."

"I think what I've got would be well suited for some of your clients."

"Can we talk about this another time?"

"Stanley Pleski for example."

She stopped halfway through fastening her bra and stared at him.

"How do you know who my clients are?"

He shrugged. "Word around town."

"Word around town?"

He took a step toward her. "But we can talk about it later." He reached around her and put his hand on her ass. He leaned over and kissed her left breast. He pulled her toward him.

"I have to go," she said, wavering.

"We can talk about that later." He ran his tongue over her nipple and slid his right hand down, between her legs. She sighed and closed her eyes and let him pull her in.

"Fuck," she said.

BEFORE

People really did talk about "units." Meaning a hundred million dollars. As in, "Rafe, you're doing a great job here. By the time you're thirty-five you should have a unit at least."

How much money did a person need? Some of his colleagues at Klamath Capital already owned vineyards. Rafe liked wine but he didn't think he needed a vineyard. He and his older brother had grown up middle-class comfortable in Westchester. Their father was sales manager for a drapery manufacturer. Mother was a school nurse. They had everything they needed.

After business school, he had joined Klamath Capital in Connecticut. He hadn't really thought about it; that was just the kind of place one went after business school. Plus, there was an intellectual challenge to the dealmaking, a high-stakes game. Like when he masterminded the undermining of an imminent leveraged buyout of a pet food manufacturer, which cost the failed prospective buyers a fortune but made Klamath twice that. And twice that again when he maneuvered the same temporarily rescued company into the arms of a hostile takeover by a competitor, which left one less pet food manufacturer in the world but was a red-letter day for Klamath Capital. That's when the firm's founder (who had once kayaked the Klamath River) started talking to him about units and vineyards. Rafe already had a Mercedes and saw no reason to buy a Lamborghini. On the personal front, he was in a relationship with a lawyer named Taylor and saw no need to upgrade that either. She was smart and laughed dismissively when people said she looked like Jennifer Lawrence (although Rafe could tell she believed she did). They got along well and talked vaguely about getting married at some point just beyond the near future. The near future turned out to include an offer by Taylor's firm to send her to open an office in Singapore. Taylor had mixed feelings, briefly, but she was ambitious and wanted to go and, once she had gone, it turned out that Rafe didn't really miss her. He was surprised by that at first. He had not known which way his emotions would go.

Rafe's brother, Paul, had been a senior at Williams when the planes struck the towers on 9/11. He had a strong sense of patriotism and a gut-level urge for action and revenge that went back to childhood playground games. He had been accepted to a Ph D program in anthropology at Yale, but he bowed out of that to join the Marines. "Going to be doing some applied anthropology instead," he said. When Rafe grew up and launched his own career, Paul had occasionally suggested that Rafe, too, might want to do something more useful with his life than help rich people pile up more money. Rafe was already beginning to suspect the same thing. But he told his brother that there was unfortunately no Marine battalion dedicated to assaulting fraudulent mortgage lenders or greedy hedge fund operators. In any case, unlike his brother, he was not exactly cut out for military life. His one brush with weaponry had been at the bachelor party of a college friend from Texas. The party had been a weekend-long event on a small ranch outside College Station, where a margarita machine was prominently installed on the house's front porch. On the Saturday night, the guests drank until they dropped, some in the house, some sprawled in the yard. At 8 a.m. Sunday morning Rafe was awakened by the groom's brother standing next to the margarita machine and shouting "How do you turn this damn thing on?" Somebody showed him, and by 9 a.m. everybody was drunk again. Which was when someone spotted a bird overhead and said they should be dove hunting. A half dozen shotguns appeared and one was thrust into Rafe's hands with the instruction to shoot at the now proliferating white birds. (Were they actually doves? Who knew?) Rafe made an intense effort to marshal his logical brain, reminding himself over and over that he was drunk, and that this was stupid, and, most of all, to keep the shotgun pointed up when he pulled the trigger. The blasts were muffled by the alcohol between his ears and his brain but did startle a few red cows grazing nearby. Rafe didn't hit any birds (no one did) but he didn't kill anyone either, so that was a success and also the most military thing he had ever done, which he did not think qualified him to serve in Afghanistan.

So Rafe stayed on at Klamath, going through the motions, despite growing qualms about what he was doing, which were amplified by a *New York Times* article he unfortunately chanced upon ("What Happens to a Factory Town When the Factory Shuts Down?") about the pet food employees he had personally helped render out of their jobs and into despair. Of course, the world was filled with moral compromises, Rafe knew that. It was possible to do some good while doing some bad (and he had done some good, he knew he had). So worse in a way was his starting to feel that what he was doing was not so much immoral as pointless. What was the point, really, of working to help people with four hundred million dollars earn another fifty? It didn't matter to them (even if they thought it did), and it certainly didn't matter to Rafe. So why was he spending sixty hours a week doing that? This line of thinking dangerously progressed to the larger question of what the purpose of life should be, which Rafe hadn't thought much about since he was twelve years old and lay on his back on the lawn at night looking up at infinite stars. (This was shortly before his first serious crush—on a blonde girl in his English class who looked alarmingly cute in glasses—took over most of his mental processes and pretty much answered the question.) He was aware that some philosophies elevated the pointlessness of life to a positive—was that existentialism? maybe, someday, he should look it up—but, in the meantime, Rafe suspected there might be something a little less pointless than his current work at Klamath Capital. Like what? Socially conscious investing? Mentoring minority business owners? Law school? (No. Ugh.) Then Rafe's brother, a year away from leaving the Marines, trying to decide whether to go back and get that Ph D or open a surf shop in Baja, was shot and killed in Helmand province by a Taliban fighter disguised as an Afghan police officer. After the funeral, Rafe made a call to a friend at Treasury and asked if there was any way they could use his services. He heard nothing for a month.

Then his friend called him back and said, actually, there was.

NOW

"I don't understand," said Pleski. "Your bank wants to share my business?"

"It's normal to use other investment firms," Catherine said, "to diversify our clients' holdings."

"You don't have to worry about her bank," Rafe said. "We split our fee with them."

"How nice for everyone," said Pleski. They were sitting at a table in the bar at the Brasserie Lipp. On the ceiling above them brightly painted images of monkeys and birds cavorted with naked nymphs. Whoever drew that, Pleski thought, must have been high on something. But Pleski liked the Lipp. So civilized. So European. There was nothing like it in Detroit. But he still didn't understand why Catherine had invited him here to meet this guy. He wouldn't have minded meeting Catherine alone, but she'd never given him a hint. It was strictly business with her, and that was probably for the best. Anyway, when was the last time an attractive woman had come to him voluntarily without a price tag attached? Well, at least that made things clear. He liked things clear. So, as a waiter trundled by with a pastry cart, he asked Rafe, "What *is* your fee?"

"Two and twenty. Standard for a hedge fund. Two percent of assets under management, twenty percent of gains."

"And if there are losses, not gains, do you reimburse the client twenty percent?"

"That isn't customary," Rafe said.

No shit, thought Pleski. He didn't know why the people he worked for took chances making their money illegally, risking jail, risking getting shot. This hedge fund racket was totally legitimate, and it was robbery, and paid better.

"So if I win, you win," he said. "And if I lose, you still win?"

Catherine was watching the back and forth, not happily.

"Actually, Mister Pleski," Rafe said, "everything is negotiable."

"Isn't it though?" Pleski said. "And you would diversify my investments how?"

"Our approach is all about information."

"Information? You gotta be kidding." He took a big swallow of his beer. French beer. Surprisingly not bad. "Newspapers and magazines are dead. Digital media is oversaturated. Every shmuck in the world has a podcast. Don't you read the papers?"

"The papers?" Rafe said. "The dead ones?"

"You know what I mean." Pleski put his glass down.

"We did have that success with Kemper Media," Catherine put in.

"A fire sale," said Pleski. "The bones sold cheap."

"You're absolutely right," Rafe said. "But we don't invest *in* information. We invest *with* information. We have sources in interesting places—pharmaceutical firms doing drug trials, staff members in American and European antitrust agencies. We expect to be the first to hear of many interesting developments."

Catherine glared at Rafe.

"So," said Pleski, "you have . . . connections?"

"It's a people business," said Rafe. "Behind every deal, behind every investment, there are people."

"Got it," said Pleski. "And people who need people . . ."

Rafe smiled. "Are the luckiest people in world."

"Okay," said Pleski, cutting it off before this guy could burst into song. "That's interesting. I'll think about it." He stood up.

"If there's anything else I can tell you . . ."

"I said I'll think about it. I can reach you through her?" He looked at Catherine.

Rafe nodded. Pleski turned and walked away. Catherine waited until he was out of earshot, then turned to Rafe, not kindly. “What the hell?”

“What the hell what?”

“I thought maybe we could do some actual business. Maybe even help you out. But your ‘cutting edge’ hedge fund? You just practically announced that its cutting edge is illegal inside information.”

“Just suiting the product to the client,” Rafe said.

“What are you talking about?”

“That phone call you made when we had lunch? A deal went through because somebody got killed? Was that a deal Pleski was involved in?”

“What does that have to do with anything?”

“Do you understand who Pleski is?”

“Yes. My client. Who you just sent running into the street.”

“He’s thinking about it.”

She stood up. “I’m going to tell him to forget about it.”

“Catherine . . .”

“This was a mistake. I work for a bank. A bank that has standards, legal and ethical. No more client introductions, Rafe.”

“Catherine . . .”

“No. No more . . . anything.” And she walked. Didn’t look back.

COMPLIANCE

Back at her office, Catherine glanced up at the screens. There were screens on every wall. All the world's markets on display, the current price of everything, updating constantly. Therefore, the results of everyone's trades, updating constantly, which certainly kept the adrenaline flowing. You were ahead, you were behind, all right there. No need to wait for quarterly performance reviews. There were reviews of your performance every fifteen seconds.

Catherine had something else on the screen at her desk. New York tabloid articles about a hit-and-run in the Meatpacking District. Tragic unsolved death of Kevin Kemper, heir to a declining just-sold media empire. The white van death vehicle stolen in Queens, abandoned in the Bronx. No leads. No mention of Stanley Pleski. What the hell had Rafe been talking about?

"Catherine." A smiling voice.

She looked up to see Michael Barnstable, her departmental vice president. Which made him, by her estimate, one of about ten thousand vice presidents in the company.

"Working late?"

Barnstable was almost fifty, long past the time when he should have made senior vice president, or executive vice president, or, God help us, senior executive vice president. Like Catherine, he was an American, which he seemed to think should give them a strong personal bond, although Catherine imagined that his wife, who was active in English-language community theater in Geneva, might disagree.

"I want to be ready for when Tokyo opens," she said. "I'm tracking some options there."

"Well," he said, perching on her desk, his expression sympathetic—he was always on *her* side—"I'm afraid I'm going to lighten your load a little. Those mining company warrants you pitched . . . we can't get involved."

"We?"

"Compliance." He shook his head. "Our official anti-business business department."

"Why?"

"Apparently that company relies on mineral rights granted by the president-for-life, and the CEO of said company just happens to be his own daughter. One of those marvelous Central Asian coincidences."

"The mineral reserves are substantial. Demand is growing in China and India. The stock is undervalued."

"No doubt. But so is the regime. Protests, torture, critics disappearing. Negative news runs. Compliance won't like it. Reputational risk."

"Ours or theirs?"

"Ours, of course. The Holborn Bank—clean and pristine."

"Not *that* pristine. We're in the other 'Stans. Including that one where the president boiled his enemies in oil."

"Yes," Barnstable said, "but this would be a 'Stan too far. Compliance has warned us. There was a memo."

"But have they even seen this yet? Have you put it to them?"

"I'd love to," he said. "I really would. But we have to pick our battles."

We. Not *I*. Their special bond, both of them being Americans—and bipeds. With genitals.

Catherine looked around the office at all the identical desks, mostly devoid of personal mementoes, of any character at all. If her colleagues had children, there was no sign of them, no photos or handmade cards or inept art projects. One desk a row over had a coffee mug with the inscription, "Kiss Me, I'm an Arbitrager." Most of the traders had gone home for the day. Orders to be executed in New York, where it was still prime time, would be handled by the bank's office there. Individual bank offices had some autonomy. Catherine knew that.

"Why not just put the order in?" she said. "See what happens."

Barnstable considered for a microsecond, then shook his head. "It's just not worth it. I'm sorry."

Jesus, Catherine thought, the son of bitch is running scared. What bonehead deals did he send up before? Is he on probation?

She smiled sweetly. "What if we made a case in writing, laid out the numbers . . .?" *We*. Not *I*.

For once he was curt. "It's not the right time," he said. Case closed. But he didn't walk away. "There's another thing I've been meaning to ask you about—a mismatch in your paperwork from last month. One side of a straddle on the DAX seems to be missing. Could you take a look and straighten things out?"

"Sure," she said. "It's just a missed opportunity with those warrants . . ."

"Let it go. Look for other opportunities. It's not like you need this one. Your P and L is excellent. I see the Kemper Media deal went through. Your client must be pleased. Mister Pulaski . . ."

"Pleski," she said. "Yes. He was pretty much counting on it." Then, casually, a random thought, since they were on the subject anyway, "Did Compliance ever raise any issues about him?"

"About Pleski? Not that I know. Should they? Has anything come up?"

From where he was perched, Barnstable could see her monitor, but the articles about the hit-and-run were gone. Catherine had hit a key to switch to the default—bond and equity tickers with a Bloomberg news crawl.

"Oh no," she said. "He's just a little . . . annoying sometimes."

"Well," said Barnstable, starting to stand—her sharp desk edge was pinching his thigh. "Aren't they all?"

GAME

It was desert all around but in this village by the Euphrates there was green, as there had been, more or less, for about five thousand years. And there was life. Small whitewashed houses. The rumbling of generators. Somewhere a bawling baby. An hour before dawn an ancient Volvo truck with a load of live chickens rumbled up and sputtered to a stop near a low-roofed house with decaying stucco walls. The driver got out to check his load of squawking fowl. A keen observer might have noticed that he was looking more at the house than at his chickens. The driver saw no such observer, and he saw nothing stirring in the house. So he turned to the chickens and told them, "Go!"

Seven other Navy SEALs emerged from beneath the birds and nodded to the driver, who stayed where he was to watch the surroundings as the seven moved to the house, front and back. A petty officer first class from Laramie, Wyoming, forced a door with his Ka-Bar and was first inside. He found a guard sleeping in a chair and killed him with the same knife, sticking it into the side of his throat, then pulling it forward through the carotid artery. Bloody but quiet and fast. Then he and three others moved into the main room, where two ISIS fighters were napping on cushions and one man was tapping at a device attached to a monitor. The man at the keyboard looked up, startled, and one of the men who was napping turned out not to be napping. With surprising speed, he pulled out a pistol and got two shots off, narrowly missing one of the SEALs, before he and the others were mowed down by four M4A1 carbines. No one was left alive but the Americans. The keyboard went clattering to the floor.

"Secure the computer," said the squad leader, a twenty-nine-year-old lieutenant from Minnesota. "We're here for the intel."

"Actually, sir," said the petty officer from Wyoming, who had moved to the screen and was looking it, "it's not a computer."

The lieutenant moved over to see it himself.

"It's a PlayStation 4," said the petty officer. "My little brother got one last Christmas." He gestured to the dead terrorist and then to the monitor. "It looks like this guy was playing *Murder City.*"

LAKE CITY

In the basement of the American mission, inside the SCIF, they were looking at the same game. Helen Sykes had a screenshot up on the display. It was a street scene from "Nova City," where the game's animated figures, almost lifelike but somehow eerily not, were going about the business of the game. Teenagers smoked joints in front of a bodega. A yuppie couple with a baby stroller hurried down the sidewalk. A gangster in a red Camaro was shooting at a police car.

"This was on a monitor," she said, "in the room where a Navy SEAL squad sent an Islamic State logistics officer to paradise."

The FBI man looked at the screen appraisingly. This was something he knew about. "That game's like a movie," he said. "Human images, sexy girls. Isn't that against their religion?"

"We don't think he was playing," said Sykes.

"It's a game," said the DS man.

Helen Sykes didn't reply. She just zoomed in past the teenagers, the yuppie family, and the gangster in the Camaro to the wall behind the police car. There was gang graffiti on the wall. "The player in *Murder City* can spray paint over graffiti," she said.

"Okay," said the DS man.

"If the game is hacked," she said, "the player can use the spray can to write his own messages on the wall."

Everyone looked hard at the screen. Rafe spoke first:

"So, if someone is online, in multi-player mode . . ."

"Yes," said Sykes. "Other players, wherever they are in the whole wide world, can read those messages."

The DS man shook his head. "A fucking computer game? Sending terrorist instructions?"

"Assume NSA is on it," said the FBI man.

"Hard to keep track of every kid in the world playing a first-person shooter," said Frank.

"I play that fucking game," said the FBI man.

"What fun," said Sykes.

"What's written on the wall?" asked Rafe. "What messages were posted?"

"I thought no one would ever ask." Sykes zoomed in tight on the wall, on the messy tags, and she read them out.

"The Latin Dukes want the Eighth Street Crew to fuck their mothers in the ass. Rodney 17 apparently just wants the world to see what a great artist he is. And Mister J," she said with emphasis, "wants Homeboy to go to Lake City and make a connection before Wednesday."

"Today's Wednesday," said the DS man.

"Well, now we're making progress," said Sykes.

"Do we know when that was posted?" asked Rafe.

Sykes shook her head. "It could have been a week ago. It could have been a month ago."

"Where's Lake City?" asked the DS man. "Is that a place in the game?"

"No," said the FBI man, who knew because he played the game.

"Lake City," Frank said. "In the past, in some communications intercepts, that's meant Geneva." Rafe looked at Frank. He had not known that. And this was not the first time Frank had known something he didn't. Frank had been assigned to work with Rafe when he arrived in Switzerland, but it had never been made exactly clear to Rafe where Frank had been assigned *from.*

"Yes," Sykes said. "Geneva has been called Lake City. That's why we're all gathered here looking at this. Us, here, in Geneva."

Ah. A moment of silent consideration. Then Rafe again: "So who is Homeboy and what is he connecting?"

"I think we should try to find out, don't you? How are things going on the Pleski front?"

"Progressing," said Rafe. "Slowly."

"Wonderful," said Helen Sykes. "Then maybe you can spare some time to help us look for Homeboy."

NEWS

In the offices of Sterling Wealth Management, Majid and his partner, Ron, were looking at a screen, too. It was a CNN newscast with a report about the bombing of an offshore oil pipeline in West Africa. There was video of flames at an oceanside oil storage facility. Oil workers had been killed along with nearby villagers swamped by a wave caused by the blast. "Local officials are investigating the cause of the explosion," the newscaster said. "They said it would cause major delays in the exploitation of newly discovered oil reserves."

"Which were being exploited," said Ron, "by Sahel Hydrocarbon?"

"Yes," said Majid.

"The company you shorted?" Ron didn't say this to Majid. He said it to Stavro, their new client, who was watching the newscast with them. Stavro looked bored.

"Yes," he replied, in the same tone he would have used if Ron had asked if he owned any socks. "What has this done to the company's share price?"

"Down twenty percent," said Majid. "And falling."

"So you'll buy shares to close out my position?"

"Yes," said Majid. "You shorted the stock just in time to benefit from this." He looked again at the screen. Flames burning steadily. Occasionally some bursting high into the sky, like fireworks.

Stavro shrugged. "These things happen. Especially in that part of the world. The safety protocols for an industrial facility there are not like those in Switzerland, or the US, or the UK." With a look at Ron, he added, "Some of your former colonies do not share your fastidious concern for risk avoidance."

"They weren't actually my colonies personally," said Ron.

"Born too late," said Stavro.

Majid changed the subject. "What shall we do with the proceeds?" he asked.

"Hold them in cash," said Stavro. "I'll have further instructions." And he left.

Ron turned to Majid. "Not much one for small talk, is he?"

"How much longer did you want to discuss the legacy of colonialism?"

Ron shrugged. "How much did his prescient investment make?"

"Two million and change."

"And he shorted the stock two days ago?"

"Yes," said Majid. "I told you when he did it. He said he had doubts about its fundamentals."

Ron pointed to the television screen. Flaming oil. Charred wreckage washing up on a beach. "That's pretty fucking fundamental," he said.

"It *is* a haphazard part of the world," said Majid.

"Sure," said Ron. "But two days, then fucking boom?"

"So . . . what? You think Mister Stavro, our client, did that?" Majid looked at the screen. "Made the investment, flew to Lagos, took a boat to wherever the fuck that is, carried dynamite in his suitcase . . ."

"I don't know," said Ron. "Maybe he has friends. Who is this guy? What do we know about him? Is his name even Stavro?"

"After 9/11," Majid said, "it came out that somebody had shorted airline stocks right before and made a fortune. The SEC investigated. The FBI investigated. Was it Osama bin Laden playing the market? No. Turned out it was an orthodontist from Omaha. Or something. Total coincidence. On any given day every stock in the world is being shorted by someone."

Ron looked out the office window. He could see Stavro walking away down the Quai des Bergues. A salesgirl standing in front of a cosmetics boutique offered him a sample of expensive soap. Stavro brushed by her.

"Does he look like an orthodontist from Omaha?" Ron said.

"I don't know," said Majid. "I've never been to Nebraska." And he turned back to look at the TV, where a shattered dugout canoe and the body of a woman, bloated and black, was washing up on a mangrove-choked shore.

THURSDAY

A driver in a stolen milk truck had run down pedestrians at an outdoor market in Rotterdam.

A small bomb had exploded by the track of the TGV running from Paris to Lyon.

Two American missionaries in Mali had been kidnapped.

It was Thursday and, inside the SCIF, Helen Sykes was running down a list of things that had happened on Wednesday. The day by which the deceased ISIS operative had commanded Homeboy to make a connection in Lake City.

"Are any of these connected to Geneva?" asked Frank.

"Not in any obvious way," said Sykes, and she continued:

Bomb threats had been called in to four synagogues in California.

An ISIS sympathizer had been arrested while making nail bombs in his garage in Schenectady, New York. Date and site of planned detonations unknown.

A confused teenager from Liverpool had been stopped at Heathrow trying to book a ticket to the Islamic State, to which no flights were scheduled.

"Lot of things happen on a Wednesday," observed the FBI man. "Any Wednesday. Welcome to the twenty-first century."

"ISIS wouldn't have known about that teenager ahead of time," said Rafe. "And it wouldn't matter if it did. Same with a lot of those things."

"I'm erring," Sykes said, "on the side of inclusivity. If you'd like to give me your definitive guidance on what a worldwide network of terrorists, with communication channels both known and unknown, knows and cares about ahead of time, I'd be happy to consider it."

The DS man smiled. He always liked to see Sykes and the Treasury preppie go at it. "Do any of those relate to a connection in Geneva?" he asked.

"Well," said Sykes, "that is the question. What do we have in Geneva?"

"Watches," said Rafe. "Chocolate. Money."

"We can probably rule out watches and chocolate," Sykes said.

The FBI man wasn't so sure. "Watches," he said. "Timers for explosives."

"You don't need a Patek Philippe," said Frank. "I like Timex."

You like Timex for *what*? Rafe wondered.

"There's one more event yesterday," Sykes said. "An oil pipeline blew up off the coast of Nigeria. Cause unknown."

"Long way from Geneva," said the DS man.

"Is it?" said Rafe.

"Pretty damn sure," said the DS man.

"In miles," Rafe said. "But money. Banks. The other thing we have in Geneva."

"What about it?" asked the DS man.

"Who owned that pipeline? Was it a public company?"

"What does that matter?"

"Because if it was public," Rafe said, "and someone knew it was going to blow up . . ."

Helen Sykes, knowing it too, finally answered one of the DS man's questions: "That someone could have made a very profitable investment."

DAX

One of the screens on the wall above Catherine's desk ran nothing but real-time quotes from the world's stock exchanges. If Catherine had looked up, she would have seen "SHLH 13.5 -22%" scroll by, and it would have meant nothing to her. She did not know that SHLH was the ticker symbol for Sahel Hydrocarbon, a company she'd never heard of, whose shares were currently tumbling. And, even if she had known that, it would not have mattered to her unless its shares were part of the German DAX index, which they weren't, because Sahel Hydrocarbon was not a blue chip German company. On reflection, though, if she had known about Sahel Hydrocarbon's decline, she might have considered it good news. Because the collapse of sketchy Third World stocks would customarily provoke a flight to safety, like to shares in the blue chip German companies that made up the DAX index. Which would make the DAX index rise, which was what Catherine had been counting on when she bought calls on the DAX while neglecting to simultaneously purchase offsetting puts, a countervailing trade that would have completed an arbitrage play that would have generated a solid but small gain or, worst case, an annoying but small loss. Small potatoes either way.

But Catherine had swung big.

She wasn't trying to cheat. She wasn't trying to swindle anyone. She was just trying to do well, to make money for the bank, which in turn would mean more bonus money for her. Her own needs were fairly basic. Her one-bedroom apartment, west of the *gare,* was, for Geneva, relatively inexpensive. She bought her own groceries and cooked her own meals. She did not have a car and did not want one. What she did want was to help her father. What she really wanted was to redeem him, but not even money could do that. He had served two years in prison because, trusting and inattentive, he had worked for a friend who was swindling everyone who walked into his office except the cleaning lady. The friend was rotting in a federal prison now and would be forever. Catherine's father was out of jail, but he was unemployed and unemployable. Her mother had left him and married a man who owned an outdoor equipment store in the Adirondacks. Catherine's father was living in a studio apartment in Flushing, Queens. The lake house in New Jersey where he had loved spending weekends, despite the occasional appearance of scavenging black bears, was long gone. The house had an expansive view of a pretty small lake, where every afternoon her father would canoe. Catherine's dream—to buy him another lake house, to see him paddling there during golden hour, to help him forget the ruin of his life. All that was required was money. And one step to achieving that was for the DAX to go up. Which it hadn't, and it was almost too late. Catherine could possibly postpone the reckoning by filing paperwork for offsetting trades that would settle in the future. Except they would never settle, because she had never actually made them.

"Catherine." It was Barnstable again, his damn smile again, walking her way again. She moved a stapler to the edge of her desk to discourage his sitting there. He probably wouldn't want to sit on a stapler. Worst case, she could pick it up and staple his ass.

He casually slid the stapler away and sat on her desk.

"Michael," she smiled. "How's it going?"

He glanced up at the screens. "Another day, another trillion dollars sloshing around. You grabbing any for us?"

"Doing my best," she said. And added, "I could be doing better." She swiveled her screen so he could see it. "Report from a minerals analyst in London. Scandium's trending up. Those mines in Central Asia . . ."

They really were a good investment, and a bargain because other investors were staying away.

"Catherine, we discussed those." Barnstable shook his head in sympathy. Verging almost on sorrow. He so hated denying her anything.

Actually, she thought, we haven't *fully* discussed them. I never got to the part where I told you I needed a big score to cover what I lost by not covering my bet on the DAX.

"It's a great opportunity," she said.

"I believe you. I do. And I personally don't give a shit if the dictator there shoots a few protesters now and then. Or tosses them in a dungeon. Or roasts them alive and eats them for dinner. But Compliance has become so chickenshit."

"We're traders. We're supposed to be allowed to trade."

"Up to a point. Corporate responsibility, blah, blah, blah." He shrugged and looked around at the other traders at the other desks. No one was paying any attention to him and Catherine. There was no money to be made by looking at them.

"Anyway," Barnstable said, "that's not what I came to talk to you about." She saw his eyes move down to the curve of her neck disappearing under her dress.

"The thing is, Catherine . . ." He paused, visualizing where that curve went. His wife was at a rehearsal for *Charley's Aunt* tonight. She was playing the aunt. "It's just . . . we still can't locate your offsetting DAX trade."

Catherine shrugged. "So it's an IT issue."

"If I take it to IT, paperwork gets generated. And that doesn't look good for the department. Or for you. The call doesn't expire until the thirtieth, so there's still time. You did make both trades, didn't you?"

"Of course. I'll track the other one down. I'm sure somebody just hit a wrong key."

"Right," he said. "Good girl." And smiled again.

Jesus, Catherine thought, what does this guy want from me?

She knew what he wanted.

Shit.

BISSE DU RO

Two days later, to his own surprise, Majid fell in love.

He was on a hike with Catherine, a weekend date they had made days before, and Catherine didn't want to break it. She was done with Rafe, again, for good, so there was no reason to break it, no reason she could think of.

The only change was the destination. Catherine had originally planned on taking Majid up the ridge of the Vuache, a ten-kilometer jaunt (if you stretched it) with a panoramic view of vineyards in the Rhône Valley and the ruined chateau of a Duke of Savoy. But that wasn't much more than a ramble, with a negligible five hundred-meter rise and fall and a pretty café in the village of Chaumont waiting at the end. Much too gentle for what the moment required. After Barnstable, and the DAX, and Rafe, Catherine wanted the satisfaction, and the distraction, of tackling something harder.

Majid didn't know where they were going, and he really didn't care, as long as it took his mind off bodies floating off the coast of Africa.

So, on Friday, after the markets closed, they took the train around the lake to Sierre and walked a few streets over to board a funicular that carried them out of the city and up three thousand feet, soaring over houses, then pastures, and then, the town shrinking below them, revealing the mountains beyond the mountains that huddled around the lake. They talked about the scenery, and Harvard, and the future of the yen. They ate dinner in an Italian restaurant that was half empty because it wasn't ski season and took a room in a hotel that looked like a low-end Las Vegas promoter's idea of a Swiss hotel. They had easy sex and both managed to fall asleep as if they had nothing to worry about.

In the morning, brisk but bright, they set out to hike the Bisse du Ro. Catherine knew what it was, but for Majid it was the day's first surprise. The path started in, of all places, a parking lot at the edge of the village, then meandered gently through trees and backyards, until, a mile or so in, they were upon it. Majid stopped.

"Is there a problem?" said Catherine.

Majid was looking ahead at the trail, if it could even be called a trail. It was a narrow ledge on the side of a cliff, with a vertical rock face above and below. Originally, it had been a channel carved into the mountain face by local farmers to capture snow melt and divert it to their fields. Where the natural ledge had been narrow or nonexistent, they had used rough timber to cantilever a trough out over the edge, with a vertical rock face above and nothing below. Now, with some modest reconstruction, it was a tourist attraction for tourists who didn't mind hiking a trail that was at most four feet wide, sometimes with a guardrail on the downhill side and sometimes without one, sometimes only a rope slugged into the cliffside wall to hold on to.

The valley straight below was lush and green and gleaming in the sun. And it was very far below.

"Is it all like this?" said Majid.

He was standing by a plaque mounted into the sheer cliff wall. It was dedicated to a local man who had died on the trail or, rather, off the trail, falling from it to his death. The plaque said, *Il a aimé les montagnes, et maintenant la montagne l'a pour toujours.*" He loved the mountains, and now the mountain has him forever.

"Is it all like what?" said Catherine. She had no concern about the trail. Even at its narrowest, it was wider than a diving board.

The section directly in front of them was actually one of the more reassuring, with wooden planking over the dirt and guard rails on both sides and, on the downhill side, not a straight drop but a steep slope where trees took root at crazy angles.

Majid nodded toward the plaque, moving only his head. He was trying to move his body as little as possible. "It says here that someone fell off and died."

"Think of it as a sidewalk," said Catherine. "When you walk down a sidewalk, you don't have trouble staying on it, do you? You just walk straight ahead without thinking. I doubt you've ever suddenly veered and fallen off a sidewalk."

Well, that was true, Majid granted, and this path was (mostly) as wide as a sidewalk. But his roots were in a desert country where things were flat, where if you did fall off a sidewalk you might sprain an ankle (or, more likely, get pulverized by a speeding Range Rover), not tumble down a kilometer through brush and rock.

Catherine was moving ahead, showing him how easy it was. As she ducked below a rock overhang, the cliff intruding on the trail from above, she called back to him, "You haven't, have you? Fallen off a sidewalk?"

"Not that I can recall," he said. If he wanted to keep talking to her, to stay in earshot, he had to follow. The key, clearly, was not to think about the drop. Put one foot in front of the other. He ducked under the rock overhang (did they have to make it *harder* with bonus obstacles?) and fell in line behind Catherine. And decided his best tactic was to keep looking straight ahead, like steering a motorcycle, where you don't turn the handlebars or consciously lean, you only look where you want to go. Looking straight ahead meant looking at Catherine, and the way she moved, and her pants tight on her body, and her climbing boots oddly sexy on her narrow feet.

She was far from the first Western girl he had had. The first had been a Moldovan prostitute in the old port area back home. In a state where engaged Western couples had been jailed for kissing on the beach, there were places in the unchic old city, nestled between discount clothing stores and auto repair shops, where prostitution was tolerated. Majid had been brought there by two older friends and was so terrified he might be spotted by someone who knew his parents that the event was a fiasco. In Cambridge things had been different. His parents weren't around. He went with the flow.

Catherine paused before a section of the trail that had no handrail on the downhill side. As feeble consolation, there were bushes there, just below the level of the trail, that might, just possibly, catch a falling body (or maybe just slow it for a moment before it broke loose and bounced down to the valley). "Are you okay?" she said. "Or do you want to turn back?"

She waited for his response, seemingly nonjudgmental. If what he said next was going to put him in one category or another, she didn't show it.

Majid cautiously turned his head and glanced over the edge. He imagined the plaque, *Majid liked the mountains, sort of, and now the mountain has his bones in a gully somewhere.*

Catherine looked back at him, her eyes bright green in the sunlight. Her pale skin. Her confidence on this ridiculous cliff. She was nothing like the girls back home. None of them would ever *lead* him. Was he weak to want to follow this one? To be with this one?

Is this what love feels like?

He moved forward along the narrow path.

SHORT REPORT

Rafe's research had commenced. The company that owned the pipeline, Sahel Hydrocarbon, *was* public. Its shares traded in London, and short positions had been taken in its stock before the pipeline exploded. Rafe got that from the short position report published by the British Financial Conduct Authority, which maintains a "public notification regime" for the benefit of all investors, in this case for investors who want to know which companies are thought by others to be on the brink of going down.

"Well, that is bloody cricket of them, don't you think?" said Frank.

"I'm not sure 'bloody cricket' is the phrase," Rafe said. He and Frank were hunched over computers in the cubbyhole office the US mission had deigned to assign to two agents whose mission they did not completely understand.

"Whatever," said Frank. "You think our pal Homeboy was one of the short sellers?"

Rafe took another look at the report. "It's hard to say. A whole bunch of traders took short positions. I guess Africa going down is considered a good bet."

"I'd take it," said Frank. "You ever been there?"

"Once. Photo safari. Tanzania."

"Nice," said Frank. "They carry you in a sedan chair? Give you a pith helmet?" Frank was there to assist Rafe, do legwork, knock on doors, show him around. He knew Geneva. He usually didn't have much to say.

"No," said Rafe. "Toyota jeep. Baseball cap."

"Ah," said Frank. "But one of those deluxe safaris, where the tents have air conditioning and flush toilets?"

Actually, Rafe's tent did have all that and a hot water shower and wireless internet, too. He had taken his parents on the safari after he started making big money at Klamath. He didn't think Frank needed to know any of this.

"We slept okay," he said. "Have you been to Africa?"

"Couple of times. Food sucks. These traders who shorted, any of them named Homeboy? Any of them in Geneva?" Frank did not specialize in transitions.

"The clients' names aren't listed," Rafe said. "Just the companies that executed the trades."

"Any of those *companies* in Geneva?"

Rafe scanned the list—JP Morgan Asset Management, BNBP Paribas, Bridgestone Volatility Partners, Banque Carouge, a dozen more.

"Maybe. I'll have to look them up. Even some that aren't based here have offices here."

"Place to start," said Frank.

Rafe scanned the list of short sales again. "Nobody went big. There's just a bunch of small bets."

"So nothing big enough to make it worth getting out of bed and going down to Africa to rig up an explosion?"

"Nothing's leaping out," Rafe said. The biggest short position amounted to less than one percent of the company's shares.

"So," Frank said, "Homeboy, whoever he is, could have been on a completely different mission having nothing to do with the stock market, and that pipeline explosion could have been caused by some idiot African smoking ganja next to an oil well. Did you see that kind of thing on your safari?"

"No," said Rafe.

"Or Homeboy could just be some kid in his parents' basement in Cleveland playing a computer game with the guy who got iced by the SEALs."

"Yeah," Rafe said. "Or he could be part of a terrorist network making money while it blows up the world."

"Could be?" Frank repeated.

"Yeah," said Rafe. "So we probably ought to check it out."

PART TWO

BIG BANG

His boyhood dream was to be a doctor, but history took care of that. After Assad's bombs killed his parents and ISIS killed his brother, he made his way to France, where he shared an apartment with five other refugees in a cinder block building on the outskirts of Neydens. Neydens is in France, but it is three kilometers from the Swiss border, just fourteen kilometers from Geneva, and Switzerland, like France, is in the Schengen Area, so there are no border immigration checks. And there is a bus.

There was a bus stop near CERN, the sprawling nuclear research complex that brought scientists from all over the world to Geneva. He had read about CERN's Large Hadron Collider when he was still in Syria. As a child, he'd been a budding science nerd, and he read a lot of popular science websites, and those sites were filled with hyped-up dire predictions that when CERN finally launched its gigantic new machine, the Large Hadron Collider, which would smash elementary particles into one another at nearly the speed of light, the resulting collisions might create a black hole that would swallow the earth.

Some days in Syria that didn't seem like such a bad idea. Like the day the men showed up at his family's apartment. Their uniforms were haphazardly matched, and they spoke Arabic in the accents of Saudi Arabia and he didn't know where else. But they had guns and they made their meaning clear—where was his brother? They had seen the antenna of the radio that was his, not his brother's, that he had extended out the window to pick up broadcasts from Lebanon and even occasionally, Allah forgive him, Israel.

The men didn't know that; they just knew that radios brought in infidel news and music, both of which were forbidden, and were very conceivably the apparatus of a spy. They assumed the radio belonged to his brother, because he was only twelve and looked younger. He didn't tell them that he liked the radio, not his brother, who preferred to read. He didn't tell them anything, because his mouth didn't work. He was frozen by fear, listening to their accents and staring at their guns. His only coherent, if not relevant, thought was that the guns were machines; he could see their working metal parts. People didn't usually think of them that way.

When they found his brother hiding in the toilet, his brother didn't say anything either, didn't say the radio didn't belong to him, didn't say that it belonged to the scared little kid standing right there, not even when they dragged his brother outside. The shots that killed him came moments later.

When the Large Hadron Collider was finally launched, it did not create a black hole, and the world was not destroyed.

This was explained when he took the official CERN tour on his first visit there. The guide, a retired British physicist wearing baggy cargo shorts that circumnavigated his pot belly, said that even if the collider did create black holes, which it didn't, they would be so tiny that their gravitational force would be negligible and they would rapidly swallow themselves up with no harm done.

He had to wonder if that was true or just propaganda put out to squelch opposition to CERN. On the other hand, he had to grant that he and the rest of the tour group were standing here in a bland white hallway, not squeezed into nothingness inside a tiny black hole. So there was that.

The tour group consisted of himself, two German families, and a French elementary school class. While the guide talked, they were looking through a glass wall at a room full of scientists looking at computers. The computers were recording the results of those non-black-hole-producing collisions—protons accelerated in opposite directions through a buried twenty-seven-kilometer loop that bridged the border between Switzerland and France (like he did!) until they crashed together at a smidgen less than the speed of light. "Only two and a half meters per second slower," said their guide. Which was pretty astounding. What was 186,000 miles a second minus two and a half meters?

Watching the results of those collisions on computer screens looked pretty boring, though. And watching people watch the results on computer screens was even more so. He thought it would be more interesting to see the collider itself up close, but it was accessible only to staff, who entered via air locks after passing retinal recognition scans (the guide said), and the radiation down there could be fatal if you didn't know what you were doing.

When he returned to CERN after that, it was always to "The Universe of Particles," an exhibit in another building that tried to get tourists interested in the big questions of physics in a world where science was losing favor. Images of the Big Bang (as if anyone could know what that looked like) were projected on the curved walls of a large darkened room, while a disembodied voice on speakers pronounced: "Our universe, what is it made of? Where did it start? What is its destiny?" He thought those were certainly valid questions. They were among the issues he had pondered when he read his favorite popular science websites before his own smaller universe collapsed. But now, by necessity, he was more interested in the darkness of "The Universe of Particles" than its potted science. On his very first visit, he had spotted some likely prospects in the waiting area outside—a group of Korean tourists busy with not only the usual cameras and selfie sticks but also a small selfie drone that followed them, its propellers keeping it hovering just over their heads, snapping photos of their adventures in Geneva. How did that work? he wondered. Did it hone in on a signal broadcast by a device one of the Koreans carried? Did it recognize their voices? Their faces? Their smell?

Whichever, the drone came to heel and was inserted into a custom carrying case as the group entered the exhibit.

He followed them inside and paused near the entrance. Now was when he needed his courage. The courage he had not had when the ISIS men came for his brother, or when he was smuggled across borders, when he cried, crouching helplessly, in a small boat pitching across the Aegean. But that was before. Now, he thought, he could do this. Because of the cat.

One of his roommates had adopted a stray cat, orange with spooky yellow eyes, three months ago. He had protested, because of what he had read on his science websites. He knew about toxoplasmosis. He knew about the parasite. But his roommates laughed at him, and the cat stayed. Now, he was certain, the parasite was inside him. And, for that, he thanked Allah.

Inside the darkened room, the voice from nowhere was asking its questions about the nature of the universe.

The Koreans, with their camera drone in its case, were reduced to snapping photos the old-fashioned way, with their fingers. This kept them very busy.

In less than a minute, he had two Korean wallets, one from a back pocket, one from a Hello Kitty bag, and he was on his way to the exit.

HELEN SYKES

Ambassadors never like the spooks in their embassies. They impose extra security protocols that mean doors the ambassadors can't walk through or rooms they can't enter—in their own embassies!—without time-wasting rigmarole. They assume positions—consular officer, deputy cultural attaché—that are nominally under the ambassadors' control but are not, which mean the ambassadors' actual complements are perennially shorthanded. Worst of all, they are involved with all kinds of spook stuff with local officials that the ambassadors aren't privy to, so an ambassador can be having a civilized luncheon with a local government official to discuss some issue of trade or politics while completely unaware that, hours before, that same official has been bribed, threatened, or blackmailed ("you don't want your wife to see these pictures, do you?") by a CIA officer, so he might be too scared, confused, angry, or flushed with excitement to have a useful conversation about soybean exports or the chances in the next election of the local social democrats.

The CIA chiefs of station aren't too thrilled with ambassadors, either, considering many of them to be overfed, half-wit millionaires who got their appointments by picking the winning side to donate to in the last presidential election. Those rarely speak the local language (the ambassadors to Britain do, barely); they know nothing of local politics, history, or customs; they have wives (in most cases) whose prime concern is still decor and the menu for the next embassy reception; and they all have the illusion that because they are the ambassador they ought to have some idea of what is going on in their own embassies, so they have to be half-briefed with harmless material at regular intervals.

For Helen Sykes, the situation in Geneva was made worse by the fact that the mission there housed not one but four ambassadors. There was the ambassador to the United Nations-Geneva, the ambassador to the World Trade Organization, the ambassador to the Conference on Disarmament, and the ambassador to the United Nations Human Rights Council. This multitude of ambassadors meant annual disputes over whom should be listed first on invitations to the mission's Fourth of July reception, and, for Sykes, three or four times as much time and effort wasted in useless interactions.

She was having more interactions with them lately than she was with her husband, another CIA veteran currently working in Peru. She sometimes wondered if, when they retired, they would even recognize each other. On the bright side, their daughter was doing great as a computer science major at Howard. (Until she was fourteen, she'd thought both her parents worked for a farm equipment manufacturer with a lot of foreign clients.)

In any case, Sykes had been in no great mood for additional non-CIA people in her life when Rafael Sassaman arrived from Washington, fresh off his recruitment and minimal training as an officer (undercover, no less!) of the Treasury Department's Office of Terrorism and Financial Intelligence. He was presentable in a preppy-meets-Wall Street kind of way and was apparently intelligent. His only flaw was that he didn't know anything. About intelligence, anyway. So Langley had told her to liaise with him, and by "liaise" they meant "make sure he doesn't do anything so stupid that it blows back on us." She had passed the assignment on to Frank Lopez, who had gone from St. Louis to the US Army and then the CIA, where he was now a case officer. He had protested that he had better things to do than babysit some rich kid playing spy. "So do I," said Sykes, and she made it an order.

When the Homeboy situation arose, it did seem reasonable (barely) to put part of it in the hands of Rafael ("call me Rafe") Sassaman because of the possible connection to financial machinations, a field in which he was experienced and which had made him prosperous enough to retire from Wall Street and dabble, an altruistic hobbyist, in government work at a GS-15 pay grade. Also in his favor: he had no doubt pulled off many machinations of his own during his career in finance, some of them at least semi-criminal, making him the proverbial one it takes to know one.

When he came to her office to tell her that the short selling investigation was at best a long shot, that there was no sign of a short bet large enough to massively profit from, and thus motivate, the Sahel Hydrocarbon explosion, she had probed, because it still seemed plausible to her, and he, after all, knew nothing. But he walked her through the paperwork he'd gotten from the Brits and, if there was a smoking short sale there, she didn't see it either. If there was truly nothing there, it was fine with her if Rafe went back to what he had been doing. She had no objection to fighting mafias and money laundering—she supposed somebody had to do it, and that somebody might as well be this guy—but she was personally more concerned with fighting homicidal terrorism. If Islamist extremism existed in Switzerland, where minarets had been banned in a national referendum, it was deep underground, but there were refugees scattered about who were worth debriefing. And Geneva was rich ground to trawl for other vulnerable sources, as the flip side of the US mission's annoying surplus of ambassadors was a surplus of diplomats from everywhere else. Sykes couldn't explain why, but Arab delegates to the Human Rights Council seemed especially prone to indulge in the kinds of behaviors they would not want their home governments, or homes, to know about.

"I can follow up anyway," Rafe said, concluding his report. "Talk to any of the firms that executed the trades who have offices in Geneva."

"Do it," she said, "and keep me posted."

Rafe nodded and left. Helen Sykes waited till he was gone, then picked up her phone and dialed a number.

"I got his report," she said. "Is there anything else I need to know?"

"I don't think so," said Frank. "But I'll keep you posted."

ALBANIA

The man calling himself Stavro had checked into the Hotel Bristol to wait for further instructions, and he should have had some by now. His original investment, plus the profit he'd made on Sahel Hydrocarbon, was safely sitting in the care of Sterling Wealth Management. He assumed it had not been a coincidence that Sterling's principal was a Muslim, but no one had told him anything about that, and, since receiving the directive about short selling Sahel, he'd had no further instructions at all. When he logged into the computer game, he saw no new messages addressed to Homeboy, only gyrating scantily-dressed female figures and cartoon morons firing guns. That Westerners spent literally millions of hours playing this "game" he found pathetic.

Not that he objected to scantily-dressed females or guns. He served an Islamic cause, but in his own way, on his own terms. He had been just a teenager in Tirana when word came of the civil war in Bosnia and the slaughter of Muslims there. While Albanians, Muslims themselves, had sympathy for the victims, most were too busy mourning their own financial calamity to do much about it. In the aftermath of the collapse of its weird and iconoclastic Communist regime, an investment mania had seized a country with no living memory of capitalism. Companies popped up offering investors returns of 10 percent a month, which seemed credible to the Albanians, who quite reasonably assumed that this was standard operating procedure for the marvelous Western system they'd been deprived of for so long. They were isolated and poor, but pictures and videos had seeped in from the outside world; across the border, Mercedes were apparently as common as goats. When Stavro's father saw that his idiot brother-in-law was reliably receiving 10 percent a month on an investment he'd made in a "diversified real estate and manufacturing company," he mortgaged their house and his butcher tools to buy into the same enterprise. What he didn't realize was that his investment was promptly paid out, pyramid-scheme style, to his brother-in-law, who was higher in the structure than he was. The pyramid collapsed soon after, burying Stavro's entire family.

Stavro went to work for the only part of the failed enterprise that had ever actually made a profit, the part that smuggled goods into splintering Yugoslavia, which had been embargoed by the United Nations because of the Yugoslav Serbs' role in oppressing and killing Bosnian Muslims. Well, people had to eat. Stavro's ruined parents needed his help. If that meant running gasoline and arms to Serbs who were killing Muslims, at least he had the satisfaction of knowing that the Serbs were being overcharged.

So Stavro learned a trade, and he made connections.

Eventually he pivoted to smuggling supplies to his co-religionists (when they had the money to pay). His name was passed around, and when Bosnian Muslims went to fight in Chechnya and, later, some joined the Islamic State, his name went with them as a man who was reliable, could cross borders, could function in the West, and was from a country that was only a semi-red flag in the computer systems of the infidels. Stavro thought ISIS was both extreme and counterproductive, although the individuals he eventually met in their finance section struck him as competent and non-fanatical, actually fairly ordinary. They might have been accountants for a state oil company whose careers had taken an unlikely turn, some kind of mix-up on LinkedIn.

And they had money from oil, from kidnap ransoms, from selling looted antiquities, from robbing banks, and from milking the unfortunate blessed residents of their caliphate, who paid taxes on property and income and everything else. ISIS cops collected fines for speeding and driving with broken taillights. It all went into the coffers.

But what to do with the money? They may have been insane, but they weren't stupid, so they wanted to invest. Do what the Westerners did, make money with money. And Stavro was happy to help.

For his standard 5 percent.

Now, since the computer game had gone silent, he was waiting. That was the backup plan—wait. He took day trips on lake boats; he found cruising relaxing. In a restaurant in the trendy Carouge neighborhood, he sat by himself and tried their special dish—shrimp in white chocolate curry sauce. They certainly hadn't had that in Albania. Which, he concluded, was no great loss. On a walk one day, he passed the Islamic Center of Geneva, a simple white house with green painted trim (and, this being Switzerland, no minaret). He didn't go in. Nor did he notice the old Peugeot with the darkened windows parked across the street.

MOHAMMED

"Is this the best car you have? Don't you have a better car?" said the man in the passenger seat. "You think this is a disguise? This is not a good disguise. Such a car stands out in Geneva. You should have a Lexus at least."

"Shut up," said Frank, leaning forward against the steering wheel. "What time is this mullah supposed to get here?"

"Soon. The class he teaches starts in twenty minutes."

Across the street, a few men filtered into the Islamic center. Immigrant workers and cleaners. Students from the university. Low-level staffers at the Arab diplomatic missions. No mullah.

"Tell me," said Frank, "does the term *Lake City* mean anything to you?"

The man shrugged. "This is a city. It has a lake."

"Did anything special happen around here on Wednesday?"

The man thought. "I ate barbecue chicken. Very good."

The informant was in his thirties and stocky and usually hungry, and his name was Mohammed. Of course. Frank had read somewhere that the five most common first names of cab drivers in New York City were Mohammed spelled five different ways.

"Tell me about the mullah," Frank said. "What does he teach?"

"The Principles of Fiqh."

"Fick?"

"Feck."

"Which is?"

"Islamic law."

"And you've been in the class?"

"No. I only heard. He is talking about jihad."

"And people are liking it?"

"Yes, of course. Do you want me to go?"

A taxi pulled up across the street, and a pudgy middle-aged man with an untrimmed beard got out. Frank could see stains on his cream-colored thobe.

"That's him," said Mohammed.

Frank picked up his phone and snapped a few pictures as the man took a quick look around, then walked into the center. "He's from Saudi," Mohammed said in an unusual (for him) respectful tone.

"What's his name?"

"Shaykh Mohammed al-Yamani."

"Doesn't that mean he's from Yemen?"

"He's from Saudi now," said Mohammed. "Do you want me to go in or not?"

"Yeah," said Frank. "And wear this."

He handed over a watch. Stainless steel. Nothing fancy.

"Don't try to adjust it," Frank said. "It's voice-activated."

Mohammed held it in his hand and inspected it, looking dubious.

"What if they look at it?"

"Then they'll know what time it is. It's not against your religion to wear a watch, is it?"

Mohammed strapped it on.

"There you go then," said Frank. "Looking sharp."

Mohammed didn't move.

"Right," said Frank. He reached in his pocket and pulled out a hundred-euro note and handed it to Mohammed, who took it without another word and went.

HELP

There was, as usual, no splash.

"Nine point five," Rafe said.

Catherine saw him as she climbed out of the pool. It was seven in the morning. He was dressed for work, in suit and tie.

"What are you doing here?" she said.

"You're not returning my calls. You're not answering my texts."

"I didn't like your business proposition."

"Then it's withdrawn."

"Good." She wrapped a towel around her shoulders and started to walk toward the locker room.

"I just need your help with something."

She turned back toward him. "My help? Really?"

"Have I ever lied to you?"

Actually, she realized, he hadn't. His suit was blue, summer weight wool. She was conscious of the contrast between his business attire and her thin covering of spandex. So much on him, so little on her, so much to undo on him, so little would be required to expose her. She was pretty sure some pornographic films started this way.

"What kind of help?" she said.

"If you were shorting a stock, lightly traded, London exchange, where would you go to borrow the shares here in Geneva?"

"Excuse me?"

"If you were shorting a stock—"

"I heard you. Why are you asking me? You know this. It's your business, right?"

Good point, he thought. He'd half convinced himself that this was why he'd come to see her. Was there *any* truth to it? Well, some, maybe.

"I'm new here. You know the local firms. Where would I go? Where would you go?"

"Oh, I don't know. To a bank? A brokerage house? Probably not one of the chocolate shops."

"I'm serious."

"No, you're not. Rafe, what we did . . ."She paused. How to finish the sentence? ". . .we did."

"Yes," he said. "We did. What we did."

Jesus, this was turning into a Beckett play. Or was it Ionescu?

"And I'm still open," he said.

"And I'm not. So please stop ambushing me with . . . stories. First about Pleski, now this."

"Right," he said, shifting gears. "Mister Pleski. Did he express any interest in my proposition?" He *did* have a job to do. And *she'd* brought it up.

"For God's sake, Rafe." She looked at the clock on the wall. It was time to shower and dress, to get to the bank. "No. I don't know. It's not going to happen."

"Okay. Fine. But you shouldn't be in business with him."

"*I* shouldn't? But *you* should?"

"He was in that deal with you, wasn't he? The Kemper Media sale. Where the kid who was holding it up got murdered in a hit-and-run."

He had to bring that up. She had read the articles. They hadn't used the word.

"Murdered? It was an auto accident. In New York. Mister Pleski was in Geneva. I saw him that day."

"So he has . . . associates. It was Pleski you called about the kid's death when we had lunch, wasn't it? When you told him, was he devastated? Did he burst into tears? I didn't hear any sobs coming through the line."

"Do you even hear what you're saying?"

"Do you?" Rafe looked so serious. Catherine wasn't used to seeing him like this. She wrapped her towel around her waist. "So Mister Pleski is a murderer, and you want him as a client?"

"I'm a startup, I can't be picky. And I'd be taking a potential liability off your hands, someone who could hurt your reputation."

"So . . . what you're saying . . . taking a homicidal client into your unethical hedge fund . . . you'd be doing that for me?"

"Well," he smiled, charming Rafe again. "I like you."

"And other men just send flowers."

She opened the door to the locker room. He took a step toward her. "You can't come in."

"Nothing I haven't seen before."

"Nothing you're ever going to see again."

REFUGEE

Stavro still had no instructions. In the evenings he took to strolling up the Rue du Rhône, pausing by the shops. The glittering multi-colored diamond necklaces in the windows at Graff caught his eye, as did the two men in dark suits with wired earpieces who stood outside the shop's door in conversation. Too chatty. Sloppy. Stavro thought they could be taken.

He lingered at the watch displays at Hublot and Richard Mille, designs that leaned heavily on displaying their innards, the gears and switches that made them work. He was thinking of buying one. It would be a nice way to remember Geneva. But for how much? Twenty thousand barely got you a band. He was considering his options as he turned into the Place du Molard one night. Passing the sixteenth-century stone tower at its entrance, he felt a tap on his shoulder. He turned quickly, automatically taking a step back.

"Excuse me. Would you mind taking a photograph?" It was a man about forty in a Savile Row suit. Average height, not tall but solid, with a neat goatee. He might have been Iranian or Armenian, or Arab. He was holding out an iPhone.

"Here," he said. "Of me, in front of the sculpture." He pointed to a large granite bas-relief set into the wall of the tower. It was headed GENEVE CITE DE REFUGE and depicted an angelic Genevan spreading sheltering arms over a poor reclining refugee.

Stavro did not see any reason not to do this. "Very well," he said, and he took the phone.

"A city of refuge?" The man smiled and pointed to the sign as Stavro lined up the shot. "How many refugees do you see hereabouts?" Stavro glanced around the square. If there were refugees from anywhere there, it was from the better districts of London or the east side of Manhattan.

"Things have changed," the man said. "Do you see whom the beautiful Genevan is sheltering?"

Stavro took a close look at the sculpture, which he had walked by a hundred times before. He was rarely surprised by anything, but now he was. The image was unmistakable. There, life-size, in stone, the pathetic refugee being protected by angelic wings, was Vladimir Lenin.

"He came here after being released from Siberia," said the man with the goatee. "He sat in coffee shops in the old city plotting the Russian revolution. What do you think the Swiss would do to him now?"

"Probably not build him a statue," Stavro said, and he snapped the picture.

"And yet," said the man, "here we are." He took back his phone and deleted the photo.

And said, "I have a message for you."

HOKEY-POKEY

Rafe was looking at a list of Swiss banks with trading desks when he glanced up and saw Sykes standing just inside the door to the cramped two-desk office. He hadn't heard her come in. Maybe they trained you to walk on little cat feet when you joined the CIA.

She looked past him to Frank, who, as far as Rafe could tell, had been sitting at his desk staring at a blank computer screen.

"We had the recording transcribed and translated," she said. "From your man who infiltrated the mullah's class on fick."

Rafe perked up. So this is what Frank did when he wasn't busting Rafe's balls.

"He said it's pronounced feck," Frank said. "Actually, sort of between fook and fuck."

"I'll keep that in mind if I decide to enroll. What exactly did your man say the class was supposed to be about?"

"Islamic law. But he said the guy had been talking about jihad."

"The guy being Shaykh Mohammed al-Yamani?"

Frank nodded.

"Who is, by the way, hard to check out," Sykes said. "His name is basically the equivalent of John Smith from Anytown."

"Probably not a coincidence," Frank said. "Did he talk about jihad?"

"No. But he did mention which hand to use to wipe your ass."

"Excuse me?"

"Islamic law," she said. "There are laws about going to the bathroom. Like how to wipe. It's recommended to use a rock."

"To wipe? A rock?"

Sykes nodded. "And when you walk into the toilet, you're supposed to go in with your left foot first. Going out, you use your right foot first."

"Like the hokey-pokey," Rafe said, breaking in. He couldn't help himself. It did sound like the hokey-pokey.

Sykes turned to him with a look that made him hope she wasn't armed.

"Maybe that was just the public session," Frank said.

Sykes turned back to Frank.

"Of the class," he said. "Just a bunch of bullshit. My guy said there was a private session afterward. He wasn't invited."

"Can he get invited?"

"He said he could."

"Do it," she said. Then, turning to leave, she looked at Rafe again. "Isn't there something you're supposed to be doing?"

Without waiting for an answer, she was gone.

"Well," Frank said, "she really told you."

CHEESE

Majid hadn't told Catherine he loved her, of course. To do so seemed too blatant, too forward (and, yes, too unlikely to get a reciprocal declaration). And, as he analyzed them (as he was prone to do), he began to doubt his own feelings. But there were feelings. He thought of Catherine when he wasn't with her. He thought about what she might be doing on nights they were apart. And he remembered the Harvard Club reception, where she had seemed so casual about running into Rafe. Perhaps too casual? Was he jealous? This was all new to him. He had never been jealous before.

The nights he spent with her now were, for him, no longer simple pleasures, mild diversions, unadorned expressions of the animal nature that God, if there was a God, had left implanted in his human creations even as they evolved into private bankers and wealth managers. He wanted to please her more than before, and he was more pleased himself, not just by the sex but even without it, just being there. He and Catherine had never talked about an "us," of course, and even though he had consistently been surprised, during a decade in the West, by how openly Americans talked about their emotions, Catherine was an exception. In that she would have made a fine Arab. He had a fantasy of his mother meeting with her mother to arrange a match. Except Catherine wasn't from an acceptable tribe, so that would have been tricky. And she never talked about her mother anyway. Another area that remained off limits.

Meanwhile, he had business to attend to, clients to service, returns to seek. The Italian fiasco had receded only slightly. He identified a winning pharmaceutical stock and successfully rode a tide of Chinese currency devaluations by some strategic swaps of yuan for dollars. Ron's family had connections in British banking and passed on, almost legally, advance word of a major merger, and Majid acted. Sterling Wealth Management was moving in the right direction. There were reasons to be optimistic.

Then Stavro came back.

"Another short?" said Ron. When he saw Stavro appear in the reception area, he had followed him into Majid's office and listened while Stavro placed his new order.

"We did rather well with the last one," Stavro said. He leaned back in an upholstered chair against the wall, under a framed beauty shot of the Matterhorn. "So why not?"

"Your money is growing nicely in our general fund," Majid said. He mentioned the pharmaceutical stock, the Chinese currency coup, the profit made on the merger. "Perhaps we should just stay the course."

"Besides," Ron said, "you can't count on another catastrophic explosion, can you? I mean, what are the odds of something like that happening again?"

Stavro looked at Ron coolly. "One never knows, does one? Fate is out of our hands. I mean, a meteorite might come out of nowhere and strike this office at any moment. Which would be a shame." He looked around at the Persian rug, the comfortable furniture, the art on the walls, at Ron. "This place is so pleasant."

For an insane moment, Majid sensed that Stavro had just threatened to bring down a meteorite on their heads if they didn't do what he asked.

"What company do you want to short?" he said.

"Bouvier Lait, the French dairy."

Majid hit a few keys on his computer. "It's big," he said. "Milk, cheese, yogurt. Number three in France, subsidiaries in Belgium and Spain."

Stavro shrugged. "But who drinks milk anymore?"

"Babies?" said Ron.

Majid carried on. "Stock up eight percent this year on projected earnings of a billion euros. Trailing P/E of nine, forward P/E eleven. It looks pretty strong. I can do more research."

"No need," said Stavro. "I think it's ready for a downturn."

"Lots of people eat cheese," said Ron. "I eat cheese."

Majid pretended Ron hadn't spoken, as if Ron was his own imaginary friend. "It would be a speculative move," Majid said.

"It's my money," said Stavro. "So it's my move. I didn't come here to argue with you. With either of you." This with a sharp glance at Ron, who apparently wasn't imaginary after all. "I do believe you work for me."

"How many shares do you want to short?" asked Majid.

"As many as you can borrow."

"That would be a big bet."

"And one I want to make. Do it by the end of the week. As before, I want total discretion, total anonymity. Is that understood?"

Majid nodded. Stavro said, "Good." And he left.

"Still not one for small talk, is he?" Ron said.

"Did you expect him to engage in a conversation about your cheese eating? Ask your preference? Gruyère? Camembert?"

"I don't like it," said Ron. "That last trade that worked out so well? Tell it to the pipeline workers who got blown up."

"You're expecting another disaster?"

"The question is, is *he*?" Ron moved to the window. "His trades are fucking weird."

"So, what, you think he's going to sabotage a gigantic milk company? How exactly? Murder every cow in France?"

"I don't know." Ron looked down at the street. Stavro was nowhere in sight. "Maybe they'll be struck by meteorites."

Majid was quiet for a moment. He was pretty sure meteorites didn't really come out of nowhere.

"We're building up our capital," he said. "We'll do this one, then we'll cut him loose."

KARL

The banker's name was Karl, and he didn't like being a banker. He had wanted to be an architect, but the best Swiss universities had not cared what he wanted. He failed to gain admission to Zurich or Lausanne. He'd considered going to Lugano, even though that would have meant studying in Italian. But his fiancée, now his wife, had urged him to take the position her father offered him in his bank. It had turned out that he was pretty good at banking or, at least, good enough at banking at a bank where his father-in-law was chairman. Now, twenty years later, he was a senior executive whose responsibilities included the bank's trading division. He still regretted not pursuing architecture—there were paths to it he had not explored, he had given up too soon. He had long since started regretting his marriage, too. But life had accumulated—children, assets, a house, a ski chalet. Dumping everything at forty-two to apply to architecture school with a bunch of twenty-year-olds was simply, clearly, not something he could do.

He could, however, tell this American to piss off.

The man had shown up uninvited at the bank this morning and flashed a credential from Washington. Sassafras, Sassaman . . . an unusual name. He had known the bank's trading desk made a minor specialty of equities with interests in developing countries. That was something Karl had proposed to his father-in-law a decade ago. It was a way for the bank to set itself apart from others, and a way for Karl to justify trips to Southeast Asia and Africa. He liked the warm weather and the perks of being wined and dined by representatives of Third World start-ups, and he liked the women they introduced him to at the end of the evenings. The bank had made money as a result of his research expeditions, so everybody was happy. Or had been until recently, when the decline in commodity prices and uncertainties about tariffs and other impediments to market access had driven valuations down. The bank had instituted cost-cutting measures that eliminated his next planned trip. "Use the internet for your research," his father-in-law had suggested. "If you need to talk to people, use Skype."

Thanks for the brilliant suggestions, sir. Never would have occurred to me.

So he was in no mood to be accommodating to any random stranger, least of all some kind of American official. The bank had dutifully followed the know-your-client rules instituted at the insistence of the United States. It had cost the bank money in time and personnel and, worse, lost it clients who preferred not to be known so had closed their Swiss accounts and moved their money to God knows where. The Caymans? Malta? Antarctica? To avoid the most onerous reporting requirements, the bank had stopped accepting any new accounts from American citizens, which meant a whole tranche of wealthy Americans retired in Switzerland were now off limits. Thank you very much, USA.

The visitor was polite and had an appealing friendly look in the American way. He could have been a tourist wandering into the office to exchange dollars for francs. But he'd wanted information about the shares of a company called Sahel Hydrocarbon. Specifically, had the bank's trading desk lent any shares of the stock to a short seller, and, if so, to whom?

Karl told him that any such information would of course be confidential.

The visitor said there were reporting requirements to which Switzerland had agreed and this certainly fell within their purview.

Karl acknowledged that such reporting requirements did now, unfortunately, extend to Switzerland, but the visitor was American, not Swiss, and if such a loan of securities had occurred, and if it did not involve any American companies or persons, the American had no standing to receive the information.

Ah, said the American, so such a loan *had* occurred.

That's not what I said, said Karl. Is my English so bad that I am not making myself clear?

No, said the American, you are making yourself perfectly clear. I won't let the door hit me in the ass on my way out.

After the American left, Karl went back to his office and found a message. The same entity that had borrowed shares in Sahel Hydrocarbon now wanted to borrow shares in a French dairy company, to short.

JOHNS

The day after Stavro left his new order with Sterling Wealth Management, Majid's partner, Ron, stepped into an apartment building elevator with an overweight man with a bad combover and a heavy briefcase. Ron was headed to apartment 4D for a session with Tania, the redheaded Romanian prostitute he'd been seeing once a week for the last two months. The pudgy man, however, seemed uncertain what button to push, and his uncertainty was confirmed when he turned to Ron and said, "Do you know what floor the hookers are on?" This left Ron undecided as to exactly what kind of ass this pudgy American was. Either he had leapt, with no plausible justification, to the conclusion that Ron was a john on his way to a hooker, and Ron was certain he looked no more like a john than any other male between thirty and sixty and less so than most. Or the man didn't care if Ron was a john or not and saw no problem with announcing to a possible resident of the building that hookers lived there, which other residents might not be pleased to hear (or be reminded of). This latter supposition was borne out by the expressions on the faces of a middle-aged couple who entered the elevator carrying bags of groceries just as the pudgy guy blurted out his question. This was an upscale building in the Champel neighborhood, occupied by doctors from the university hospital and diplomats and college professors. But this was also Geneva, where there was no law barring prostitutes from practicing their trade anywhere they could afford the rent.

"Four," said the woman, sourly, as she and her husband got off at three.

Ron didn't say anything. He got off at the fourth floor and so did the other man, who followed Ron to the door of 4D and said, as Ron rang the buzzer, "You here for Vanessa, too? I don't want to go second."

"No," Ron said. Tania opened the door. She was wearing a short yellow dress and dark eye shadow. She gave Ron a kiss on both cheeks. "I'm here to see Tania," he said.

Tania led them into the living room, where a bar was set up. The couch was from Ikea but comfortable. The windows were large and let in plenty of light. "Is Vanessa expecting you?" she said to the pudgy man.

"Yes," said Pleski. "I called. I'm Mister Jones."

Just then Vanessa entered from a bedroom. She was from the Congo, with dark skin and high arching eyebrows. She was wearing a bathrobe and her hair was pulled back straight. She gave the man a quick appraising look, then said "Bonjour" and reached out her hand. He did not take it.

"You looked different in your picture in the ad," Pleski said.

"My hair was down, not like this."

"You looked better in the picture."

"If you like," she said, "I can let my hair down."

The man's phone rang. He answered, "Yeah?" Then, "He's here already?" Then, "I have an appointment for the next hour. Can't he wait?" Then, "Shit, okay."

He rang off and turned back to Vanessa. "It's going to have to be a quickie. That, plus the deceptive advertising, I think three hundred francs is too much. I think one hundred should do it."

"No," said Vanessa. "It's three hundred. You may leave if you like."

Pleski considered for a moment. "Fuck it. Let's go," he said. Vanessa shrugged and walked into her room. He followed.

Through all this, Ron was sipping a cognac. He was in no hurry and he enjoyed talking to Tania beforehand. There was such a thing as being civilized.

"Unpleasant fellow," he said. "Do you get many like that?"

"We get many like everything. Some men are aggressive. Some men just want to be hugged. Some like to sit and talk about politics in Bucharest. There is no extra charge for that." She smiled.

So did Ron. He liked Tania and, through her, he liked Vanessa, who just then yelped from the other room. It might have been nothing more than surprise, or possibly even pleasure, or, more likely, feigned pleasure, but it might have been something else. Ron turned toward the sound. "Is she all right?" he asked.

Tania listened. "If she was in trouble, she would call my name."

They heard Pleski's voice through the wall: "It's my money. I'm the customer. You do what I say. Isn't that how this works?"

"Should I go in there?" said Ron.

They didn't hear anything else. "Not unless she says my name," said Tania.

Vanessa did not. But Ron had already come to a decision. Customers were customers, but he didn't like being pushed around. He'd had enough of that at school. And he wasn't a prostitute. He wasn't going to be treated like one.

DUE DILIGENCE

"Stavro," Ron said into his phone. "S-t-a-v-r-o. He said he was a partner in a computer services company." Ron looked down at his desk, at the form Stavro had filled out on his first visit to Sterling. "Hyperion Limited. Apparently it was active in Africa, places like that. *Is* active. It's supposed to be privately held, a partnership. Well, don't you do business in Uganda? He said they do business in Uganda. Uganda isn't that big, is it? All right, just do me a favor then, ask around. No, there's not a problem. I don't think there's a problem. It's routine. Due diligence."

Majid had walked into Ron's office. He listened as Ron finished the call. "And do give my love to Evelyn." Ron put the phone down and saw Majid looking at him. "I went to school with him," Ron said. "Decent bloke. Works in the City."

"Due diligence?" Majid said.

"Overdue diligence," said Ron. "Don't you think we should know who the fuck this guy is?"

"You just said. Decent bloke, works in the city."

"Not him. Stavro."

"Oh. You mean the man whose investment saved our company?"

"He's a phantom," said Ron. "I don't like it. I don't like *him*."

"Fine. You want to send his money back? Close up the fund? Sell the furniture?"

Ron didn't answer.

"Why not?" said Majid. "Maybe I can get a job driving a streetcar."

"You can work for a bank. You could go home."

"I'd rather drive a streetcar," Majid said.

He had decided long ago that he didn't want to go home. For a well-educated Emirati, Dubai was a comfortable cocoon. Which was not what he wanted. The endless round of family and a few old friends. The old traditions—camel racing, falconry, tented retreats in the desert. The new tradition—going to the mall. And then what? Camel racing, falconry, tented retreats in the desert, and going to the mall. The West was a cornucopia of excess, some of it disgusting—commercialism, exploitation, depravity. But it had a dizzying variety of upsides. You could make a fortune. You could go bankrupt. You could be mugged by a drug addict. You could invent a cure for drug addiction. You could take a walk in a park without recognizing half the men crossing your path and the obligations you owed them or they owed you. You could vote for a Communist. You could vote. You could fall in love with a fearless woman on a terrifying mountain path. Dubai, with all its modern trappings, its highways and high-rises and high-end shopping, presented itself as the West without the faults of the West. But it was a simulation and a flawed one at that. It built its ski slope inside a shopping mall. A developer had admired the architecture of the Chrysler Building, so he built a copy of it. And right next to it he built another copy of the Chrysler Building, two Chrysler Buildings obviously being better than one. But neither was as good as the original.

He had never discussed any of this with Ron who, despite his own minor flight from England to the Continent, had never made a major change in his life. He could get the same single malt in Geneva that he drank in London. His French was execrable but it didn't matter. Switzerland, for him, was much the same as England, only with the rough edges (poverty, homelessness, hooligans, immigrants) sanded off.

Ron hit some keys on his computer and looked up. "There is some good news. The shares of Bouvier Lait are up. Our friend Stavro is losing money on his bet."

"Not to point out the obvious," said Majid, "but if he loses money we don't make any. We're in for twenty percent of gains, not losses."

"I don't like him," Ron said.

"You've mentioned that, a few dozen times."

"Are you still selling short for him, even into the rise?"

"I am. No orders to stop. I'll be borrowing more shares to sell tomorrow."

"I'll do it," said Ron.

"You will? You don't like him."

"Correct. So I want to get this over with and be done with him."

"Fine," said Majid. "Remember, use one of the nominee accounts. Discretion. Anonymity."

"I heard him," said Ron. "I know what to do."

After Majid left, he began tapping on his computer.

INTERESTING

Afterward, Catherine thought about this day. A lot. Majid had lunch with her. He'd been acting different since their hike on the bisse. More intense. Breaking unspoken boundaries. Talking about taking a trip together. Maybe going to Lebanon. His sister, he told her, was a student at a university there, making an escape from home the same way he had. This was all new to Catherine. She hadn't known that Majid had a sister. Why was he suddenly talking about his family? And asking about her family? Her family was private. She didn't talk about her family. Lebanon, he said, was beautiful, and much of it was safe despite what one heard. There was an inn he could take her to, in the mountains, overlooking the Mediterranean. Not far from the famous cedars of Lebanon, with fresh fish brought up every day from the sea. Hot days, cool nights. In the winter there was snow. Majid's talk of romantic inns had the unintended consequence of making her think of Rafe. The absurd visit he had made to her at the pool, with the ridiculous excuse that he needed a how-to about short sales. What if she had invited him into the locker room with her? It was usually empty at that hour. And let him peel her bathing suit down, over her breasts, over her belly, over everything. And then him throwing her back onto a bench. And she looked up, and there was still Majid talking about the cedars of Lebanon over his poached fish, and the sister she'd never heard of before. Amina. He was sure that she and Amina would like each other. *Who? What? Why?*

She ordered another glass of wine.

And then, back at the office, there was Barnstable again, and the damn incomplete DAX straddle again. It was crashingly clear that she wouldn't be able to put off the reckoning much longer. End of quarter reconciliation was bearing down like a beast. Would they have her arrested? Doubtful. She hadn't gone out on this limb for personal profit. She had done it to profit the bank, so the bank would reward her, so she could take care of *her* family. But nobody was going to profit, because the trade was a total loss. So no jail, almost certainly, but she'd be fired, and hardly sent off with a glowing recommendation. And what then? She had no idea.

And she was only rescued from the awful conversation with Barnstable by the appearance of Pleski of all people, her day piling up into one enormous tower of shit. But Barnstable had stepped aside when he arrived, because Pleski was a valued client, and Pleski suggested that Catherine leave the office with him to talk about his account over a drink, and she seized that escape, only hoping that Pleski wouldn't start talking about his sister and taking her to visit the mountains of, where was it, Detroit? But Pleski, settled in a bar with her, actually did want to talk about his account and asked about the mining company investment she had told him about. It was off the table, she said, an issue with Compliance, she had fought it but been overruled.

"By who," asked Pleski, "that guy you were talking to when I came in?"

"Yes," she said. "My boss. Mister Barnstable. But I may be leaving the bank and opening my own firm, making my own rules, maybe you could bring your account . . ."

Pleski was already shaking his head. He liked dealing with a big bank, he said. International branches. Lots of prestige. Why would she leave? Because of that guy? What was his name? Barnstable?

"He's very conservative," she said. "Very intrusive. Questions everything. My investment choices. My clients."

She never meant to get into this, and she wouldn't have ordinarily, not ever. But with Majid being weird and the DAX options about to blow up and the wine at lunch and now martinis with this guy, and . . .

"Your clients?" Pleski said. "What about your clients? Even me?"

She looked at him through her buzz, this ugly man. She'd never asked him. Maybe she should just ask him. About what Rafe had said.

"Some crazy story," she said. "About Kevin Kemper."

"Kevin Kemper?"

"The kid in New York. Who got killed in the traffic accident."

"What about him? What about that?"

"The timing of the accident. How it all worked out, with the deal closing."

"Who's talking about this? That guy, Barnstable?"

Pleski looked angry. She didn't want to mention Rafe. Not to this man. She didn't want to mention anyone, but she was already down the road. Too late to rewind.

"Just him? Anybody else?"

She shook her head. "No," she said. "No."

"Interesting," Pleski said.

Interesting. Afterward, Catherine remembered that most of all.

COINCIDENCE

Rafe hadn't had much luck tracking down the source of the borrowed shares in Sahel Hydrocarbon. If there was a hidden mastermind behind the play, that mastermind remained hidden, having borrowed the shares he/it/they had sold piecemeal from a dozen brokerage firms, firms that could have been anywhere. Rafe had inquired politely at several plausible firms in Switzerland and had doors slammed in his face, not always so politely. He could ask the Swiss authorities for help, but they would hardly consider it a matter of urgency. There was nothing illegal about short selling and no actual evidence that any short seller had committed industrial sabotage or any other crime. And Switzerland might not be the right place to look anyway. If an American firm was involved, Rafe might in theory have gotten a clue from perusing Suspicious Activity Reports filed by financial institutions with Treasury's Financial Crimes Enforcement Network, but that hardly seemed worth the effort.

"Why not?" asked Frank as they sat side by side at computers in their little office.

"Because fifty-five thousand reports are filed every day. Banks cover their asses. Every time a kid walks in with a piggy bank and can't document the source of the pennies, they report it."

"Brilliant," Frank said. "Building a haystack so no one can find a needle. You think Homeboy's bank filed a report when he walked in? If Homeboy used a bank. If there is a Homeboy."

Rafe didn't answer. He was scrolling through documents on his screen, saw one, and stopped. "Wait a minute," he said.

"No rush," said Frank. "While you've been running around getting nowhere, I've been catching up on my *Murder City*."

Rafe looked over to see if that was what Frank was doing over there, actually playing *Murder City*.

He was.

"I'm not finding any clues," Frank said. "Though I did just steal a Ferrari."

"I queried the British firms that shorted Sahel," Rafe said.

Frank didn't look up. On his screen he was shooting at a cop. "Did they tell you to go fuck yourself nicer than the Swiss did?"

"If ignoring me is nicer, yeah. But one of them did reply. It said the transaction was routed through a bank in Cyprus . . ."

"Greek side or Turkish?"

"Turkish."

"Natch."

"For the benefit of an LLC in the Turks and Caicos."

"Wild guess—anonymous?"

"Very."

On his screen, Frank was reaching for a howitzer in the trunk of his convertible. "You know," he said, "for a change, you might enjoy playing this game. Things actually happen in it, things actually get accomplished." He fired the howitzer and blew up a gas station. "See?"

Rafe didn't. He had turned back to his screen. "The same firm just reported another short sale, routed through the same bank in Cyprus."

"More Sahel Hydrocarbon? Now? After the stock cratered? Kind of too late, isn't it?"

"It would be. But this is something else. Not Sahel. A French dairy. But the pattern's the same. Same London firm. Same Cyprus bank. It's a pretty big coincidence. Except for one thing. The client isn't an anonymous LLC. It's a firm in Geneva."

That registered. Frank looked up from his game, hitting pause so he wouldn't be killed. "In Geneva? Here? 'Lake City'?"

"Yeah."

Frank got up and walked over to look at Rafe's screen. He read the name of the Geneva firm. "Sterling Wealth Management?"

"I know someone there," Rafe said.

Frank looked at Rafe with a look that was either respect or suspicion.

"You know someone there. You know the babe at the Holborn Bank. You're personal friends with everyone we investigate?"

"We're not *investigating* Catherine. But yes, we all went to Harvard Business School. That's sort of the point of my being here."

Frank pointed to himself. "Missouri State. Lower class of crook." Spoken with pride. "So, are you going to see your Harvard pal at Sterling Wealth Management? Maybe have a drink and sing old school songs? Boola boola?"

"That's Yale," Rafe said, wondering briefly what they sang at Missouri State. "Anyway, it could be a coincidence."

"Lot of coincidences going around," Frank said, and then, a distant memory triggered, he started to hum "Let's Do It for the Bears."

TOXOPLASMOSIS

The Syrian lingered outside the windows of Ladurée, watching the customers seated on pink cushions sip coffee and eat macarons, the house specialty. They came in dozens of colors that were laid out in a display case like a rainbow. An expensive rainbow. A menu posted in the window offered to sell a box of twelve (each easily consumed in two bites) for thirty-two euros. The Syrian and his roommates in Neydens could eat for days for thirty-two euros. In Syria, his family, what was left of it, could eat for a week.

He himself had had three-day-old bread and cheese for breakfast, and he was hungry. He bore no resentment toward the well-fed customers in Ladurée, and he didn't think it would be just for them to resent him, even though they would. Stealing was forbidden not only by their laws but also by Islam, which prescribed the penalty of having one's hand cut off. But suicide was also forbidden (despite the suicide bombers having found, or claimed, an exemption), and it took money to buy food, and it took food to stay alive.

He was working in daylight now, not just in the dark interiors of CERN. His roommate who had adopted the cat had moved on without it, and the roommate who replaced him had taken a dislike to it (it made him sneeze) and wanted to get rid of it. He said cats were *haram*. Alarmed at the prospect of losing the cat, the Syrian had protested that that wasn't true. The Prophet Himself had liked cats. He had a favorite named Muezza who sat on His lap while He preached. The Syrian hadn't known any of this before (he'd never paid much attention to the religion classes in school), but he quickly discovered it by searching the internet on a cell phone he had stolen. It was the same cell phone he'd used to learn more about the parasite that lived inside the cat, more than he remembered from his childhood reading. It was called toxoplasma gondii and was way too small to be seen by the human eye. It reproduced in the body of a cat and, when it did, its eggs were expelled in the cat's feces, where they were picked up by other scavenging animals. The parasite most preferred to be picked up by rats (not that the parasite had consciousness and will, but it acted as if it did). Once inside a rat, the parasite wanted (or "wanted") to get back inside a cat, which is the only place it can breed. (Sex, the Syrian thought. Sex.) To accomplish this, it somehow migrated to the rat's brain and rewired the rat's natural impulses. Normally, rats fear and flee from the smell of cat urine. Rats with the parasite in their brains lose that fear. Normally, rats have no romantic interest in cats. Rats with the parasites in their brains misassociate cat urine with the presence of a potential mate (again, sex). So rats with the parasite in their brains do not run away from cats. They run toward them. So that cats can eat them. So that the parasite can get back inside a cat. Which is where it wants to be. So it can reproduce. (Sex.)

Honestly, the Syrian thought, if Allah wanted toxoplasma gondii to thrive, it would be a lot simpler to just put them inside cats and leave them there. But he supposed Allah must have His reasons.

And then, crucially, there was the matter of the parasite and humans, who could pick it up by consuming contaminated food or by just being too close to a cat. Once inside a human, the parasite gets to work on his or her brain. It can't achieve its goal of getting back inside a cat, since cats don't eat people. But, in that futile effort, it does succeed in making infected people, like infected rats, act recklessly. Which in humans can be both a negative and a positive. Studies had shown that infected humans are more likely to drive too fast, to abuse drugs, to commit suicide. On the positive side, they are more likely to be less fearful, to act boldly, to be aggressive, to be entrepreneurs, to be successful in business.

To work as thieves, even in broad daylight.

The Syrian stepped around the corner and started to walk along the river.

RAISINS

Loitering on the quay near the office of Sterling Wealth Management, Rafe wasn't sure what he expected to see. If Majid was involved in this, would he come waltzing out arm in arm with a bearded fanatic brandishing an ISIS flag and a backpack bomb?

Not very likely.

And maybe there was no *this* anyway. Banks in Turkish Cyprus, which wasn't even really a country, were widely known to be, uh, accommodating to clients who valued discretion. So Majid might have made a transaction via that route not for a terrorist but for a *normal* discretion-seeking client—a normal rich tax cheat or a normal married man hiding assets from the wife he was planning to divorce or a normal kleptocratic government official from any one of a hundred countries. Or Majid could simply be pursuing a deal for the benefit of his own fund that he didn't want visible to competitors who might copy (and dilute) his trade or to law enforcement officials who might interpret it ungenerously. Rafe knew all about that. During his dealmaking days at Klamath Capital he had not to his own knowledge committed any actual felonies but he sure as hell had threaded through a lot of loopholes, which he hadn't even needed Turkish Cyprus to accomplish. It required less identifying information to establish a shell corporation in Delaware than it took to get a library card. Which was convenient and very useful.

It was actually sort of amazing that anyone ever paid tax on investment income anywhere.

But Rafe hadn't uprooted his life and volunteered for government service because he yearned to chase tax cheats or philanderers. He had no objection to going after hardcore criminals (hello, Mister Pleski) but even that had not been his prime motivation. He had joined because of the death of his brother. His first motive, even in his own mind, was to somehow avenge his brother's death, but beyond that, Rafe came to realize, was a desire to be *like* his brother. Not like him in killing terrorists in Afghanistan, which had been his brother's purpose, but, like his brother, to *have* a purpose. Things had always come easy for Rafe. He had coasted through college and business school and then into finance, following paths that obligingly laid themselves out in front of him. Some boys want to be basketball players or astronauts; very few dream of growing up to structure leveraged corporate buyouts. Rafe had never had a calling. His brother did. And so, in a horrible funhouse mirror way, did the fanatic who killed his brother, who was willing to die himself (and did, thirty seconds after Rafe's brother did) in the service of a vision, preposterous as it was. Rafe had read about an academic article about the Koran's supposed promise of seventy-two virgins awaiting martyrs in paradise. "Virgins," the article said, was a mistranslation. The author, an expert in the language of the Koran, explained that the word actually meant "raisins." Or grapes. Thus grape juice. Which, to nomadic Arabs in the seventh century, wandering in a parched desert, would sound paradisiacal, Islam's version of God enticing Abraham to the Promised Land with a vision of flowing milk and honey. Virgins were probably at hand in the seventh-century desert, refreshing liquids not so much.

Of course the scholar who wrote that paper had had to publish under a pseudonym, so he would not be targeted, like Rafe's brother, by a suicidal lunatic who sincerely believed that the murder would entitle him to a place in a post-death paradise where he would enjoy the company of seventy-two virgins who were actually grapes. Except, of course, they were actually nothing, because the entire thing made no sense.

Just like Rafe's working to make millions of dollars for billionaires had made no sense.

In case rampant senselessness needed another example (which it didn't), Rafe just then noticed, near him on the quay, a Roma woman of unknowable age, in a flowing brown dress and white head scarf, kneeling on the sidewalk and bowing in a supplicating manner with a plastic dish on the pavement in front of her. It was against the law to beg in Geneva, so she wasn't begging. She didn't have a sign. She didn't say a word. She was just resting semi-prone here on the quay with her plastic dish available as a repository for any passerby who suddenly felt overburdened by small currency. If cited by the police nonetheless, she would be fined one hundred francs, which of course she would only be able to raise by more non-begging begging.

Which was just one more thing for Rafe to ponder as he lingered outside his Harvard classmate's office trying to decide if and how to go in and question him about why he was shorting shares in a French dairy company—and also, by the way, as long as they were talking, had he previously shorted shares in another company as part of an international terrorist conspiracy? Maybe, as a conversational icebreaker, he could ask Majid what he thought of Harvard's chances against Yale in football this year.

It was ridiculous. Except it wasn't. So he crossed the street and started to walk toward the office building. And stopped when he saw Majid walking by the river. He was with Catherine, and they were having an intense conversation. They paused, then sat on a bench across the street from Rafe. They were looking away from him, facing sightseeing boats threading around the islands in the Rhône, sitting close to each other, the way lovers would. Or, in this case, the way lovers do. Catherine, after all, had told him. Now Majid was saying something, and Catherine turned her head to look at him, which put Rafe in her peripheral vision. He ducked into the doorway of a store. He didn't want them to think he was spying on them, even though he was, sort of, spying on them. Catherine had her handbag slung over a shoulder and was leaning into Majid, listening intently—*since when had Majid ever been that interesting?*

*

That's when the Syrian made his move.

He'd been lingering with some German tourists a few yards away. They were watching the boats in the river. He was watching the woman on a bench, seeing her handbag loose on her shoulder. It would slide off with a grab, if he only had the courage to do it. Which he now felt sure he did. He could feel the virus from the cat inside him. The Christians were right. God moves in mysterious ways. He watched as the woman leaned toward the man she was with. Shamefully flirting where anyone could see. Her thoughts perhaps on licentious behavior. As his own, shamefully, started to be. She was beautiful, a Western goddess. And the man with her looked Arab. How did they come to be together? What kind of things did they do together? The Syrian had never seen a woman naked. He had never . . .

He smashed the thought down and darted away from the river rail and, passing behind the bench, grabbed the woman's bag and ran.

*

Catherine jerked around and yelped. Majid jumped up but didn't give chase, first looking down at Catherine to see if she was all right. She was shouting, "My bag! Son of a bitch!" So Majid started to run, but by then the thief had darted across the street and was sprinting down the opposite sidewalk, heading toward the doorway where Rafe, who had seen it all, was standing. The thief reached him and Rafe lunged, missing the man but getting hold of the strap of Catherine's purse. The thief strained against it, and the strap broke, and the bag ended up in Rafe's hand as the purse snatcher kept running and veered off into the maze of narrow streets that led away from the river. Rafe did not follow. He stood there holding the bag, looking slightly surprised, as if it had fallen from the sky and landed on him. This had all happened in seconds. And then Majid was beside him, and then Catherine was there, too, looking at Rafe, looking at her bag.

"Here," Rafe said. He held it out to her.

"Rafe?" she said. "What are you doing here?"

"Shopping," he said.

"Here?"

Why not here? Rafe turned and looked at the shop in whose doorway he'd been sheltering. It was a high-end cosmetics boutique.

"For mascara?" said Majid.

"Were you following me?" said Catherine.

"No," Rafe said. "Don't be ridiculous. If I want to see you I know where to find you." He was still holding his arm out, the purse in his hand. "Do you want this or not?"

She took it.

"I think the strap is broken," Rafe said. "But otherwise . . ."

Catherine was examining the bag for damage and, it appeared, possible contamination. A boat with an orange sail glided by on the river behind her.

"Thank you," she said. "My passport's in there. Losing it would have been a major hassle." She pulled the passport out, looked at it, and put it back. Then looked at the cosmetics in the shop window and said, "You weren't shopping, were you?"

"No," Rafe said. Then looked at Majid. "Actually, I was on my way to see you."

"Really?" said Majid. "What about?"

STUPID

"What did you tell him?" Ron asked.

He and Majid were in Ron's office an hour later, after Rafe had gone. Ron was leaning back in his desk chair, cream leather, ostentatiously relaxed. He'd seen Rafe go into Majid's office, and he'd seen Rafe come out. He hadn't heard their conversation.

It had not been the most pleasant conversation Majid had ever had. After a rehash of the attempted purse snatching and some rote pleasantries and mild averrals by Rafe that he had not been spying on Majid and Catherine, Rafe produced proof of the latter, proof being the question he had come to ask Majid, which was: did Majid frequently route trades through a certain bank in Turkish Cyprus?

Majid would have preferred that Rafe had been spying on him and Catherine.

To Rafe's question, he had said maybe, they used a lot of banks here at Sterling Wealth Management. And counter-questioned: why did Rafe want to know? Was he looking for a friendly bank for his own new firm?

Well, Rafe had said, not exactly. And smiled and got sheepish, the guileless American. Rafe could pull that off. The girls in Cambridge had liked it—Catherine had apparently liked it—a friendly down-home face among the tight smiles of naked ambition that everyone else there wore without shame. They had not come to Harvard Business School to learn how to bale hay. But did Rafe wear it easily because he actually was a guileless American? If there had been any doubt about that in Cambridge, it was augmented in Majid's office by Rafe's answer to Majid's question.

Actually, Rafe said, during his years on Wall Street after business school he'd kind of cut a corner or two here and there, not really his fault, not really that bad, except the government became aware and didn't see it that way, and it could have gone hard on him, but he'd had a good lawyer who argued that Rafe, with his special expertise in finance, and in cutting corners, could maybe help out the government from time to time. The government had gone for that, on a provisional basis anyway, so he was here in Geneva to get his own venture up and running, really, but also the government did call on him for favors now and then, and this thing had come up with Majid's name on it (and by Majid he meant Sterling Wealth Management), and, since he knew Majid, his dropping by today was one of those favors. For the government.

What thing was that? Majid had wondered.

Well, it seemed that that bank in Turkish Cyprus had been the vehicle, via a fairly circuitous route, for the short sale of a French dairy stock for the benefit of Sterling Wealth Management—whose tasteful offices Rafe made a point of admiring, by the way—and, the thing was, a similar trade routed through that same bank via the same circuitous route a couple of weeks ago involving another short sale was of interest to the government because it was linked to some bad people the government had a special interest in.

Well then, Majid had logically suggested, the government should go talk to those bad people and not send Rafe to question Majid about some kind of connection that was obviously a total coincidence, although Majid was always happy to see an old friend.

Well, Rafe had said, he was sure that the government (its official representatives, not him) would love to do that, talk to those bad people, but the trade had been made in the name of an untraceable LLC—actually, come to think of it, the kind of blind entity a firm like Sterling Wealth Management might set up for a client who wanted to be untraceable—and, since the peculiar routes of the two trades were so idiosyncratic, and so identical, and one trade was made by Sterling, it was just possible that Sterling had made the other trade, too. And by Sterling he meant Majid.

The two trades were identical, Majid had pointed out, except that they weren't. They differed in one very significant aspect—one was blind, and one led to Sterling Wealth Management. If Sterling Wealth Management had something to hide about the first trade, and the two trades were somehow linked, why would Sterling Wealth Management make the second trade openly traceable? That made no sense. It would be stupid.

"That's what you said?" Ron asked Majid, the two of them in his office, Ron sitting, Majid standing, after Rafe had gone. "Stupid?"

"That's what I said." Majid moved close to Ron's desk. Put his hands on it. Leaned forward. "But stupid isn't the only explanation, is it?"

Ron did not reply.

"I told you to make the Bouvier trade blind, like the other one. You said you would, like the other one. But you didn't. You put our name on it."

From Ron, still no reply.

"Honestly, sometimes I think you *are* stupid . . ."

"Excuse me?"

"But I don't think you were being stupid. I mean, you *were* being stupid but you thought you were being smart."

"Why don't you sit down?" Ron said.

Majid didn't move, still hovered over Ron's desk.

"I don't like him," Ron said.

"You've mentioned that."

"I don't think we should be in business with him."

"You've mentioned that, too."

"But we still are in business with him."

Majid closed his eyes and shook his head. "So you didn't talk to me again. You didn't have it out with me. You just, in your own great and unmatched wisdom, decided to deliberately leave a trail to lead the authorities to our door?"

"I *did* talk to you again," Ron said.

"And I told you that, after this dairy business, we'd be done."

"I thought this might give us a gentle shove in that direction. Make sure we didn't forget. Either of us."

Majid sighed, removed himself from Ron's desk, and sank into a couch.

"You've never had any difficulties in life, have you?" Majid said. Behind the couch, on the wall over his head, was a photo of Ron with his rowing club at Cambridge.

"What has that got to do with anything?"

"You don't need to succeed here, in this little company of ours. You always say you don't want to go home, but if our firm blows up you don't have to. You can go play remittance man somewhere else. Singapore, Hong Kong . . ."

"I don't really . . ."

"You can afford to be stupid."

"I think our discussion of my intelligence is finished."

"Do you?"

"Yes. What did you tell him next?"

"Well, I didn't tell him we suspect we have a client who fucking blew up Africa."

"That's good."

"Do you think so? I would have thought you'd disagree. I pleaded client confidentiality. I pleaded coincidence. I pleaded lack of stupidity."

"Did he believe it?"

Majid sank deeper into the couch and shook his head. "I have no idea."

BALLOONS

"Did he believe it?" Helen Sykes was leaning back in the chair behind her desk, a manifestation of insouciance that went against every other visible aspect of her persona. On the wall behind her was a colorful print of red balloons floating over the Eiffel Tower. Rafe wondered if she had taken over someone else's office in the embassy and hadn't bothered to redecorate (which would, come to think of it, be in character after all).

"Believe what?" Rafe said. "That I did some crooked deals myself and avoided jail by agreeing to work for the government?"

"I'd believe it," said Frank. He was sitting against a side wall beneath a photograph of German children folk dancing. "Nothing personal," he added, nodding toward Rafe. "I mean, you were making what on Wall Street, five million a year? Ten million? You took a big pay cut going into government work. Maybe you had some extra motivation."

"Actually," Rafe said, "that *is* personal."

Frank shrugged. "It's not like I would hold it against you."

"Good to know. What got *you* into government work?"

"The retirement plan. Have you checked it out?"

Sykes cleared her throat. "If you don't mind my interrupting, I believe you're both here for the same reason I am, and we can all celebrate over drinks some day when we've succeeded in removing evil from the world. Mister Sassaman, I believe you came in here to report, not thumb wrestle with your colleague."

"Yes," Rafe agreed. "I did. And my report is that Majid—"

"Majid," said Frank, smiling.

"Mister Hassan," Rafe said, "had a point. He is not stupid. If he had gone out of his way to cover his tracks in the first trade, if there was a *reason* to cover his tracks in the first trade, he would not have exposed them in the second."

"Everybody makes mistakes," Frank said.

"Big mistake," Rafe said.

"Does Mister Hassan work alone?" Sykes asked.

"No," said Rafe. "He has a partner. I haven't met him."

"Maybe his partner makes mistakes."

"Or maybe," Frank said, "his partner is more averse to dealing with terrorists than your college pal."

"They're in that company together," Rafe said. "If the business goes down, they both go down."

"Sometimes partners have different points of view," Frank said.

Sykes considered. "It would be useful to see their books," she said.

Frank nodded. So did Rafe. "Don't you have ways to do that kind of thing?" he said.

"Yes," Sykes said. "We do."

BOULANGERIE

There were four of them—a Tunisian, two Moroccans (from Brussels), and an Englishman. The Englishman had a tattoo on his right temple of a dragon or a lion (or possibly a cocker spaniel, it was hard to tell), and he was new, so the Tunisian had doubts. Could he be trusted? Was he devout? These questions he had raised to the Moroccans, who shut him down. They themselves had been raised in the West, they said, and no one questioned their devotion. And they knew converts like this Englishman. They had seen for themselves that converts were among the strongest believers.

But this afternoon the Englishman wasn't praying. None of them were. They were sitting in a rented Renault parked next to a boulangerie in a small town near Lille, in the north of France. The boulangerie was popular, there were people walking by the car nonstop, occasionally glancing inside. It was not the ideal place to be parked. The men were concerned about drawing attention—three Arabs and guy with a weird tattoo. But this spot had the best view of the back of the dairy.

They had been surprised by the size of the place. It was at least fifty meters square, with giant silver silos erupting like launch tubes from its mass. The men in the car had taken a crash course in the configuration of milk processing—pre-stack tanks, pasteurizers, separators, and the rest. They wanted to make their intervention after pasteurization for sure and preferably after homogenization. Either way, they had to get inside.

Now, parked in this inconvenient spot, ameliorated only by the pleasant scent of fresh baguettes wafting from the boulangerie door, they watched truckers and warehousemen moving in a repetitive choreography of receiving and shipping at the dairy's loading docks, gleaming silver tanker trucks filled with raw milk arriving and refrigerated containers of finished products departing from docks at the far end of a long row. What they didn't see were any guards on the site. They did see Arabs among the workforce. That was the clincher. The Englishman had wanted to be the one to go in, but the Tunisian, short and slight and two days beardless, would do it. The other three would handle the chemical, drive the car, provide surveillance and backup if necessary, and, when it was done, help to make the announcement. If the dairy was shy about spreading the word, they would make sure the world knew anyway.

The loading docks looked like the best point of entry. Slip behind a tractor-trailer and in through an open door; there were dozens. It would be no problem getting a gray shirt and pants. Close enough to the factory uniform. The Tunisian was ready. He had pickpocketed the ID of a worker who was drunk after work at a café on a Friday when he should have been at mosque. More shame on him.

None of them noticed the woman in the boulangerie who had been looking out through the shop window. She was a suspicious woman to begin with, and the country was still on alert. It was always on alert. Why would four men be sitting in a car so long? Especially men like that? She had made the call on her cell phone, and she was still watching when the police car pulled up, no lights, no sirens, blocking the rented Renault, and two policemen got out, and the men in the Renault saw them and got out and ran.

RESEARCH

It was bound to be an awkward conversation, but Majid knew it was inevitable. Stavro had been stopping by periodically to see how their short selling of Bouvier Lait had been going. The stock price had not dipped, it was still mildly up, and that was the first tack Majid took with him. The truth could wait. "I'm afraid you're making a losing bet," he said. "I don't see any sign of weakness. You can cash out your position now with a moderate loss, and that is my recommendation."

Stavro, as usual, was a man of few words. "I thought I'd made myself clear. Increase my short position. Keep borrowing and selling."

"The firms we're borrowing from are getting nervous. If the share price goes any higher, there will be a margin call."

"So be it. I have enough cash in my account to cover. It's my cash, my risk, my order. I don't even understand why we're having this discussion."

Ron was watching the discussion from his customary chair along the side wall of Majid's office. He was holding himself back, which wasn't easy, especially when Stavro started playing the "I'm the boss" card again. But he knew the tide would have to turn soon. He wondered how Majid would handle it.

"Actually . . ." Majid said.

Ah, thought Ron, here it comes.

"There is another problem."

"Oh?" said Stavro. "What kind of problem?"

"There was an inquiry concerning one of the channels we've been using to make your trades."

"An inquiry?"

"It concerned the Bouvier Lait short sales . . ."

Stavro waited.

". . .and also the Sahel Hydrocarbon transactions."

Stavro, stone-faced, asked, "What kind of inquiry?"

"It was looking for a possible connection."

"Who made this inquiry?"

"Someone working with American authorities."

"American? Not Swiss?"

"No."

Stavro held for a moment in his seat, the guest chair facing Majid's desk. His right thumb and forefinger touched his lower lip, for him a display of wild emotion. "I told you to make these trades anonymously."

"We did. The trail didn't come to you, it came to us."

"But to you presumably means to one of your clients. How many clients do you have?"

"Many."

"How many?"

"That's really not your business, is it, Mister Stavro?" This came not from Majid but from Ron. Stavro turned his head to look at him.

"I suspect I am your major client, Mister . . ." A brief pause, eyes boring in on Ron. "What was your name again?"

Ron announced it proudly. "Mayfield."

"May Field." Stavro made it two words, neither of them his favorite. "It seems to me, Mister May Field, that there is an excellent chance that a trail that leads to you leads to me."

"Well," said Ron cheerfully. "That's another reason for us all to call it a day, don't you think?"

Stavro glared at Ron, then turned back to Majid. "How did this trail come to exist?"

"Our name," Majid said, "our *firm's* name, was accidentally listed on a trading record where it should not have appeared."

"Accidentally?"

Majid held firm. "Accidentally," he said again. Not for the first time, Ron admired his partner's determination and tact. He'd made a good choice going into business with Majid. If only the world hadn't gone insane.

"It may all be for the best." This was Ron again. Stavro and Majid turned back to him, Majid thinking, "Stop! Stop!" He couldn't see a way to grab Ron and drag him out of the office.

"For the best?" said Stavro. "Why would it be for the best?"

"Well, as my partner said, the Bouvier share price shows no sign of dropping. And there's no reason to think it will. So it looks like this isn't a winning bet, and . . . oh . . ." As if a thought just struck Ron, a random thought, out of the blue, not unlike an unexpected meteorite. "Did you happen to see, by the way, the news this morning from a town outside Lille?"

"No," said Stavro. "What news was that?"

Majid had no idea where Ron was going with this, but he knew it couldn't be anywhere good. "Ron," he said, "can I talk to you for a minute?"

Ron acted like he didn't hear the question. He was on script now.

"Three men," he said, "with terrorist connections were picked up by police there. They're being held."

"Such news happens every day," Stavro said. "We live in an unsettled time."

"The weird thing," Ron said, "is there was no obvious reason for them to be in that town. It's a small place. No military bases, no nightclubs or concert halls or newspapers or tourist sites, you know, the kind of places terrorists usually go after. The only thing that town has, really, is a single industrial installation."

Please don't be, Majid thought. Not that.

"A milk processing plant," Ron said.

Oh no, thought Majid. Oh no oh no oh no . . .

"A big one," said Ron, and he smiled. "It belongs to Bouvier Lait."

Why did he have to smile?

"That sounds like a very small news item," Stavro said. "How did you happen to come across it?" For the first time in the conversation, possibly for the first time ever, Stavro seemed interested in what Ron might say next.

"Well," Ron said casually, "Bouvier Lait. I mean . . ." He gestured at Stavro, at both of them. "Bouvier Lait."

"So . . . you've been researching?"

"The best investment guidance," Ron said, "is the product of diligent research." He had read that somewhere, some big firm's ad.

Stavro nodded, almost pleasantly, then, also apparently struck by a new thought, turned back to Majid. "This 'accidental' listing of your firm's name on one of my trades. How did that happen? Can you enlighten me?"

Afterward, Majid was afraid he had hesitated too long before answering. He was very careful not to look at Ron. "A bank from which we borrowed shares, they know us there, so the person entering the trade, she knew it came from us, she didn't look at the name of the anonymous entity on the form. The order came from us so she just assumed it was in our name."

Majid stopped there. It was already a very long explanation. Possibly too long, he thought. His only consolation—Ron didn't leap up during his speech and take credit for the "accident."

Majid looked at Stavro for his reaction.

There was, as usual, none.

REHEARSAL

Barnstable looked across the dining room table over the remains of his Saturday lunch (baguette, paté, tomatoes) at his wife. He could see the streak of undyed gray in the central part of her hair. She was only forty-three. "I just wanted to let you know," he said, "how sorry we all are for your loss."

"That's very kind, detective. Are you sure you don't want to come in and have a nightcap before you drive back to the station?"

"Well," Barnstable said, "I am on duty. But I guess that would be all right."

"I think it would be more than all right," his wife said, and she winked. "I make an excellent breakfast. Wait. Let me say that again. I'm supposed to be seducing you. Did I sound like I was trying to seduce you?" She picked up her tea and took a sip.

Barnstable looked up from the script in his lap. It had been a long time since his wife had tried to seduce him, so he wasn't sure how to answer the question. "Who wrote this script?" he said. "It sounds like a bad TV cop show."

"Jeffrey, our artistic director. He wanted us to try something original this season."

Barnstable knew who Jeffrey was. The little gay guy who got his rocks off tormenting the husbands his loyal corps of actresses dragged to productions of their amateur English-language theater troupe. Half-assed Noel Coward was bad enough, but this . . .

"Original?" he said. "The woman murdered her husband. It's completely obvious. Where's the mystery?"

"It's a mystery if I don't *act* like I murdered my husband."

"Fucking the investigating detective isn't acting like you murdered your husband?"

His wife put down her teacup. "If you don't want to help me rehearse, I can find someone who will."

Barnstable looked out the window. It had been raining all morning, but now there were breaks in the clouds, some shafts of clear autumn light.

"If you don't mind," he said. "I'd like to take the boat out." He had a fourteen-foot daysailer in the marina at Eaux-Vives. It was probably the smallest boat there, but it was fun to handle, and he liked being on the lake—it was pretty and calm and quiet—and, bonus points, his wife almost never wanted to go with him.

"In this weather? Isn't the Bise happening?" The Bise was the cold wind from the northeast. He'd mentioned it to her a few times and now she just liked to use the word. But she was right. The Bise was blowing. But, hey, wind and sailboat—wasn't that a *good* combination?

BOOM

His body didn't wash up until Sunday afternoon. The cantonal police had been leading the search since late Saturday night, when Barnstable's wife called to say he hadn't come home, but the body washed up on the French side of the lake, in a cove near Yvoire, so the postmortem exam was conducted by the *médecin légiste* in Annecy. She found a large contusion on Barnstable's left temple, but, as statements taken from his widow and the supervisor at the Eaux-Vives marina, relayed by Swiss authorities, established that he had been sailing alone, she concluded that he had most likely been caught unaware by the boom, perhaps while jibing. The marina supervisor also made the point that the deceased had not been an expert sailor. In fact, far from it. Plus, the Bise had come up strong not long after he set sail, far stronger than the forecast had anticipated.

MAJID

Saturday morning Rafe woke up thinking about Majid. He woke alone. Since Catherine had brushed him off, he had not pursued anyone else. Anyway, who? He was still new in Geneva, still feeling his way around. The American mission wasn't exactly alive with hot prospects, more likely anti-prospects, a dour bunch. In bars and cafés, he had spotted attractive women from a half-dozen countries, but he wasn't even sure he was allowed to date women who weren't American, for security reasons. Not that there was much to be wormed out of him that would be of interest to an enemy intelligence service, or even a cocktail party. Workwise, the Pleski matter had been put on hold for Homeboy, and that had led to Majid, and to Majid's protestations of innocence and coincidence. Which Rafe was inclined to accept, because . . .

Because why? Because Majid's explanation had been logical, and Rafe believed in logic. Because, the issue of Catherine notwithstanding, Rafe liked Majid. But so what? Rafe was working in intelligence now (up to a point). It occurred to him as he spread blueberry jam on his breakfast croissant that he should be making more of an effort to think like someone who worked in intelligence. So—what did he really know about Majid? He was from Dubai, which, from all Rafe had read and heard, was a ridiculous place. Majid apparently felt that way, too, because he had left Dubai geographically and seemingly in every other way as well. At business school, he hadn't seemed much different from any other aspiring master of the universe (except, perhaps, a little less self-satisfied). Now he was a wealth manager, a cog in the Western financial system. Could that all be a cover, an act? Could his fine suits and silk ties conceal a fanatic? Or, more plausibly, be not a disguise but just the uniform of a money handler without morals, servicing whoever walked through his door. Even criminals and terrorists. Even ISIS. Wasn't that exactly the sort of person Rafe was supposed to be on the hunt for?

Rafe sipped his coffee and looked out his living room window, which, in the Swiss custom (or was it a law?), was large and matched by an identical window on the opposite wall, insuring natural flow-through ventilation. In the evenings, on the street below, Rafe could see streetwalkers. He lived in the Paquis, between the train station and the lake, which was considered unsavory (although, in almost any other city in the world, it would be considered upscale, even deluxe). Looking at the street in the bright morning light, he recalled a prostitute with dyed orange hair he had seen last night, and that made him think of sex, and women, and Catherine. And then sex again. And then sex with Catherine. She was so tightly wrapped, and she came undone so completely. The contrast so strong that being with her had been like being with two women. ("But I only had to buy one dinner." *Thank you, Groucho.*)

When he'd seen her with Majid just before her purse was snatched, their conversation had seemed intense. He hadn't seen Catherine smile. (But when had Majid ever been witty?) If their relationship was fraught, there might be reason to hope that Catherine would reconsider her attitude toward him. Although, she had accused him of stalking her. He'd had his story ready, and it was even true—he had come to see Majid. If only he hadn't been hiding in the doorway of a fucking cosmetics store.

And that led him back to Majid again. Catherine led to Majid. A possible terrorist explosion in Africa led (maybe) to Majid. Rafe finished his coffee and decided he would go see Majid. About Catherine or terrorism? He considered the question, then decided he didn't need to decide. He would just go and have a conversation. Something might become clear.

Did Majid work Saturday mornings? Well, he'd find out. It was a pleasant walk anyway, along the lake and then the river, at least until he reached the President Wilson Hotel, where he was nearly bowled over by a rampaging group of German high school students on a field trip, their teachers strolling ahead, oblivious. The sun was warm, but wind was up on the lake, blowing frosty from the permanent snow on the mountains it skimmed on its way to Geneva. Rafe walked by the scene of the purse snatching, the bench where Catherine and Majid had been sitting, the cosmetics boutique. He paused to look in the window. What *was* all that stuff? Did Catherine shop in a place like that? She always smelled like fresh spring flowers. It had to be a scent, but it did not smell like any perfume Rafe had ever encountered. Did that mean it *wasn't* perfume, or was it a perfume so expensive that it didn't smell like perfume?

Let the CIA figure that one out.

He took the stairs to the third floor of Majid's building. He always took the stairs, free exercise without going to a gym, feeling virtuous. The door to Sterling Wealth Management was unlocked. The reception area was empty.

"Majid?" Rafe called. The door to Majid's office was shut. Rafe knocked. No answer.

"Majid?"

There was one other office, Majid's partner's, Ron something. Rafe rapped on that door and it swung open. There was nobody inside.

He didn't see it at first. He had already started to turn to leave when his eye went to something flesh-colored on the dark gray carpet. If the carpet had been beige he mightn't have noticed.

It was a hand, with a silver ring on the little finger. Stupidly, he thought that Ron something might be taking a nap, and he started to back away. But then—on the floor? It could be a heart attack. Rafe moved into the office. There was a phone on the desk. He could use it to call an ambulance.

And then he saw the rest of Ron. Sprawled on his back. Not moving. It could have been an oddly-placed nap, or a heart attack. Except for the blood pooling behind his head, a dark and blotchy puddle.

QUESTIONS

The police found Majid at Catherine's apartment. They didn't say how. Geolocation on his phone? They did say they had been to his apartment first. They treated him with the respect owed to a well-to-do Arab resident in Geneva, of which there were many—the diplomats, the tourists, the "Gulfies" who took over entire floors of the most expensive hotels with their wives and children and Malaysian nannies in the summer when their homelands were unbearable.

When Majid asked why they wanted to see him, they asked him to step into the bedroom, away from Catherine, so they could have a private conversation. There were two of them and they were very polite, a large man in his fifties with a gray crew cut and a small woman in her thirties who took lots of notes. But she looked up from her notebook so that both she and her partner could watch Majid's reaction when they told him his partner was dead.

If Majid's reaction—surprise, disbelief, perhaps a little lacking in visible sorrow—was to their minds incriminating, the detectives did not show it. They answered his first questions. Where? The office. When? Probably late last night. How? That was being examined. Why? They turned that question around. Did Sterling Wealth Management keep cash on its premises? No. Did Sterling Wealth Management have any clients who were *mécontents*? No. Did Ronald Mayfield have any personal enemies? None that Majid knew. Did he know anyone who might know? No. Where was *he* last night? Here, with Ms. Cole.

This last question was asked separately of Catherine a few minutes later. She had been asked to stay in the living room, and the male detective remained with Majid while the woman went out to talk to Catherine, who affirmed that yes, Majid had been here all night, with her, following dinner at an Italian restaurant around the corner. No, once they returned to the apartment he hadn't gone out for groceries or cigarettes or anything, and what was this about anyway? The woman detective looked up from her notebook and told her. Catherine's reaction was a blank puzzlement. She didn't know Ron Mayfield. She had never met him. But he was dead? That was terrible. But why were the police here? How did he die? Were they saying he was murdered? The detective said the death was being investigated, and she had one more question. How did Majid and his partner get along? Catherine actually had no idea. But she said, "Fine. Just fine." As she was saying it, she realized it was actually probably true. She had never heard Majid say a negative word about his partner. (On the other hand, she couldn't recall his ever saying anything about him at all.)

The detectives left, with a request that Majid meet them at his office so he could tell them if anything was missing. And perhaps answer a few more questions.

"Majid," Catherine said. "I'm sorry. This is crazy. It's awful."

Majid nodded. Ron dead? It *was* awful. They had not been close, but they had been partners in the firm, and often dined together, and rarely fought, or even disagreed, until the recent business with Stavro. Which Majid had resisted cutting off.

"Do they think he was *murdered*?" Catherine said.

"I don't know," he said. "I'd better go." He found his jacket and walked out. Without kissing her, which was odd, because lately he'd been kissing her a lot.

Outside, Majid started to walk toward his office, then turned off at an angle, down a small street with *tabacs*, minimarkets, and bars. He wanted to think before he saw the detectives again. Or wanted to stop himself thinking. Thinking about the last meeting he'd had with Stavro and Ron. Ron who was dead, probably murdered (what else could the detectives' questions have meant?). In their last meeting with Stavro, how obvious had it been that Ron had sabotaged Stavro's project? Or tried to, by giving up the firm's, and thus Stavro's, anonymity? Not to mention the "research" Ron had conducted into Bouvier Lait and into Stavro's background and god knew what else. And how had Stavro taken Ron's snarky comments, in their earlier meeting, about the likelihood of convenient and profitable industrial catastrophes? And about cheese, that idiotic comment about cheese. And, finally, icing on the cake, Majid's own very long hesitation when Stavro asked who had been responsible for the de-anonymizing "accident." Why had he hesitated so long? Why hadn't he just shrugged and said "Clerical error, sorry"? And case closed.

But so what? What if Stavro *knew* what happened? What if Ron or Majid had flat-out *told* him what Ron had done? Did that necessarily mean that Stavro would *kill* Ron? (This is what he was thinking. This is what he didn't want to be thinking.) Why not just fire Sterling Wealth Management and take his money elsewhere? That's what a displeased client, a *client mécontent,* would do. It happened all the time. That would be the likely, the logical, thing for Stavro to do. And so, with that unlikely happy thought in mind—that his partner was dead but hadn't been murdered by their suspicious client (hooray!)—Majid turned left at a newsstand and resumed heading toward his office. And then hesitated again. Yes, an unsatisfied client would simply change firms, but that would be a *normal* unsatisfied client. What about a client who had guaranteed the success of an investment by blowing up an African oil field (and Africans with it), and who suspected, correctly, that Ron Mayfield *suspected that* and had taken a step against him that could be a preface to other steps that would send law enforcement his way and shut down his homicide-based investment program and perhaps him as well? Thus *not* your normal client. But—shifting gears again—that was ridiculous, wasn't it? Things *did* explode. Africa *was* haphazard. And look at Stavro's second short sale, Bouvier Lait. No catastrophes there. The cows all happy and healthy. The stock price up.

But—damn, the mind could keep spinning—why had Stavro insisted so strongly on anonymity? What was that aborted terrorist gathering that

Ron had dug up on the doorstep of a Bouvier Lait plant? And why had Rafe Sassaman, his old friend from Harvard, now some kind of US government operative, suddenly popped into his life asking questions about Stavro's trades?

And why had he himself stared so long at news footage of the African explosion and its victims and promised Ron, willingly, that they would cut Stavro loose?

So many questions. And so troubling. As Majid finally resumed walking toward his office again, he knew only one thing for sure—he was not going to discuss any of them with the Swiss police.

MOVIE

Catherine didn't find out about Barnstable until she got to work on Monday. Nobody had called her to tell her he was dead. He hadn't been especially well-liked in the office, and why would anyone call her in particular? "We thought you'd want to know that the middle-aged middle manager who's been hitting on you is suddenly dead." There was no reason for that, even if anyone had noticed the strained non-relationship between them. At 9 a.m. Monday, the office operations manager made a brief announcement. A tragic sailing accident. Their esteemed colleague. The funeral to be held in the United States. She'd send an email when word came of where donations could be made. People were already eyeing their terminals. Markets were open.

Catherine sat at her desk but didn't look at her terminal. Two people dead in two days. She hadn't known Majid's partner, but Barnstable had been a fixture in her life, even if an unwelcome one. She picked up the stapler she had placed to prevent him from perching on her desk. She wouldn't need it for that anymore. Now she could use it for stapling.

Barnstable would never try to look down her dress again. Or question her about the incomplete DAX straddle, which had been more worrying, more of a problem. The pressure was off, all because of a freak sailing accident. Which brought to mind—this wasn't the second death in her world lately, it was the third. There was the Kemper kid in New York, killed in a traffic accident that Rafe said her client Pleski was responsible for. Mister Pleski, another gem. Mister Pleski, whom she'd had drinks with a few nights ago, mainly to escape (frying pan to fire) an unwelcome conversation with Barnstable. Whose name, she now recalled, had come up in her buzzed cocktail conversation with Pleski. She'd mentioned how Barnstable had blocked the mining shares trade she had pitched to Pleski. How Barnstable had been an intrusive pain in the ass, even implied that he'd been asking questions about Pleski and the fatal Kevin Kemper accident. Which Barnstable had not been doing. That had been Rafe. Had she *believed* Rafe's crazy assertion that Pleski was the kind of man who could arrange a fatal accident if it suited him? She didn't. She hadn't. But . . .

She sat at her desk and saw nothing in front of her, not the terminal, not her colleagues, not the infinite ticker that told her who was winning and who was losing. She saw none of it. Because Rafe had said Pleski killed people and now Barnstable was dead. And she had as good as told Pleski that Barnstable was suspicious of him. If she had said Rafe, not Barnstable, would Rafe be dead? Only if what Rafe had said was true. But that was something from a bad movie, not the real world.

But she had said Barnstable to Pleski. And Barnstable was dead.

HERE

Helen Sykes wanted to hear all about Rafe's discovery of Mayfield's body. He was in her office again. The red balloons above the Eiffel Tower. Sykes at her desk. Frank leaning back in his chair against a side wall. The smell of bad snack room coffee and hot copying machines wafting in from the hallway. I really need to get out more, Rafe thought. Although he'd just been out and it hadn't been pleasant. He'd never seen a dead body before. People in finance, as a rule, generally had their heart attacks when they were on vacation, not in the office. Lots of bodies got shipped home from St. Barts.

"So," said Sykes, "what did you do then?"

"I called the police."

"On your cell phone?"

"No. The phone on the desk." He had stumbled through that call in his lousy French but had managed to get the point across, all the while staring at the body, at one point imagining that it moved. But it didn't. Then looking away, at anything else, the jumble of papers on Mayfield's desk.

"Did you give them your name?" This was Frank, from his chair, casual, nonchalant. So how was your weekend?

"Not on the phone. They asked me when they got there."

Sykes's tone changed, got a little sharp. "So you waited there for the police to arrive?"

"What was I supposed to do? Jump out the window?"

"Walk down the stairs," Frank suggested. "Isn't that how you got in?"

Rafe ignored that. So did Sykes, or at least Rafe thought she did until she said, "So you managed to get us involved in a murder."

"Good going," said Frank.

Rafe held back—what was wrong with these people? "I don't think they think I killed the guy. I went there to see an old friend. That's what I told them. And it happens to be true. If that matters. I think they saw it as a break-in gone bad. There was a blow to his head . . ."

"You didn't mention your mission?" asked Sykes. "Your recent special interest in your old friend? Your investigation of your old friend's firm?"

"No. I'm know I'm new at this spy stuff, but that didn't seem wise." He wanted to be out of there. He wanted to take a walk that didn't end in finding a dead body. When he went to the phone on Mayfield's desk, he had stepped in the pool of blood. He was pretty sure there was still some blood on the bottom of his shoe.

But Sykes and Frank weren't finished.

"You *think* they saw it as a break-in gone bad?" asked Frank. "What led you to think that?"

"What else could it be?"

"It's not a bank, is it?" said Sykes. "They don't keep cash in that office, do they?"

"No," said Rafe. It seemed like a long time ago that he had resolved to think more like an intelligence officer, but it had only been breakfast. "Oh," he said, remembering. "We were speculating. *You* were speculating"—he looked at Frank—"that someone might have blown up the firm's anonymity. That maybe it was done on purpose, by Majid's partner . . ."

"The late Mister Mayfield," said Sykes.

"So if there really is a Homeboy, and Mayfield did do that, and Homeboy knew that Mayfield was rocking the boat . . ." Rafe had an image of Homeboy, an outraged homicidal character in a video game.

"The question," said Frank, "is what kind of investigation the police will be pursuing. A break-in gone bad? The jealous husband of some woman Mayfield was fucking? Or something else?"

"Did they give you a hint?" asked Sykes.

"They wouldn't tell me anything, would they?"

"They might if they thought you knew something," said Sykes. "They might if they wondered why you were really there."

"I was really there to see my friend."

"The thing is," she said calmly, "is you were there to see your friend because we're investigating your friend's possible connection to a terrorist organization."

"Which if they knew, or suspected"—this was Frank again—"might lead them to look at us."

"For what?" said Rafe. "Investigating terrorism?"

"Investigating terrorism by breaking into the office of someone we suspected of helping to finance it," Sykes said.

"And killing Mayfield when we got there?" This was veering into very strange territory.

"Cops can get crazy ideas," said Frank.

"I didn't tell them anything to make them suspect me, or us," Rafe said. "I'm not an idiot."

"Good to know," said Sykes. "New topic: did your friend Majid ever mention the name Stavro to you?"

Rafe paused. That name . . . Stavro . . . "No. I don't think so. No."

"You don't think so, or he didn't?"

"He didn't. Why? Who's Stavro?"

"A client. A client that Mister Mayfield was interested in when he died."

That's right, Rafe thought. He knew that. When he had averted his eyes from Mayfield's body to the papers on the desk . . .

"The papers on Mayfield's desk," he said, "they were about someone named Stavro."

"Were they?" said Sykes.

"You knew that. You just said."

Sykes shrugged. "We only know that someone named Stavro was a person of interest to Mister Mayfield and therefore to us."

"Possible Homeboy," said Frank, cheerfully.

What the fuck was he so happy about? Rafe thought. The cartoonish image of homicidal Homeboy was melting away. He asked Sykes, "How do you know what was on his desk?"

"The Swiss police. We have relationships."

"It just happened," Rafe said. "I just came from there. The Swiss police are still arriving."

Sykes and Frank exchanged a look. Unprofessional, Rafe thought, his new intelligence officer skills suddenly on full alert. He didn't know why. He only knew that he caught that look and saw something in it that he wished he hadn't. If only he were back in Connecticut tearing apart companies and destroying employees' lives.

But not literally.

"You said we had ways," he said.

"What?" said Sykes.

"When we talked about Sterling Wealth Management the other day. You said we had ways to see its books."

Sykes looked at him, expressionless, saying nothing. The fucking red balloons in the picture on the wall behind her.

Rafe said, "I assumed that meant spy cameras, tapping lines, electronic intelligence."

"Correct," Sykes said.

"But you know what was on his desk when he was killed."

Rafe stopped. He could have gotten up and walked out right then. Out of the embassy. Out of this job.

He didn't.

"Was it us?" he said. "*Was* it a break-in gone bad? *Our* break-in?"

Sykes said nothing.

Frank spoke from his chair against the wall. "Nobody would have expected him to be in the office late on a weekend night."

Rafe looked at him. Was this an explanation? An excuse? "Who was it?" he said. "Was it you?"

"I was in Chamonix," Frank said. "With a lady friend."

"But it was us," Rafe said. "We have contractors, black operatives . . ."

Frank and Sykes exchanged another look. Sloppy.

"We do intelligence," Rafe said. His voice rising. Not professional. He didn't care. "We investigate. We analyze. We report. We don't kill people."

"We killed the ISIS officer whose computer game led us to Homeboy," Frank pointed out.

"That was . . ." Rafe searched for the word. "There."

Sykes sat back in her chair, looked Rafe straight in the eye. "Unfortunately," she said, "*there* is here now. There is everywhere. I thought everybody knew that."

0.0

There was another Harvard Business School alumni reception, and they all went. Rafe because it was part of his job. He was mortified by his job now, but there were still homicidal terrorists out there. He might get over it. And, if he didn't, a Harvard Business School alumni reception was an excellent place to network, maybe get a different job, back in finance, which was definitely not a dance of angels, but at least in finance he never had to step over actual corpses.

Majid and Catherine came because it was better than sitting home alone, even alone together, each unable to tell the other, both exhausted from dwelling on the suspicions that their clients, with varying degrees of their own complicity, had murdered his partner and her boss. Unlike Catherine, Majid was mourning. He'd had to speak to Ron's father several times, including the call that broke the news. He'd had to make the arrangements to ship Ron's body home ("Will it be the intact body, monsieur, or just cremains?")—so mechanical, so industrial, so awful. He and Catherine had spent one night together since the deaths, their natural reserves deeper than ever, their conversation insanely banal (the future of the Euro, *really*?), their sex a failed attempt to escape from thinking into sensation. Neither thought to question the other's coldness; each assumed it was coming from themselves.

The three classmates sat together at a round table at the edge of the gathering. An older alumnus was drunk and making a fool of himself hitting on a handsome bartender half his age. A young alumnus was handing out business cards, so uncool. Rafe was pleased, despite everything, to see no sign of emotional connection between Catherine and Majid. In fact, he saw her looking at him, Rafe, a few times with an odd intensity, very un-Catherine-like. He wondered but had no way to know it was because she wanted him to tell her more about Pleski, to help her confirm or deny. She wanted to know but didn't want to ask. Majid also wanted to know more than he could ask. How much did Rafe know about the trades he'd made for Stavro, what did Rafe know about Stavro (who was he? was he a killer?), was he in legal jeopardy himself, should he sprint out of the reception (no thank you, not another crab cake) and head straight to the airport for the Emirates flight to Dubai? He was drinking Scotch.

Rafe couldn't talk, really talk, to Majid either. "Hey, these guys I work with, or guys who work for the guys I work with, they killed your partner. Didn't mean to. Sorry."

They all left the reception early, no better off than when they arrived.

Ten hours later, before dawn, Catherine was at the Piscine de Vernets, suited up and alone. She came out of the locker room and tested the board, stepped down to adjust the fulcrum, remounted. She intended to start with something simple, a front one-and-a-half, a dive she had done a thousand times, a dive she could do without thinking. No thinking of any kind. She took three steps, jumped, bounced, rebounded, and then she was in the empty air she knew so well. She went into the pike position but her momentum was wrong. Her butt went forward and her head moved back, an unthinkable mistake, and then there was the water, too soon, where she landed, on her back, with an ugly and noisy splash.

PART THREE

OKORO

And then nothing happened.

Rafe and Frank and their unseen colleagues, above and below, discovered that there were a lot of people named Stavro. It was an especially common name in Latvia and Greece and Albania, and a lot of Stavros had departed their homelands for pretty much everywhere, including Geneva, but none of them had any discoverable connection to Sterling Wealth Management. The documents on Ron Mayfield's desk had been notably lacking in specifics. It looked like he had been trying to track down a Stavro too.

In a conversation with Frank and Helen Sykes, it was considered whether Rafe might simply ask his friend Majid if he had a client named Stavro, but, if he did, and Majid passed the query on, Stavro might disappear. If Stavro was Homeboy, they wanted to observe him, track him, get to know his friends and connections, perhaps blackmail or threaten and turn him, not drive him away.

Rafe thought every day about quitting. And wondering at the end of every day why he had not. His colleagues were ruthless, monomaniacal about their mission. They had killed, and they had shrugged off the killing. They were not . . . nice.

Not *nice*? What had Mao said? A revolution is not a dinner party. And neither, of course, is combating terrorist fanatics who think nothing of blowing up teenage concertgoers or French cartoonists and who enslave and rape women who practice the wrong kind of Islam and behead people for listening to Beethoven or not growing beards. If Ron Mayfield had been killed by accident (and surely no one on Rafe's "side" had broken into that office intending to kill him), that was one death against thousands, against tens of thousands, in a worldwide battle. And it was a battle. And Rafe, unlike his brother, had never been in a battle (except with a few birds in Texas). And maybe he *liked* the idea that he, a former overpaid Wall Street drone, was now a combatant in the battle of the century. If he was fighting that battle at cocktail receptions in Geneva, not mountain ranges in Afghanistan, if he risked nothing except feeling bad about an accidental casualty (collateral damage!), well, he was too old to join the Marines and he was not going to charter a jet and parachute solo into the Hindu Kush. And, anyway, Helen Sykes was right. There was here now. There was everywhere. He had a friend whose grandfather had joined the Navy in World War II, when everybody served. The man owned a women's clothing store in Detroit. The Navy trained him—to be a dentist—and he spent the entire war at the Great Lakes Naval Station near Chicago fixing the appalling teeth of draftees from Appalachia. When the war ended, he went back to selling ladies' dresses in Detroit. One served where one could. And Rafe was doing more than that. Wasn't he?

Catherine took a week off from the Holborn Bank and flew to New York to visit her father. She slept on the couch of his post-prison apartment in Flushing and was pleasantly surprised to see that he was not miserable, that he was adjusting to his new life. He had part-time work as a bookkeeper for a Sri Lankan immigrant who owned a piano moving company that may or may not have been officially licensed. He had joined the New York City Trivia League and played Wednesday nights at a bar on 38th Avenue. He also seemed to be in some sort of relationship with a middle-aged Chinese woman named Karen whom Catherine saw twice while she was there, but he didn't tell, and she didn't ask. As for money, he had taken his Social Security early, and he was surviving.

Catherine did not see or talk to Pleski in Geneva before she left for New York, and, back at the bank, there was still no word from him. There was cash in his account, and, now that Barnstable was gone, when she moved to invest it (with other clients' funds) in the Central Asian mining company warrants, nobody objected. Had Barnstable been lying about Compliance's concerns, or had he been playing some game of his own? No way to tell. Even better, when her new boss queried her about the missing half of her DAX straddle, she told him she had devised the strategy with Barnstable and that Barnstable was supposed to make the part of the trade that was missing. Hadn't he done so? (She was shocked, shocked.) No, said the manager, who didn't seem surprised. Apparently, Barnstable had been generally regarded as even less competent than Catherine had suspected. So the DAX loss was written off as a posthumous Barnstable fuckup, unrecoverable and best forgotten. Which left Catherine free and clear—and a little surprised, but not unpleasantly so, at how easily the lie had come to her.

Majid didn't hear from Stavro. He was apprehensive about their next meeting—what would he say to Stavro, what would Stavro say to him? He dreaded the phone call, dreaded seeing Stavro walk though his door, but days went by, and he had other things to worry about. Even with Stavro's money in Sterling, the firm's situation was still precarious. One client, a fellow Emirati, had suddenly become devout (only God knew why), and Majid had to scramble to convert his portfolio to halal-compliant investments. Another client, a conservative Texan now residing somewhat ridiculously in an Alpine chateau, decided he wanted to go all in on gold, and Majid had to dissuade him from taking physical possession. There was also, of course, the reputational effect of his partner's death. Conservative investors (and they were all conservative) tended to shy away from firms with dead bodies in their offices. Hands needed holding, calls and meetings conducted, condolences accepted, and the unfortunate passing of Ron Mayfield minimized as random and inexplicable.

Meanwhile, by doing nothing, Majid maintained Stavro's short position in Bouvier Lait. The stock didn't dip, but it had stopped climbing. He had no further instructions, and no news was good news. Feeling better, he finally invited Catherine to dinner, and Catherine, feeling better, accepted. Autumn was full upon Geneva, the days crisp and blindingly bright, the mountains hanging awesome above the shimmering lake. Restaurants displayed notices that "La chasse est arrivée." Majid didn't especially like venison, but he gladly went with the local culture, one in which terrorism and murder felt remote. The meat was beautifully served, of course, and tough and tasteless, of course, despite the valiant effort of a heavy sauce to compensate. Catherine wisely went with the trout. She seemed more relaxed than he had seen her recently, in fact more relaxed than he had ever seen her. After dinner, they went back to her apartment, and the sex was enthusiastic. His feelings for her came back whole, and her kisses and embraces after sex gave him encouragement that she had never given him before. Arriving at work the next morning, Majid walked by the door to Ron's empty office with only a small shudder. And this too shall pass, right, right? Majid was looking out his window at the sunshine on the lake when a visitor arrived. He was a tall man with dark skin, a shaved head, narrow nose, and a penetrating gaze. His khaki sport jacket was clearly off the rack, but that didn't rule him out as a potential client. Some Africans, even wealthy ones, had their own standards of dress. Majid introduced himself and shook the man's hand and asked what he could do for him. His visitor took an appraising look around the room, then returned his gaze to Majid. "I am Emmanuel Okoro with the Nigeria Police Force, here to investigate some investments made in an oil company operating in my country. I was hoping you and I could have a chat."

ICE CREAM

As usual, Mohammed wanted to meet Frank at an ice cream place. Frank supposed he hadn't had access to a lot of hot fudge sundaes growing up in Yemen. And France, which had taken him in as a refugee, gave him a food allowance but not enough for treats. His favorite was the one on the Place du Molard but that was crowded (and expensive), so Frank tried to steer him to a smaller shop behind the *gare routière*. Where Mohammed was now enjoying butter pecan ice cream with caramel sauce, paid for by the United States government, while Frank was saying, "You were supposed to be recording the meeting. Why didn't you record?"

"The watch broke," Mohammed said. "It's not my fault."

"So we'll give you another one."

"And I walk in with a new watch? Every week at the private session with a new watch? No. Too suspicious. These people are serious. The shaykh already looks at me very hard."

Frank sighed. What's to see? he thought. A poor refugee adrift in Europe. One of millions. Frank didn't think this guy was any more dangerous than the caramel sauce. But he had a connection to the shaykh. And to the people in the shaykh's private sessions.

"What did they talk about?" he asked.

"They are angry. Very angry."

"And what are they going to do about it?"

"I don't know. They speak carefully. Even in front of me. But I think something will happen. And if they trust me they will tell me."

"Is there anyone there named Stavro? Does anyone ever mention that name?"

"Stavro?" Mohammed put down his spoon and thought. "I don't know. People don't say names. Or maybe they make one up."

He picked up his spoon and dug in again. "Do you want me to keep going?"

"Yeah," Frank said. And Mohammed waited while he pulled out another hundred-euro note.

AASIM

When the police showed up and confronted the men in the rented Renault, the Englishman had escaped by running into the boulangerie and out its back door. The others—the Moroccans and the Tunisian—had scattered on the street. There were only two cops and only so many ways they could give chase. By the time they had rounded up the Arabs and come into the boulangerie to talk to the proprietor, all they could get from him was that a man had run in and run out. Which way had he gone from there? The proprietor shrugged. He had been busy with customers.

The Englishman, born Trevor but since his conversion Aasim, made his way back to the shabby apartment in an immigrant quarter of Lille that had been rented for the operation by someone he and the others had never seen. He couldn't be sure that the Arabs wouldn't give away the address—in his own previous career as an armed robber he had more than once turned in mates to get a break—so he was in and out quickly. Just long enough to grab the hidden cash and two jugs of the chemical. There was still a way to accomplish the mission. He went to a mini-mart and took a close look at some bottles. It was easy enough to buy syringes and needles from an indifferent chemist.

He took a train to Rouen, bought some samples, and experimented. Plunging the needle straight down through the plastic cap left a hole—actually, not so much a hole as a disturbance in the smooth blue plastic—that was small but noticeable. Better to inject at an upward angle beneath the bottom edge of the cap, where it overlapped the neck of the bottle.

The hole/disturbance was masked by the overlap and, once the cap was unscrewed, lost in the threads. He practiced doing it smoothly and quickly. After a couple of hours, he had it down to seconds.

Then he started to travel, by local train and bus, east toward Reims, then arcing south toward Paris. He knew that in Paris it would get the most attention. For Parisians the rest of the country scarcely existed. He had to pick unbusy hours to go into stores. Mid-morning was good. Late night had even fewer customers, but the emptiness and the hour led store clerks to pay special attention to a lone man with a face tattoo. So, mid-mornings.

With a preference, of course, for stores that didn't have security cameras in the dairy aisle.

After five days he had been to a dozen stores and injected thirty bottles. No one had told him why they all had to be Bouvier Lait, but he assumed there must be a good reason.

Then he waited.

FCIID

First Rafe, now this Nigerian. His gaze was intense, unnerving.

"Chat?" said Majid. "About what?"

He just wanted to know, the Nigerian said, if Majid knew anything about investments in a company called Sahel Hydrocarbon. "It has an operation in Nigeria." Was Majid by any chance familiar with it?

Majid took a moment, sat in one of his two visitor chairs, invited his visitor to sit in the other. This was where he had his opening conversations with potential clients. What were their goals? What was their time horizon? Their risk tolerance? Yes, Sterling Wealth Management could serve them well. This kind of thing was exactly their specialty.

Their specialty was not dealing with African cops investigating a client's role in sabotage and murder. So:

"Sahel Hydrocarbon? I'm not sure. What about it? What kind of investment?"

The man's gaze was still on him. "It is related to a criminal case in my country. An act of sabotage. It might not have been heard of here, in Geneva, in Europe. But people died. It was a terrible thing."

"But how is that related to an investment? I don't understand." Majid saying this at the exact moment that he absolutely, with certainty, all doubt and denial vanquished, finally did understand completely.

"I would not presume to tell you, as it is your business, that there are ways an investor can make money if a company has trouble. If its share price goes down." The accent strong but the language clear, concise, elegant. The

Queen's English that was no longer spoken in England. Majid had heard it before. There had been a Nigerian student at Harvard who'd said he was a tribal prince.

"Of course. One sells short or buys a put option. You think someone made such an investment that profited from this criminal act?"

"I do. And not just I."

Not just he? Who else? Who else?

"And why have you come to see me about this?" Majid said. The obvious question. Was it too obvious to ask? No, it would be suspicious not to.

"I cannot divulge the sources of our intelligence, of course. But we have sound reason to believe this investment was made in Geneva."

Majid made a gesture with his hands, opening his palms and pulling them apart. A gesture of volume, the wide, wide world. "There are six hundred and eighteen investment firms in Switzerland." (Where had he said that before?)

"*Geneva*," said the Nigerian. "Not Switzerland. Certainly there are fewer here. Are you aware of anyone who made such an investment in Sahel Hydrocarbon?"

"No," said Majid. "No, I'm not."

Okoro's gaze again, laser point on Majid. But Arabs know how to gaze, too, Majid thought. And how to resist gazes. He looked blandly back at Okoro. "I don't see how I can help you."

"Very well," Okoro said, still staring. "If you hear of anything, if you remember anything, let me know, please. You can reach me at this number." He handed Majid a business card printed boldly in black and green and red:

EMMANUEL OKORO

DETECTIVE/PEACE AMBASSADOR

THE NIGERIA POLICE

FORCE CRIMINAL INTELLIGENCE & INVESTIGATION DEPT (FCIID)

THREE MILLION NAIRA

Emmanuel Okoro had been born in Nsukka, in Enugu State, after the failed Biafran war. The Igbo separatists had fought bravely (and had brilliantly appealed to world opinion—that image of the starving child), but the central government, with outside aid, had prevailed. The official postwar policy was "no victor, no vanquished," but on the streets of Nsukka it certainly felt like they had been vanquished. Emmanuel's family's savings were gone, half his cousins were dead or disappeared or absorbed into strutting gangs, preying on the impoverished. His father had been invalided in the war, shot in the left knee. Persevering through a painful limp, he spent most of his time in Lagos, eking out naira by selling plastic bags of allegedly clean water to drivers stuck in go-slows. He hauled the water in a small green wagon. When it was stolen, he switched to lighter goods—handkerchiefs, T-shirts, belts. (It was said a Lagos driver could leave home stark naked and, with purchases from vendors in traffic jams, arrive at work fully clothed.) Emmanuel, back at home with his mother and sisters, worked streets as well, selling his mother's bean cakes and firewood he hacked from the bush at the edge of the city. His father had been a schoolteacher before the war, and his family valued education—Igbos generally valued education, it was a point of pride. With the money he earned and the little his mother could spare, Emmanuel paid fees to attend a state school. When older boys tried to get him to smoke *wee-wee*—marijuana—he resisted. The drug was also called "igbo," which he found personally offensive. He wondered why it didn't bother anyone else; they were all Igbo. They should all have their eyes on something bigger, something better. He certainly did.

But why a police officer? To serve justice? He had seen friends bullied in school (but never him, he would fight back fiercely no matter how hopeless), and market women extorted by gangs, and newspaper headlines about businessmen shot dead by robbers on the Obolo-Idah Road. Or to avoid injustice? He had seen plenty of that, too. Police constables demanding money from motorists at checkpoints. A taxi driver who accidentally splashed mud on constables dragged from his car and forced to sit in a puddle up to his waist. The police an ambiguous force, combating injustice and committing it. It was complicated. Life was complicated. Grow up in Nsukka, Enugu, Nigeria, and you learn that.

After police college, his first posting as an assistant superintendent was up north in Hausaland, where a violent band of Chadian rebels, on a sojourn in Nigeria to raise money for their cause, was robbing and killing. Roadblocks were established. Real roadblocks, not the pay-to-pass variety. A car full of Chadians was stopped, and they leapt out and escaped into the bush. Okoro was present when their car was searched. There were cartridges for AK-47s. And bean cakes. And a receipt for a car repair. Okoro went to the mechanic, who told him the men who had brought the car in were picked up by another man on a white scooter. Okoro got a warrant to detain the mechanic and installed him by a window in the police station. He dispatched constables to round up every white scooter they could find and direct the drivers to pass by the window. The mechanic saw and identified the scooter of interest. Its driver was arrested. Under physical interrogation (police justice/injustice), he eventually told where the gang was living, and several of the Chadians were arrested.

Okoro was still a young officer, but he already knew enough not to celebrate. He applied for a transfer. And a visitor came to see him. An emissary from one of the arrested men's mothers, he said. She was devastated by the arrest of her son, the emissary said. She was sure it was a mistake. She was sure her son and his friends were innocent. She was bereft. In her grief she had sold enough of her cows to raise three million naira, which would be given to Okoro if only he could see his way to weaken the so-called evidence against her son and his friends and get them released.

Okoro declined. Whatever kind of police officer he would turn out to be, he was not the kind to let murderers go free. He sent the emissary away. And checked on the status of his transfer.

When the emissary went to Okoro's superior, and that man accepted the money, and certain evidence was mislaid, and the prisoners were released, and they came looking for Okoro to get their revenge, he was already on his way to his new post.

BY FRIDAY

Stanley Pleski had a problem. It was in a dark gray Tumi suitcase sitting on the floor of his hotel room, next to the minibar. It was $675,000 in cash.

He handled larger sums than that, frequently. But this had come from Miami via DHL (risky but successful) with an urgent message attached. The sender needed clean money by Friday for a down payment on a Singer Island condo. There was another bidder for the unit, and the sender's wife wanted this unit, and this unit only. And the Florida real estate people had been infected by the anti-money-laundering virus and needed to see the right kind of paperwork with the money. Next fucking thing you knew you wouldn't be able to buy a candy bar without presenting documents with your fifty cents or however much a fucking candy bar costs nowadays. The sender didn't actually say all that in his message but Pleski got the drift. The main point: make this clean by Friday.

There was no "or else" attached, but there didn't need to be. Pleski didn't think his life was at stake, unless the sender's wife was a much crazier cunt than he imagined. But this was a client Pleski didn't want to lose. His regular fee was half of 1 percent, not much in this case, but a lot from this client over the course of a year. And Pleski had a lifestyle to maintain.

But by Friday? Nowhere near enough time to cycle the funds through a stamp or art auction. Or one of the real estate gambits he ran in jurisdictions where real estate agents hadn't been deputized by anti-money-laundering authorities. (There was one property in Malta he had bought and sold for clients a dozen times, everybody on both sides always showing a profit.) The quickest way to launder was through a casino (buy chips, then cash them in—winnings!) but that required a compliant casino manager, and the guy he worked with in Interlaken had recently been fired, and Pleski hadn't even begun to try to groom his replacement.

And so his thoughts turned to his banker, Catherine, non-erotically this time. Although, speaking of erotically, that doofus he'd seen hanging over her desk the last time he'd seen her clearly had more on his mind than banking. Barnstable, that was his name. When he'd taken Catherine out for a drink, she'd talked about him. About what a pain in the ass he was. How he'd blocked some good trades. And, worse, he'd been asking questions about him, Pleski, that Pleski didn't want anyone asking, ever. Since then he'd read about Barnstable on the local English-language news site. Dead. Killed in a tragic accident on the lake while sailing alone. Apparently he'd been one shitty sailor.

Good to know.

He called the Holborn Bank and asked for Catherine Cole and made a date to see her.

NEWS

One child sick in Beauvais. Her pediatrician prescribed rest and fluids, and then the child started to vomit uncontrollably.

An elderly woman in Compiègne rushed to the hospital with convulsions. Suspected meningitis. Died twelve hours later.

Four children sickened after having cake and milk at a birthday party in Roissy. This led to the first official inquiry.

Two of the party victims died. The first news stories appeared.

MISSIONS

Catherine had been perfectly content with Pleski out of sight and out of mind. And then this phone call with his request to meet. She would go, but she was running scenarios for the conversation when she got there. How maybe someone else could take over his account. Lead off with that. Make up some excuse. She was transferring to a different department (or different planet). This other colleague would be a better match for his needs anyway. Win-win, everybody happy. Pleski would have to agree. How could he argue? No, you're *not* transferring to another department? How could he claim to know? Tell him how sorry she'd be to lose him as a client after their pleasant and successful business relationship. But she was certain he'd be just as happy working from now on with what's-his-name, whom she could recommend without reservation. Now get the fuck out of my life.

He proposed meeting over a drink at Les Armures, in the old town. It figured that he'd like the traditional places, and Les Armures had tradition in spades. Location on a cobblestone street. You could break an ankle getting to the front door. Inside, a massive stone wall and ancient wooden rafters overhead. (One modern appurtenance: a bronzed letter of thanks from Bill Clinton for hosting him and Hillary, those two probably attracted by the same Swiss schmaltz that attracted Pleski.)

He was waiting when she arrived, seated beneath a crossed pair of antique rifles on a whitewashed wall. He had a Scotch, she ordered coffee. This was going to be simple, and unfogged. She had a mission.

But so did he.

She had just begun, "Mister Pleski, there's something I—" when he cut her off.

"I need a small favor."

"I'm sure the bank will be happy to help with anything you need, but I'm going to be moving to a different department, so—"

"Fine, whatever. Just one last lick before you go."

Last lick? This already didn't sound good.

He explained, as casually as asking for a fifty-dollar loan: One of his associates, who happened to own an all-cash business (*all cash*? People nowadays were using credit cards to buy Tic Tacs) needed a bank check to consummate a real estate transaction, a check from a source that would satisfy the nitpicky demands of the real estate organization, which his friend was not able to satisfy in the short time available.

"Well," Catherine said, setting down her coffee, "I don't know if you'd call the Holborn Bank 'nitpicky,' but we do have to satisfy certain regulatory requirements in vouching for a source of funds."

Pleski leaned forward confidentially. "You know what? I don't think you do."

What was this? Catherine looked at him. There was a mole on his right cheek that he really should have checked out. Although it wouldn't break her heart if he didn't.

"We don't?"

"*You* don't," he said. "You're on the inside there. You know how things work. I'm sure you could sidestep some of the formalities. I mean, you know the right people. Maybe you've got some special relationships . . ." He gave a knowing smile, almost a leer. What did he think, that she was fucking her way through the executive ranks? She tried to maintain a neutral expression—she always tried with Pleski—but he must have seen something that made him back off.

"Or maybe you don't," he said. "I don't know. But you're a smart girl. I'm sure you can find a way to make this happen. This is Switzerland. They used to make millions of dollars disappear all the time. And then reappear. All kinds of magic tricks with money."

She couldn't deny that. "But that was before," she said. "There are new rules." Not to mention the bank's own internal security measures. No disc drives or thumb drive ports on the computers, an AI program scanning attachments to employee emails for suspicious content, mainly designed to prevent the theft of proprietary information or client data (although she certainly wished someone would steal this client).

"Rules?" said Pleski. "Made to be broken." He drained his glass and signaled the waiter for a refill. "I need this done. And right away. Six hundred seventy-five thousand US. That's not even big money in this town. A rounding error. I'll give you the cash and—"

"No," she said. "That's not how things work."

"How things work?" Pleski's tone changed. Now he was laying out facts, simple and plain. "You've been handling my money for a year. Handling it *happily*. You and your bank. Taking your fees, taking your commissions, taking your salary and bonuses and skiing at Zermatt and vacations in the south of France. How closely did you ever look at my sources of funds? Ever?"

"You always presented documentation."

"Sure," he said. "You want documentation for this batch, too?" He picked up a napkin. "I can write something on this. You can put it in a file."

"That's hardly the same thing."

"Maybe it is."

"I don't think so," she said. But starting to think so. Oh shit.

"You know," said Pleski, "if anyone ever looks at all that other documentation, takes a hard look, and something's not right, the bank would be shocked, surprised, and appalled, right? How could such a thing happen, the bank being so upstanding and all? So they'd look: Who's the exec on the account? You. Who went rogue? Who takes the fall?" He pointed a fat finger at her.

How closely *had* Pleski's sources of funds been checked? she wondered. That wasn't her department, but she was supposed to notify Compliance of any red flags, and Pleski, from day one, looked like he was wrapped in a red flag. Or two, or three. But his account had been a good one, for the bank and for her.

But not anymore. She stood up. "I'm sure there's nothing to worry about," she said. "I can't help you with this."

"Sit down," Pleski commanded. "I think you may need another drink. And not coffee." He hailed a waiter. "Scotch for the lady."

She didn't want to sit, but she did. She needed to hear what was coming next.

Pleski lowered his voice. "Remember our deal with Kemper Media? *Your* deal? How it was stuck but went through because that kid in New York had an accident?"

Catherine nodded. Waiting.

"You called to tell me about it. You said it was good news, bad news. Good news that a kid got killed? Kind of callous, don't you think?"

"It was an accident," she said.

"That's right. It was an accident. And then there was that guy who was bothering you, messing with you—I saw him—and you told me about him. Barnstable."

Catherine nodded again, getting numb now. Heading into nightmare territory.

"And then he had an accident, too," Pleski said.

Catherine noticed he left out one thing—that she had also told him that Barnstable was looking into him, Pleski. The way Pleski was telling it, it was all on her. Barnstable was her problem, not his.

"I don't understand what you're saying," she said.

Her Scotch arrived. She drank a swallow.

"I'm just saying it's a funny thing, you practically insinuating I had something to do with what happened to that kid, like I'm some kind of hit man or something, and then making a point of telling me this Barnstable character was bothering you, almost like you were asking me for a favor."

What favor? Catherine thought. Like I asked you to murder Barnstable? Oh, right, that.

"Just like I'm asking you for a favor now," Pleski said.

Catherine wished she was recording this, so she could play the tape back later, parse the words, parse exactly what he was saying.

Pleski was still talking. "If anyone starts looking into the Barnstable accident, who was going around town saying what a pain in the ass he was? Not me. I didn't even know the guy."

Catherine said nothing.

Pleski reached under the table, and pulled out a Tumi bag. "Here," he said. "Six hundred seventy-five k. You can do it. I know you can."

Then he pointed to the menu she hadn't touched. "Do you want to eat?"

SMILE

The Syrian was cruising tourists in the old town when he saw the woman come out of a restaurant with a man. The beautiful woman whose purse he had tried to snatch by the river. She was with a different man this time, not the one who looked like an Arab. This man was Western and he looked like a pig. How many men did she go with? Was she a prostitute? Or was this just the way of things here in Switzerland? Go with one man one day, another man another? If so, what was the difference between that and a prostitute? She didn't seem to be flirting with this man, however. She looked nervous as she and the man stopped outside the restaurant door. He was holding a heavy bag, holding it out toward her. The narrow street leading away from the restaurant toward the cathedral was in shadow, and the Syrian started toward it so the woman would not see him.

But he was too late.

The woman turned her head in his direction. He got ready to run, ready for her to scream, to shout for the police. But she didn't scream or shout. She only smiled. She smiled at him. He froze, not understanding. Did she think he was somebody else? Or did she smile at every man she saw, even men who had tried to rob her?

The ugly man was still talking to her, but she was still looking over his shoulder, at him. Then she tilted her head toward the bag the man was holding, like she wanted him to notice it. Of course he had noticed it. Bags were his business. She looked straight at him, and she nodded and then looked at the bag again. What did she want? Why hadn't she shouted? Why was she pointing this bag out to him?

He had thought he was beginning to understand the West but clearly he had no idea.

Then the ugly man turned to see what the woman was looking at. He spotted the Syrian and he looked at him like he was nothing, like most people did, and the Syrian ran away.

RINGO

Rafe was sleeping when she knocked on his door. The knocking, in his dream, became Ringo Starr trying to wake Paul McCartney so they could finish recording "Octopus's Garden," a song he had liked when he was six. His dreams never made any sense. She knocked again and called his name. Then he was up. "Catherine?" He walked to the door in his underwear.

She walked in wearing a maroon dress—office wear—and, incongruously, what looked like slippers. She was carrying a small suitcase.

"Are you moving in?" he said. "Did you change your mind?"

"What? No."

Actually, he realized, he'd never asked her to move in. He'd just asked her to see him again, to be with him again (and, sure, to have sex with him again), maybe to give his life something it was lacking, although he'd never actually said that. But now, half awake, he liked the idea of her coming to live with him. They could both just get back into his bed. She could unpack in the morning, then they could make plans for the future, maybe a bigger apartment.

"You remember my client, Pleski?" she said. She had come inside and was standing by the couch.

"Pleski?"

"The one you said was a crook? The one you said was a murderer?"

He was more awake now. "I think I just said that was a possibility. Why?"

Good question. Why he was standing here in his underwear discussing

Pleski in the middle of the night? They should at least sit down. "Do you want to sit down? Do you want a drink?"

"Anything but Scotch," she said.

"I have vodka."

"Vodka." She sat on the couch and Rafe went to the kitchen. While he was pulling the Russian Standard out of his refrigerator, he looked back at her. She'd always been a little high-strung. *Animated*, he used to think. *Lively*. Now she just looked like a nervous wreck.

He handed her a glass and asked, "What's in the suitcase?"

She took a swallow. "Six hundred seventy-five thousand dollars. In cash. I saw the man who tried to snatch my purse. I tried to get him to steal this, too. But he ran away."

"What? Why?"

"I wanted it to go away. It's from Mister Pleski, what's in the suitcase. If I don't launder it for him by Friday, he'll implicate me in money laundering. And a murder." She took another swallow. "That's what he said. We were at Les Armures." She took another swallow.

"Murder? What murder?"

If Catherine heard him, she didn't let on.

"Of course he can't do that without implicating himself, so it doesn't really make sense, but he might get caught, there's always a chance he might get caught, and then . . ." She paused. "He brings me into it."

"Into what? You didn't kill anybody." He thought for a moment—was there any chance she *had* killed someone? No.

"No. *I* didn't. But money laundering . . ." She looked at him, raised her eyebrows. "Isn't that why you were so interested in him, and in me?"

"You know why I was interested in you."

"Yes, in Cambridge. But then five years go by with nothing. And then here I am, doing what I'm doing, and suddenly you're back."

"I didn't even know you were in Geneva."

"But I was, and you found me. And then you were investigating me."

I was, Rafe thought.

"No, I wasn't."

"Fine," she said. "Let's both believe that. Then maybe you can help me." She held out her glass. "Do you have any more vodka?"

He went and got the nearly empty bottle and sat on the couch next to her.

"Help you how?"

"Majid told me. He said you got into trouble in the States, some funny business, so you know that side of things."

Majid told you? Thanks a lot, Majid.

"And now you're doing favors for the government, so you know that side, too. So you can help me with this." She stretched out a leg and kicked the suitcase.

"Launder more than half a million dollars? By Friday?"

"Fair is fair. You fucked me to get to Pleski."

"No," he said. "Catherine, no."

"No?" She pointed to the open bedroom door, the unmade bed beyond it. "I was standing right over there, pretty much naked, when you asked me to introduce you to him."

"To help you. To help you get rid of him."

Apparently that did not dignify a response.

"Besides," she said, "you owe me." She drained her glass and looked at him with an expression he hadn't seen before. "If you're right about him, I think I saved your life."

"Saved my life?" Was he still dreaming? Would Ringo be walking into the room with the lyrics for "Octopus's Garden"? ("Lads, think I should sing this one.")

"I told Pleski that someone was asking about him and that fatal accident in New York. But I didn't tell him you were the one doing the asking. I kind of told him it was somebody at the bank."

"And . . .?" Rafe waited. Her voice was firm, her tone casual, like she was telling someone about a funny thing that happened at work. *And then we found a box of condoms behind the copier.*

"And then he was killed. In an accident."

"Who was killed?"

"Aren't you listening? Do you have any more vodka?"

"I'll look in a minute. Did Pleski tell you he killed him? That somebody from the bank?"

"He didn't *say* it . . . He . . ." And then she broke. Small tears, her head bobbing. Rafe put an arm around her.

"But you think he did?"

"I don't . . ." A sob. "I don't know. But if he did, it wasn't you, because I said it was somebody else."

"That doesn't make sense. Whoever it was at the bank, you said it was an accident, accidents do happen."

"That kid in New York, was that an accident?"

Rafe hesitated. "I don't know."

"So you don't know either."

Rafe didn't answer, wondering what he did know, about this or anything. He leaned over and opened the suitcase.

"See?" Catherine said.

He saw. Bundles of hundred-dollar bills. Six hundred seventy-five thousand. In the overall scheme of things, not really very much.

He closed the case and sat back into the couch.

"Okay," he said. "I have an idea."

Catherine nodded, crying now without tears.

He put both arms around her, and she didn't resist. She leaned into him. He kissed her, and they stumbled their way to the bedroom.

OBLIGATION

It didn't take more than a few minutes online for Majid to anticipate what would come next from Detective/Peace Ambassador Emmanuel Okoro. The FCIID, the Force Criminal Investigation and Intelligence Department, was elite, but elite what? The Nigeria Police Force was notoriously corrupt, world-class corrupt. Google "Nigeria police corruption" and get sixteen million results: "Police Abuses Rife," "Nigeria Police: Protectors or Predators?" "Survey: Police Most Corrupt Institution in Nigeria." Majid found some photos of the FCIID headquarters in Lagos. On a ramshackle side street called Alagbon Close, the low-rise structure looked like a derelict motel, with hand-painted signs pointing the way to various offices and bureaus and warning lesser officials not to park in their superiors' spaces. Looming ironically over the mess was a half-completed high-rise intended to replace the current offices. It had been abandoned mid-construction following exposés of massive corruption. If the police couldn't get their own new headquarters erected honestly . . .

Okoro returned a day after his first visit. He walked in like he commanded the place. The formality of his language made his words sound scripted, a memorized text, but delivered by a talented actor. "I know you were lying when I was here last time," he said. "There were a small number of other candidates, other firms, that might have facilitated the transaction in Sahel Hydrocarbon, but I have seen them now and eliminated them as possibilities. That leaves only you."

Majid was still seated behind his desk. Okoro had not given him time to rise. He was standing just inside the door. "Only me *what*?" Majid said.

"Don't insult me," Okoro said, "and I will not insult you. This is simply business. There are obligations to meet. And one obligation has not been met. I represent a party in Nigeria to whom it is owed."

"I thought you represent the police."

"I do that also." Okoro smiled. "It simplifies things when all parties are one."

And just then, of all times, Majid's computer dinged with a WhatsApp message. From Stavro: "News in France. People dying from poison milk. So sad. Bouvier Lait shares will fall."

Now? Majid thought. *Now*?

He blanked his screen and stood up, ready to continue playing dumb, but Okoro didn't give him a chance.

"I make assumptions on your behalf," Okoro said. "A new client came to you, previously unknown, with a substantial sum of money. His credentials, if he presented any, were bogus. You didn't know, or you didn't care. Perhaps this lovely office is hanging by a thread. Perhaps you are just greedy."

Majid started to say something, to object, but did not.

"He asked you to make an investment that would prosper if Sahel Hydrocarbon shares went down. And they did, because of an act of industrial sabotage. Which your new client knew was going to happen. Did you think the man who came to you did that himself? That he gave you his money, then jetted to Lagos to set explosive charges?"

Of course not, Majid thought.

"Of course not," Okoro said. "There were others involved. There had to be. Middle Easterners, as you may have guessed. But not just them. Nigeria is a complicated place. They needed someone there to ease their way. And someone did. For twenty percent of the profit. Which he has not received. Which is why I am calling on you. May I sit?"

Without waiting for an answer, he sat. And Majid's computer went *ding* again. Majid ignored it. Now he was standing and Okoro seated, their staging reversed.

"Perhaps you did not know," Okoro said. "Or you did not want to know." He paused, playing the drama. "But now you know."

Finally, Majid spoke. "First of all, even if any of this is true, you must be aware that I cannot tell you anything about my clients or their transactions."

"Excellent," said Okoro. "You have stopped denying."

"I am not confirming."

"You are."

"Even if any of this is true," Majid repeated, "I can't hand over a client's money just because you tell me to."

"So talk to your client. Explain the situation to him."

Talk to Stavro? Majid thought. Ron had talked to Stavro, and Ron was dead.

"Explain what? Who are you? A police officer who is not a police officer? From Nigeria? This is Switzerland. What kind of authority do you have here?"

"Perhaps I should talk to him myself. You could arrange an introduction. I imagine you would prefer that anyway, to retain whatever ignorance of this you still possess."

Majid realized: He doesn't know who Stavro is. He wants me to lead him to him.

None of this had been covered at Harvard Business School.

Okoro looked at his watch and stood. "Think," he said. "Think carefully. I'll be back. Remember that you are an accomplice to murder."

"Then so is your principal," Majid said. "Then so are you."

"But we have not violated Swiss finance regulations. The Swiss may not care about the deaths of a few Africans, but they care about those. Should that be exposed, all this"—he gestured around the office, its art, its furniture—"goes away."

Who cares? thought Majid. Then thought: I do. Then thought: Do I?

He watched Okoro walk away through the reception area. And saw, sitting on a couch, waiting to see him, Rafe. *Now*? Majid thought. *Again*? Who else would be dropping by today? Interpol? The KGB? The Mounties?

His computer was dinging with more messages from Stavro.

"Rafe," Majid said. But Rafe wasn't looking at him. He was looking at Okoro's back as Okoro walked out of the office. He stood and picked up a Tumi bag on the floor at his feet. "Here," Rafe said. "Hold this for me." He handed the bag to Majid, then followed Okoro out.

MINCHA

Okoro walked along the river, passing the doorway of the cosmetics shop where Rafe had sheltered, passing boutiques, passing banks. Rafe maintained a discreet distance behind him. Okoro turned left to cross the Pont de L'Île, stopping to read the marker commemorating Julius Caesar's destruction of a previous bridge there in 58 B.C. Rafe stopped there, too. Julius Caesar? Who knew? Then he fell in again behind Okoro. Fifty feet apart, they passed the island's old clock tower, crossed the second bridge and reached the river's south shore, where, one following the other, they bore right onto the Quai de la Poste.

A block on, Okoro turned left at the post office, and Rafe's phone rang. Caller ID blocked.

"What the fuck do you think you're doing?" It was Frank, never one for pleasantries.

"Frank?" Rafe kept his voice low even though, having turned the corner himself now, he could see that Okoro was too far ahead to hear him.

"Yes. Frank. What the fuck do you think you're doing?"

"I'm following a guy who was at Sterling Wealth Management," Rafe said, wondering why Frank would be asking him that question just now, exactly now.

"So are we," Frank said. "The place is being watched."

"It is?" Rafe looked around, at business people, tourists, shoppers. "I don't see anybody."

"That's the point," Frank said.

"Okay," Rafe granted, "but I was close enough to this guy to hear him talk. He sounds Nigerian."

"To you? He does? You know what Nigerians sound like?"

"There was someone at business school, a Nigerian prince."

"Harvard again," Frank said. "Thank god for Harvard."

"If he's from Nigeria," Rafe said, "he could be involved. He might even be Stavro."

"Brilliant," said Frank. "Now will you please back off and get the fuck out of the way?"

Up ahead, Okoro turned again. Rafe reached the corner where Okoro had turned and looked around it and saw a building unlike any other he had seen in Geneva. It was a large Moorish edifice topped by a dome, with walls striped pink and gray. He saw Okoro walking directly to it. Then he saw the six-pointed stars on its iron gates.

"Shit!" he said.

"What?" Frank said. "Shit what? Have you stopped? Have you backed off?"

"He's heading for a synagogue."

Frank's tone changed instantly. His anger gone, now a finder of facts, but one in a hurry.

"Is he wearing a backpack?"

"No."

"Carrying anything? A suitcase?"

"No."

"Bulky jacket?"

"No. He's going inside."

"Stay back. People are coming."

Frank clicked off. Rafe put his phone in his pocket and followed the Nigerian into the synagogue. It was cool and dimly lit, a large sanctuary with balconies above, on the left and on the right. There were arches everywhere painted with the same pink and gray stripes as the exterior. Rafe hadn't been in a synagogue since his friend Richie Nodel's bar mitzvah in Larchmont. This one was much nicer.

A few men wearing prayer shawls and yarmulkes were gathered up front by a raised platform, chanting and bowing. No one was looking back toward the entrance, where Rafe had stopped inside the door. A dozen feet away, the Nigerian reached into a wicker basket, picked up a yarmulke, and put it on his head. As he did, he turned and saw Rafe. He nodded. Rafe nodded back. This didn't seem like correct spy-tailing protocol, but it would have felt weird not to.

Then two men Rafe had never seen before walked quickly into the sanctuary. One was dressed as a banker (conservative suit, powder-blue tie), the other as a tourist (dad jeans, passport pouch hanging on a cord around his neck).

People are coming.

Frank's people.

Rafe wondered if it was one of them who had accidentally killed Ron Mayfield.

They walked toward Okoro, spreading out as they did, so that when they reached him one was on his right and one on his left. A tactical formation.

Rafe was close enough to hear what they said.

"Synagogue security," said the banker. "Do you mind telling us what you're doing here?"

"And keep your hands where we can see them," the tourist said. "I'm sure you understand."

"Yes," said Okoro. "It's terrible what's been happening at synagogues."

"So," said the banker, "what are you doing here?"

"I've come for the mincha," Okoro said, pronouncing the last syllable like he was clearing his throat.

"The mincha?" said the banker.

He doesn't know what that is, Rafe thought, and "mincha" sounded like something that synagogue security should know about.

"The afternoon prayers," said Okoro.

"Why is that?" asked the tourist.

"Why are there afternoon prayers?"

"Why are you here?" said the banker, more aggressive now.

"Why else?" Okoro shrugged. "I'm Jewish."

And Rafe's phone dinged with a text from Majid:

"What do you want me to do with this bag of money?"

FOR CATHERINE

"This is for Catherine?" Majid said.

"Yes," Rafe said. "For Catherine." Repeating what he had texted back to Majid, which was why Majid had told Rafe to come right over, and why Majid still hadn't replied to Stavro's texts (although he didn't need much encouragement to put off Stavro), and why Rafe had left the synagogue with the Nigerian and Frank's people still there (although he had also been very strongly urged to get the fuck out by angry looks and gestures from both the banker and the tourist).

The bag of money sat on the floor between them, Majid at his desk and Rafe in the chair where Okoro had been.

"She's being pressured," Rafe said, "actually sort of blackmailed, by a client who wants it laundered. By Friday."

"How do you know this?" Majid asked.

"She told me. She came to my place last night."

"Last night?" Majid had texted Catherine last night, twice, early and late. She hadn't responded.

Rafe nodded, knowing he hadn't needed to share that detail, but had wanted to.

"And she feels compelled to do it? Why?"

"She can tell you about it if you call her. But she's pretty upset."

Too upset to talk to her current lover but not to one who was "ancient history"? But this was not a question Majid wanted to discuss with Rafe.

"What is this client sort of blackmailing her *for*?"

"He's been laundering money through her at the bank. He says she's complicit."

"Is she?"

"He says he can make the case. Also . . ."

"What?"

"There's a murder."

Majid's eyes widened. "A murder?"

"A possible murder," Rafe amended.

"He's saying Catherine killed someone?"

"No," Rafe said. "But *he* might have."

Majid took a breath. A client who was a murderer? There was a time, say two weeks ago, when he would have thought the idea far-fetched.

"He says Catherine is involved?"

"He's saying crazy shit, but Catherine doesn't want him saying anything. She wants to do this favor for him and make it go away, make him go away."

Majid looked at the bag of money. "She came to you," he said. "Why don't you do it?"

"Do it how? I'm not a bank. I'm not a hedge fund."

"You said you were a hedge fund. At the Harvard Club party. That's what you said."

"I said I was setting it up. Early days."

"Fuck you," said Majid. "That story you told me last time, about doing some favors for the government because you got in trouble. That's all you're doing, isn't it? You're working for the government."

"If I am," Rafe pointed out, "I'm definitely in no position to launder money." Which was a good logical point—an anti-money-laundering federal agent shouldn't be laundering money. It was the opposite of the job description. Rafe tried to remember everything he had said to Majid and if it could all be reconciled.

"*If* you are?" said Majid, probing the weak spot.

"Look," Rafe said, "all that matters is that Catherine needs help, and I'm not in a position to help her, and you are."

Actually, Rafe had realized when he'd heard Catherine's problem that there might be a way he could help. There was enough on Pleski to bust him now. All Rafe had to do was make the call. True, his bosses in Washington wanted to get more from Pleski, to get leads on more of Pleski's clients, so busting him now would be premature. But Rafe could justify it, and nabbing him before Friday would moot the problem of laundering this cash. The government would seize it. Treasury agents somewhere would get a nice new surveillance van.

But Pleski could point a finger at Catherine. And the Holborn Bank, to save itself, would be only too happy to sacrifice her—"one bad apple."

So no.

"Six hundred seventy-five k," Rafe said, pointing to the bag. "It's not even that much."

Majid nodded. "Does she know you were coming to me?"

"No. She already thinks I'm shady. Do you want her to think you're shady, too?"

Good question, but Majid would have to put answering it on his to-do list. First, if he decided to launder this cash (and he would—for Catherine), he had to do it by Friday. Meanwhile, he would have to see what Stavro wanted and deal with that. And then there was the Nigerian cop who wanted money for his corrupt boss in Africa. On the plus side, so far next week was wide open. Maybe he could take a vacation, if he wasn't under investigation, or under arrest, or dead.

He got up from behind his desk and picked up the bag.

"I'll take care of it," he said.

SUPERHIGHWAY

"Who is he?" Rafe asked. "What did you do with him? Where is he?"

In a secret sub-basement, bleeding?

They were in Sykes's office again. He'd come straight from Majid's.

"We had a chat," Frank said.

A chat? Rafe didn't think that word was in Frank's vocabulary.

"He's a cop," Frank said. "From Nigeria. You were right about the Nigeria part."

"A Jewish cop from Nigeria?" Rafe turned to Sykes. "He said he was Jewish."

"It's a big and varied world," she said. "I guess you couldn't see it all from Connecticut." She took a sip of the bad embassy coffee and grimaced as she swallowed, as if she hadn't learned from the previous thousand cups. "He's an Igbo. Some of them think they're descended from one of the Lost Tribes. The State of Israel officially disagrees." Which apparently was enough about that. She changed the subject. "He went to see your friend, Mister Hassan, for the same reason you did. He's investigating the pipeline explosion."

"How do you know?"

"He told us," Frank said. "He figured we had that in common. He didn't buy that my colleagues were synagogue security."

"Nobody would," Rafe said.

"Plus he saw you following him from your pal's office. He wanted to know why we employed such amateurs."

"Next time I'll borrow one of your guys' disguises."

"Your wardrobe wasn't the problem. Anyway, he figured we were most likely investigating the same thing."

"We ran him," Sykes said. "He is a detective."

"Did you tell him who we are?" Rafe asked.

"Not in so many words. And he was too discreet to press the point. But he wanted to share information."

"Did you? Will we?"

"God no!" Sykes said in a rare fit of animation. "With Nigerian police? Do you know anything about the Nigerian police?"

Rafe shrugged.

"Traveler tip," Frank said. "If you're ever in Nigeria and get robbed and the police show up, run like hell or they'll get whatever the robbers missed."

"Switzerland just turned over three hundred million dollars from the bank account of one of their military dictators," Sykes said. "We think that's less than ten percent of what he stole."

"Fine," Rafe said, feeling sufficiently educated on Nigerian kleptocracy. "So what did we tell Detective Okoro?"

Frank smiled. "Have a nice day."

"It is worth noting," Sykes said, "that whatever his motive was in visiting your friend about the pipeline explosion, the fact that he went there of all places indicates that you were on the right track."

"About what?"

"About your friend. About his firm using the same route as Homeboy did for his Sahel Hydrocarbon trade, the same British brokerage and the same bank in Turkish Cyprus. That is a pretty big coincidence."

"Right," said Rafe, and added without pausing: "Except it's not, really."

"It's not?" Sykes looked at him. "Those were your words—'a pretty big coincidence.'"

Rafe remembered. He had said that, but to Frank, not to her. Was Frank taking notes on their conversations? And reporting? Every word?

"Yeah," he said, "but that was early days. I've checked around, and that particular route—that brokerage, that bank—it's pretty well known." Sykes looked at him skeptically. "And widely used," he added.

"By whom?" Sykes asked.

"By people who don't want people to know their business. I talked to people in London. That route, it's like a down-low superhighway."

"Is that so?"

"Sterling Wealth Management uses it. So do a dozen other firms. Here, London, New York. Any of them could have been working with Homeboy. If there is a Homeboy."

While Sykes considered what he was saying, Rafe realized that, for the last minute or so, everything he'd said was a lie.

BECAUSE

As he drove back to his apartment from the embassy, Rafe wondered why he had lied to Sykes and Frank. The circuitous route Majid had taken for his trades was not a widely-used down-low superhighway. As far as Rafe knew, it was something that Majid had done, and Majid alone. Yet the lie had popped out, smoothly and confidently. It had felt so right.

But why?

As he turned right toward his apartment at the giant chair with the broken leg, he considered the possibilities.

Because it simply felt good to lie to Sykes and Frank, neither of whom he liked or trusted? That was true but was hardly sufficient. Unless he was ten.

Because he didn't want to find Majid lying dead on the floor the next time he stopped by his office? That was a better reason, but Rafe thought Frank and his people would more likely want to get information from Majid than murder him (and he didn't even think they had killed Majid's partner on purpose).

Because he and Majid were now co-conspirators in an illegal money laundering scheme, which Majid might mention if push came to shove, with unfortunate consequences for Rafe himself? Well, yes, but that was a selfish motive, and Rafe didn't like to think of himself as selfish.

Because he and Majid were at least semi-friends who had hung out at parties in Boston and gone to Red Sox games together? There might be something to that, Rafe thought, but it was definitely outweighed if Majid was part of an international terrorist organization.

Because Majid didn't seem like an international terrorist (even though he had rooted for the Yankees)? Well, wasn't it part of a terrorist's job not to seem like a terrorist?

Because Rafe felt he owed Majid something because he had just fucked Majid's girlfriend? But, hey, she had been his girlfriend first.

This last thought led to a short but intense non-Majid reverie about Catherine and the night they had spent together after she'd brought him the bag of cash. It had been like their first times in Cambridge, hot and abandoned. He parked near his apartment and sat in his car for a moment, savoring the memory, as the sun went down over France. Whatever happened next, he wanted it to include more of that, more of Catherine. Primal was simple. Primal was clear. Primal was good.

As if in emphasis, a heavy beer truck roared past and streetlights burst on as he opened his car door and stepped out onto the sidewalk in front of his building.

Where Detective Emmanuel Okoro was waiting for him.

BOYFRIENDS

Catherine was home alone, waiting. She wasn't exactly sure what she was waiting for. She thought Rafe might call. With news about Pleski's money. With a suggestion that he come over and spend the night. She didn't entirely regret last night. It had made her forget her problems. There was that to be said for basic instincts. But starting up again with Rafe would be another kind of problem. She looked around her apartment. The white walls. The practical furniture. The de rigeur Montreux Jazz Festival poster. The books neatly arranged on shelves. Finance books, a literary anthology from college, short stories by Alice Munro, all those stories about lonesome Canadian women. Lonesome, but they survived. When unreliable men entered their lives it never turned out well.

The doorbell rang.

It was Majid. She opened the door, and he stepped inside and looked around as if he suspected someone else might be there.

"You didn't call," she said. "You usually call."

"I didn't want to talk on the phone," he said. He moved into the living room but remained standing.

"Why not?" Because he wanted to confront her about Rafe in person? But how could he know? And even if he did, he had no claim on her. She thought that had been clear.

"I did something for you," he said. "Rafe asked me to."

"What?"

"Took care of a problem with some cash. Something best not talked about on the phone."

Was he worried about being wiretapped? Should she be? Because of Pleski? But Majid wasn't involved with Pleski, at least until now, so what would he be worried about?

He sat on the couch. She sat on the white chair opposite.

"Rafe asked you to do it? Why you?"

"Because he thought I could do it more easily than he could."

"But you're . . ." She hesitated.

"Honest?" he suggested. "Not like him? I appreciate the confidence."

How odd, she thought. Every man in her life jumping in to help her with this. Rafe and Majid and, hey, what about Gary, her boyfriend in the eleventh grade? Would Gary be helping out, too?

"He said he didn't tell you he was coming to me," Majid said. "He didn't want you to think less of me. Or maybe he didn't want you to think more."

"Majid . . ." She didn't know what to say. Was that an accusation? That she preferred dishonest men?

"I don't think less of you," she said.

"I hope not," he said. "I hope nothing has changed between us."

She said nothing.

He waited a moment, then pulled an envelope out of a small portfolio he was carrying. She hadn't noticed he was carrying it.

"This is documentation of cash in an escrow account," he said. "Proceeds from the sale of a villa in Sardinia. The money is in the Barbadian branch of an Italian bank. Six hundred seventy-five thousand dollars waiting to be claimed by the seller, a trust established in Nevada. The name of the trustee has been left blank. You can fill it in as you wish."

She took the envelope and said, "Thank you."

"Do you want me to stay?" he asked.

Catherine looked at the attractive, kind, and considerate man sitting before her.

"Not tonight," she said.

And his phone dinged with a text. From Stavro. Summoning him to a meeting.

RELIGION

Okoro invited Rafe to have a coffee.

"Why?" said Rafe. He was still standing next to his car. He shut the door and locked it.

"Because your friends were not very helpful to me."

"What friends?"

"The ones I met after you followed me to the synagogue."

Rafe didn't see any point in denying further. Besides, he was curious.

"They said you were Jewish."

"I am."

"You're wearing a cross," Rafe pointed out.

Okoro looked down at it and smiled. "I am also Catholic. And Episcopal. God does not make distinctions. Why should we?"

Rafe didn't know how to begin answering that one. He let Okoro lead him down the street to a small bar with a metal counter. There was a table with two chairs by the window. They got coffees and sat there. Through the window, on the street outside, they could see the prostitute with dyed orange hair talking to a man in a gray overcoat.

"Interesting neighborhood," Okoro said. "The sex trade and cheap hotels." He took a sip of his coffee. "The Chinese tourists love them."

"The prostitutes?" Rafe asked. If Okoro was in no hurry to get to the point, Rafe saw no reason to rush him. He sipped his coffee, too.

"The cheap hotels." Okoro pointed through the glass to a middle-aged Chinese couple walking into a one-star hotel carrying three shopping bags apiece. "They save their money to come to Switzerland to buy prestigious goods. Watches and jewelry and handbags to impress people back home. Why stay in an expensive hotel? You can't take the hotel back to Guangzhou to show your friends."

"Where are you staying?" Rafe asked.

"That same hotel," Okoro smiled again. "It is all my estacode can afford."

"Your estacode?"

"My expense allowance," he said. "A police term. I suppose you have heard I am here on police business."

"How did you find me?" Rafe asked.

"You are not a very good spy. I saw you following me from the investment office. When I was finished with your friends I waited outside the American mission until I saw you come out. Then I followed you. Your tradecraft needs a little work."

Rafe said nothing. As he recalled, he'd been lost in thought when he left the mission. Not that it would have made a difference if he hadn't been.

"I think we should be cooperating," Okoro said. "I think we are all on the same side. Your associates did not trust me because I am Nigerian, and all Nigerians are corrupt."

"So I'm told," Rafe said.

"But two hundred million Nigerians? How could all of us be corrupt? Not one honest man anywhere? Is that even possible?"

Rafe shrugged. He was beginning to think anything was possible. "What are we all on the same side of?" he asked.

Okoro took another sip of coffee. "Solving a crime. Industrial sabotage and murder. Motivated by financial profit and enabled by a cynical investment manager. You were at Sterling Wealth Management. Your colleagues who followed me—without my noticing them, unlike you—had obviously been watching Sterling Wealth Management. So you and I and they all suspected that Sterling and its principal, Majid Hassan, were involved in the scheme. My suspicion validated theirs. Your suspicion validates mine. Together, we can apprehend the murderers. Mister Hassan will be our starting point."

Rafe hesitated. He could start telling this man the same lies he had just told Frank and Sykes. Had they believed him? They might have, because they only suspected Sterling in the first place because Rafe had fingered it, and now he was unfingering it. But this guy must have his own source of information. He hadn't been led to Majid by Rafe.

He took a middle ground. "Nothing has been established," he said.

Okoro finished his coffee and put down his cup and leaned forward and looked at Rafe. "It's curious," he said.

The look made Rafe uncomfortable. "What is?"

"I don't know who you are," Okoro said. "You followed me from Sterling, and I saw you leave the embassy, so it's logical to assume you are some kind of American agent. But you came to the Sterling office carrying a small suitcase. Investigators calling on suspects don't bring suitcases with them. So perhaps you are something else. What were you doing there?"

"You know I can't tell you anything," Rafe said.

"What was in the bag?"

Rafe stood up. "Thank you for the coffee," he said. "If you have any more questions, you should go back to the embassy."

Okoro was still looking at him. Did this guy ever blink? "You asked about my religion," he said. "I'll tell you what I believe. I believe I was created by God and deposited on this earth for a purpose. My purpose is to pursue criminals and murderers and bring evil to justice. I am curious. What is yours?"

PARTNERS

Stavro was waiting for Majid at the Grand Hotel Dolder in Zurich. Majid took a morning train from Geneva and then a taxi to Römerhof through the center of the city. Zurich, like Geneva, had a river and a lake, but it was darker, sterner, more German. At Römerhof he boarded a bright red car of the Dolderbahn, the old cog-wheel railway that carried him up through the forest on Adlisberg Hill to the grounds of the hotel. It would have been faster to drive straight there from Geneva, but Majid was in no hurry to see Stavro, and he'd thought he could use the time on the train to think about what to say to his client. In the event, though, he had mostly just stared out the window. Riding the Dolderbahn, he watched the teeth of the turning pinion mesh with the teeth of the rack as the car hauled itself up the steep slope. Technology from a simpler era. Simpler but no less violent, he knew. Majid had once stayed at an inn near Ypres in Belgium. The innkeeper, while serving him steak frites on dishes decorated with cheerful yellow daisies, had pointed to the gently sloping hill behind his establishment. It was covered with grass, freshly mowed, and occupied by the children of another guest playing tag, and, one afternoon in 1914, the innkeeper said, twelve thousand soldiers had been killed there.

They had been killed, however, without the involvement of an investment advisor in another country.

Stavro was waiting at a table between tall white columns on the hotel terrace, smoking a cigar and drinking coffee, with a copy of the *Financial Times* in front of him. He looked so calm, so smug, that Majid decided to be direct. Could this guy be unsettled? "Somebody came by the office looking for you," he said.

"Is that so?" Stavro took a puff of his cigar and laid it in an ashtray, careful not to disturb the ash, which was too short to brush off. "Was it the person working with American authorities who inquired about my trades? The one you told me about when I last met with you and your partner?" Which seemed to jog a memory in Stavro. "Oh, I heard about his passing. My condolences."

His *passing*? What does one say upon receiving condolences from one who might have murdered the party in question? *Not now*, Majid thought, *not now*.

"Thank you," he said. "It was somebody else. An African. A policeman from Nigeria."

"What did he say?" Stavro seemed mildly interested. He had picked up his cigar but was just holding it.

"He said he represented someone in Nigeria who was entitled to a share of your profits in the Sahel Hydrocarbon investment."

Majid watched for Stavro's reaction. A waiter appeared. Would the new arrival care for a beverage? "Pellegrino," Majid said. The waiter bowed away.

"What did you tell him?" Stavro said.

"I said I couldn't discuss my clients. It seemed like he wanted to meet you."

"Did you tell him how to find me?"

"How could I? I don't know how to find you. I thought you were staying in Geneva. Why did you want to meet here?" Majid waved a hand toward Zurich below them—heavy stone buildings punctuated by church spires, trams on the avenues and tourist boats on the Zürichsee.

"Change of scenery," Stavro said. "Plus Geneva does seem to be getting rather crowded with people interested in my business."

"As for that . . ." Majid began, but Stavro cut him off. "Yes, as for that, have you liquidated my position in Bouvier Lait?"

Majid nodded. He had. Stavro's messages had been clear. And

Majid had seen it as part of cleaning up, a prelude to being done. And he thought (*rationalized?*) that closing out the position, buying shares at the new lower price to replace the shares they had borrowed, meant there was no additional profit to be made by any additional drop in the price. So nothing to motivate any more deaths, any more poisoned children. Closing the trade an ass-backward way of saving lives. Probably not worthy of a medal, though. Or even a pardon. The waiter brought Majid's water.

"Excellent," said Stavro. "You are holding the profits in cash?"

"I am."

"I want to withdraw them. Not my initial investment. Just my profits to date." Stavro reached into a jacket pocket and pulled out a folded paper and handed it to Majid. Majid opened it and saw the names of two banks, two account numbers. "Send ninety-five percent—of the profits—to the bank listed first and five percent to the other."

"And the share claimed by the Nigerian?"

"I know nothing of any Nigerian," Stavro snapped. "After you've made these transfers, with what remains you should . . .'

This time Majid interrupted. "You should transfer it all. I'll be closing your account."

Stavro looked at him as if he had just suggested he withdraw his money in cash and throw it in the lake.

"Why would I do that?"

"Since the death of my partner," Majid said, "I'm refocusing the business. I'll be working with a handful of banks, advising their clients exclusively." Did that make sense? Majid wondered. It sounded plausible.

"No," said Stavro.

No?

"You may work with those banks if you wish. But you will also retain my account. And I'm ready to make another investment. Another short play." He was puffing on his cigar again.

"I'm afraid I can't . . ." Majid began.

"You can. I know it, and you know it. So just do it. I want to short a cruise line. The same procedures as before. The same anonymity. And, this time, no clerical 'accident' that unveils your name or mine."

"A cruise line?" That wasn't just ominous, it was also dumb, which almost cheered Majid up. "Cruise line shares are bottomed out. It doesn't make sense to bet on their dropping further."

"*Most* of them have bottomed out," Stavro agreed. "But one has recovered. Medallion Cruises. Small ships. Safe countries. Rigorous health measures. There's pent-up demand for cruises, and Medallion is getting the business. Its stock is up, but I think too high." He puffed on his cigar and smiled. "I mean, ships *are* prone to mishaps."

The smile was terrible.

Stavro gestured to the Zürichsee below them, and Majid looked down there again. The boats he could see all looked pretty stable. Nothing was foundering or blowing up or getting poisoned. A car ferry was chugging to Horgen. The waiter came and laid down a bowl of mixed nuts and wondered if Majid would like to see a menu.

"No," said Majid. The waiter thought he was talking to him and backed away. But Majid was talking to Stavro. "There are plenty of firms that can handle your business. Dozens right here in Zurich."

"No doubt," said Stavro. "But how many are run by a Muslim?"

Majid took a breath. Then asked, softly, "What does that matter?" Already fearing that he knew the answer.

Stavro took his time replying. He summoned the waiter back and ordered a cognac and then took more time before he leaned forward toward Majid.

"You have no way of knowing this, of course," he said, "but I'm working with people who are Middle Eastern. Like yourself . . ."

"I don't see how that matters." Majid tried to sound as if he actually didn't.

Stavro continued as if Majid had not spoken at all. "Like your mother in Dubai. Like your sister at university in Beirut. I'm told Amina is a very intelligent young woman. Studying civil engineering. Unusual field for a girl."

Stavro reached into his jacket again and pulled out a photograph of a young woman standing in front of a yellow brick building on the campus of the American University of Beirut. She had flowing black hair and was wearing a white blouse and tight jeans and talking to a young man carrying a book bag. They were both smiling. Majid stared at the photo as the waiter brought Stavro's cognac. "She looks lovely," Stavro said. "But her clothes . . ." He shook his head. "Not very modest."

Majid looked up from the photo. "Why do you have this?"

"My associates like to know who they're working with, and they're comfortable with people they can relate to—fellow Arabs, fellow Muslims. There was no other reason to pick your firm to be our partner. It's not very successful."

"I'm not your partner."

"No? Would the American authorities believe that? The Swiss?" He shook his head sadly. "You know, some people think all Arabs are terrorists." He lifted his gaze and stared directly at Majid. "Isn't that ridiculous?"

Then he picked up the photo and slid it back into his pocket.

PARTNERS II

Catherine supposed it was true what people said. How pleasant your job was depended on how good your boss was. Her new boss, newly transferred to Geneva, was worlds away from Barnstable. He was sixty years old and a native of East Tennessee with a trace of its warm drawl still in his voice, and he generally dealt with Catherine the same as if she'd been a man, or an animate lump of clay. On an occasion when he'd summoned her into his office and closed the door behind her and she started to tense up for whatever was about to come, what did come was his polite request to be able to call on her to give career advice to his college student daughter who was thinking of going into finance, since she (Catherine) was a woman and might therefore have insights on women in the field. So he had taken notice of her gender after all, but that was as far as it went. She supposed it was also true what people said about that—that fathers of daughters treated female colleagues differently, better.

It also didn't hurt that she had been on a roll lately. The Central Asian mining warrants had paid off, and she'd uncovered a successful play in the retail sector. The stock prices of major retailers, at least the ones that had survived internet shopping and pandemics and the resulting bankruptcies that consumed half the field, had recovered to appropriate levels. So there was no upside in equities, but Catherine had found one in debt. Through tedious old-fashioned research, she identified a tranche of corporate bonds that was, purely by chance, heavy in retail. Its price had plunged when retail did, yet had not recovered when the stocks did. She moved into it for her clients and the firm and, when it caught up to where it should be, was rewarded with a handsome gain, and a bonus.

This (and the preceding mind-numbing research) had been almost enough to take her mind off Pleski and his threats and his suitcase of cash. The latter had been handily dealt with by her little platoon of boyfriends (another situation she preferred not to think about), so when she got word that he had come by the office and was waiting to see her in the fishbowl, she headed downstairs thinking he had come to appeal once more to remain her client (no way) and, failing that, a greasy but welcome farewell.

*

It turned out that Pleski had a different view. For some time now he had been knocking himself out giving the boatloads of cash he received from his clients a spin or two in the washing machine before he took them to Catherine and her bank. The casino dodges, the real estate phantasms, the diamonds from India that were actually broken teacups, even fucking rare stamp auctions where he could barely stay awake to make the necessary bids. It was all very tedious, and he wasn't getting any younger. If only there was an easier way to handle at least some of the jobs, say by simply handing the cash to an accommodating banker and letting her do the work. Which, come to think of it, Catherine had just done for him once, so . . .

Catherine stared at him and sternly shook her head. "I am not *accommodating*. I was coerced. It was a one-time situation. You made that very clear."

Pleski smiled and scratched his jaw, his stubble rustling. "I don't see what your problem is. There could be something in it for you."

"No."

"Your call then. You can just do it for fun."

A couple of traders were walking by the fishbowl, paying no attention to what was going on inside. Catherine stood up. "We're finished here." They were alone in the room but she lowered her voice. "Those threats you made. You can't do anything without implicating yourself. And you have no proof I ever knowingly did anything to help you. Because I didn't."

"Well," he said, looking up at her, "as for *before*, I was kind of bluffing there. You probably could have called me on it. But now . . . those documents you gave me? Laundering the six hundred seventy-five k? Your fingerprints are on them, figuratively—and literally. And if anyone takes a look at that transaction . . . the address of the 'villa in Sardinia' that was the source of funds? It's a Chinese restaurant. In Sardinia. No kidding. Italian chop suey. Who knew?"

Catherine said nothing.

Pleski was enjoying himself. "Whoever created those documents was a little sloppy. Was it you? Friends of yours? I don't know. But I'm pretty sure it violates the sacred code of the Holborn Bank for an employee to be involved in something like that." He paused. "Not to mention Swiss law."

Catherine, still standing, said nothing.

"I'll have some more cash for you soon, so put your thinking cap on." He hauled himself out of his chair, never the easiest task, and walked to the door, where he turned back for a final word. "See you then, partner."

DADDY'S GIRL

Majid was numb on the train back from Zurich. Had Stavro just threatened to harm his mother and sister if Majid didn't keep working with him? Had Stavro just acknowledged that he (*they?!*) were working for terrorists? Had Stavro just asserted that if the scheme went down or Majid blew the whistle he would be implicated as a terrorist himself?

And wasn't that very likely to be true?

Yes, yes, yes. And yes.

The train passed through tidy Swiss towns and tidy Swiss fields and stunning mountains. There were always mountains in view. Majid knew that some of them were partially hollowed-out—civil defense shelters or secret armories. The Swiss hadn't fought a war in two hundred years but they believed in being prepared, with an army of citizen-soldiers who kept their weapons at home. It occurred to Majid that that might make it possible for him to obtain a gun himself, perhaps from a disgruntled or mercenary citizen-soldier (*were* there any disgruntled Swiss? they seemed pretty satisfied to him). And then what? Shoot Stavro? Would that make his situation better or worse? "Terrorist Financier Shoots Terrorist Accomplice!" Not good.

This being Switzerland, the wireless service on the train was excellent. Majid opened his laptop and searched for Medallion Cruises. Its website was beckoning and bright. *Exciting Destinations! Your Travel Dreams Come True! Fun for the Whole Family!* There were videos of happy customers in shipboard hot tubs and night clubs and smiling during shore excursions to beaches and Roman ruins. A live webcam was trained just then on the boarding ramp of a Medallion ship about to set sail after a stop in Villefranche-sur-Mer. The Mediterranean sun was beaming on passengers returning from a day on the French Riviera. They were wearing straw hats and sunglasses and carrying beach gear and shopping bags. A couple in their thirties was boarding with two children. The mother, her hair wrapped in a yellow scarf, was carrying a boy of two or three who was collapsed asleep against her shoulder. The father was chasing after a girl of six or seven with bright red curly hair and a T-shirt that said "Daddy's Girl." She was making a game of their walk up the ramp, running from her father, then waiting to be caught, screaming with delight when she was, then breaking away again. She was adorable. Daddy was laughing.

Fun for the Whole Family!

I mean, ships are *prone to mishaps.*

Majid was still watching the webcam when his train pulled into Geneva.

PART FOUR

TO ACT

"I believe I was created by God and deposited on this earth for a purpose. My purpose is to pursue criminals and murderers and bring evil to justice."

That's what the Nigerian had said to him, and he couldn't stop thinking about it. How nice for the man. Every morning you wake up and look around for evil and then go after it. Rafe supposed that could be dangerous, but at least it was clear. It was simple. You always knew what to do. Assuming, that is, that you could recognize evil when you saw it. Evil just seemed to be so damned amorphous nowadays. Homeboy and Pleski certainly fit the bill. But what about Frank and CIA goons? And Majid? And Catherine, who, despite what she said, might have turned a blind eye? And Rafe himself, the newly-minted money launderer? How had that $675,000 he'd taken care of been earned? Off whose backs? From whom stolen, extorted, swindled? (Which brought to mind his own previous career, where he had bought and sold and shut down companies for the benefit of wealthy speculators, never mind whose jobs might be lost, whose lives might be ruined.)

Rafe drank his morning coffee and looked out the window at the street below. No sign there of last night's hookers. A Sudanese immigrant opening a tobacco kiosk. A postwoman pushing her wagon on early rounds. Both with duties simple and clear. Rafe thought about what his purpose might be. Worst case: this could be his purpose, to think about his purpose. He remembered a story he'd read in high school, "The Beast in the Jungle." Poor son of a bitch in the story kept waiting for something important to happen in his humdrum life, for the "beast in the jungle" to appear. But his beast in the jungle was that there was no beast in the jungle. A clever irony but sad as hell.

He set down his coffee cup, thinking "Stop thinking." Just act, and purpose will (may?) follow. Or at least keep him too busy to dwell on these thoughts.

He stood up, ready to act, and was saved from thinking the next thought, asking the next question—"act at *what*?"—by the ringing of his phone.

It was Catherine.

Majid called a few hours later.

*

Diving had made Catherine brave. She had taken it up because she wasn't. She'd been a shy child. A normal mother would have taken note of that and helped ease her daughter's way into the world. But Catherine's mother had been self-involved, trying to establish herself as an abstract artist, too busy painting and hustling around galleries to devote much time to Catherine. She figured school would socialize her daughter; it had socialized *her*. Catherine's father, more attuned, encouraged Catherine to join after-school activities and often carted her there himself, leaving early from the office where his employer was busy swindling hundreds of people of millions of dollars (what had her father known? had he suspected? had he turned a blind eye?). She liked dance classes, but when her school required a sport and soccer was king, Catherine backed off. Too many people in bumping confusion on the field. Swimming was an option. Better. And from that she migrated to diving, where she could be even more alone. But diving forced one to be brave. The twisting dives where you lost orientation, the reverse dives where your head flew inches past a concrete platform. The ten-meter! She was surprised by how brave she could be. It was a happy surprise, and it gave her confidence. She could make friends. Or leave them. She could endure the competition of business school, and break up with a wrong fiancé, and take a job in a foreign country. She could start an affair with Majid, and now seem to have another one going as well. So why, she wondered, had she lost her courage with Stanley Pleski? He couldn't implicate her in money laundering without incriminating himself. As for being an accomplice in the death of her idiot boss, who for all she knew had died solely because he was a lousy sailor, which he very likely must have been . . . it was ridiculous. So why had she agreed to help solve Pleski's "problem"? Because the return of Rafe had knocked her off balance? Because she had been happy that Barnstable was dead? Because she had somehow known that Pleski's money was dirty and had turned a blind eye? Because she was her father's daughter?

Alone in her apartment with a glass of chilled vodka, she tried to sort that out. And quit trying when she realized it didn't matter which of it was true or if all of it was or none of it. All that mattered, now, was what to do now. She knew what she wanted to do, and she knew she could. She had done dives like the reverse one and a half, with twists. She had made a nervy bet in the bond market and won. She would get Stanley Pleski out of her life.

Also, she should probably drink a little less.

She did not tell all that to Rafe when she called him. The story of her life could wait for another time. Or never.

She went to Rafe because he had helped her before. Well, he and Majid, but Rafe had put it together, and Rafe had some kind of connection with the US embassy or law enforcement or something. (She'd never gotten to the bottom of that. Every time they talked she was either too upset or they were jumping into bed. Or Rafe evaded.)

So she called Rafe, and they met at a bland modern café near the university, with peace and love posters on the walls and students working on laptops. She ordered a coffee and told Rafe everything she knew about Pleski. She said she would tell it to anybody, that she would go public, even at the cost of her job and whatever revenge Pleski could exact. "I don't care," she said. "I just have to stop it." She was clear-eyed and calm.

Rafe put down his own cup and looked at her, seeing her in his current state of mind not as his lover, not as a woman whose cream silk blouse he wanted to pull off her, but as a person with a problem that he could help solve by dint of his experience and knowledge and position. It was like being back in the office in Connecticut looking at a complicated deal. He knew how to resolve complications.

"You don't have to go public," he said. "I have an idea."

Catherine looked skeptical. Or disappointed. "Like your last idea? Just do what Pleski wants?"

"No," Rafe said. "Not that. Not that at all."

He asked her some questions about the Holborn Bank and about her new boss, and she answered them.

He told her what he needed and asked if she could get it. She said she wasn't sure, there were security procedures.

She said she would try.

*

"Do you know about the camel races in my country?"

"No," Rafe said.

"About the jockeys?"

"No," Rafe said.

He was meeting with Majid in late afternoon, sitting on a bench near the rose garden in the Parc de la Grange. He had met with Catherine just hours before. His head was still on her problem. He did not know why Majid had summoned him to talk about camel racing, but he didn't mind. Majid had said it was important. It seemed that once you resolved to act, there was suddenly plenty to do.

"Nobody goes to them," Majid said.

"The camel races?"

Majid nodded. "There are hardly any spectators, but they are very big, very important, for the owners of the camels. Wealthy Emiratis with big stables. Bragging rights and big bets. Lots of money changes hands. Plus, it's an ancient tradition, which means something there."

"Okay," Rafe said. Majid could take his time with this, whatever it was.

"The races can be very close," Majid said. "A matter of inches. And camels run faster with less weight on their backs. The lighter the jockey, the better."

Rafe nodded.

"So," Majid said, "the jockeys used to be children."

"Children?" Rafe said.

Majid nodded. "From Pakistan and India. The camel owners bought them from their parents."

"*Bought* them?"

"The parents were impoverished. They needed money. Also, the camel owners might have lied to them about providing their sons with education." Majid shrugged. "Or maybe they didn't."

Rafe wondered—was his next task going to be rescuing enslaved children?

"Then some articles were written in the international press, exposés, and the government was embarrassed, so it banned the practice."

Okay, so not that.

"Who rides the camels now?" Rafe asked. "Monkeys?"

Majid shook his head. "Robots. With mechanical rotating arms holding whips. The camels' owners drive their cars around the outside of the track while the animals are running. The camels are racing, and the Mercedes are racing. The owners have remote controls telling the robots when to swing their whips."

"That sounds very bizarre."

"It is. The robots wear jockey caps and jerseys with the colors of the owners' stables."

"The robots have heads?"

"Knobs," Majid said. "Just big enough to hold the caps."

He was silent while Rafe tried to visualize that. Nearby, an old man trailed by a young nurse was leaning over to smell some of the roses.

"What do you think?" Majid asked. "Does that make it all right?"

"Does what make what all right?"

"Doing the right thing after doing the wrong thing. The robots came in and there were no more child slaves."

Rafe considered. "What happened to the children?"

"Some were sent home. The government put some in schools, I think. I don't know." Majid looked off in the sky at nothing.

"You want to replace children with robots," Rafe said.

Majid looked down from the sky and nodded. "I can't undo what's happened. People dead in Africa. Children dead in France. But I can stop it from happening again, maybe. I can help. If I'm allowed to."

"Allowed?" Rafe said.

"By the authorities. Your authorities."

"I'll talk to them," Rafe said. "But they aren't the only ones investigating this. That Nigerian police officer. He talked to me."

"The Nigerian? He's a crook."

"He is?" Rafe turned on the bench to face Majid full on. "How do you know?"

"He came to me and demanded a share of the profits. He said they were owed to a corrupt cop in Nigeria who helped set up the explosion there."

Rafe sat back and thought. Okoro a crook? *Not* put on earth to bring evil to justice? Could that be true?

It could.

But did it matter?

"What is it?" Majid asked. "What did he tell you?"

Rafe looked back at Majid, decision made. "It doesn't matter," he said. And it didn't. He had things to do.

LIES

People lied. Helen Sykes knew that from years of experience. And she counted on it. If people didn't lie, she would be out of business. The CIA would be out of business. Every time an informant told them something, the informant got that thing by lying to someone else. Unless, of course, they were lying to the CIA and telling the truth to the other party. Or lying to both (which was probably the most common). At this moment she was wondering about the truth of the story being told by the man sitting in her office. The fact that he was a member of her own team didn't change anything. That might have given him the benefit of the doubt except for the fact that he was right now telling her that he had lied to her before.

"That's not what you said yesterday," she said. "Yesterday you said exactly the opposite." As usual, there was nothing on her desk, nothing extraneous to devote her attention to.

"Not *exactly* the opposite," Rafe said.

"You said there was nothing special to link Sterling Wealth Management to Homeboy's trades. That lots of firms used the same shady brokerage and the same shady bank. That any of those other firms could be handling Homeboy's business."

"It was a 'down-low superhighway,' you said." This came from Frank. "We were back to square one, you said. We were nowhere, you said." Frank was sitting in his usual chair along the wall. The chair Rafe had was more comfortable, but it didn't feel more comfortable.

"I've had another talk with Mister Hassan," Rafe said.

"Your friend Majid," Frank said. He turned to Sykes. "They both went to Harvard. Has he mentioned that?"

"One question before we go any further," Sykes said, still looking only at Rafe.

He waited.

"What was in the suitcase?" she said.

Oh shit, Rafe thought. He knew he looked surprised. He hoped it looked like the surprise of someone who found the question surprising because it made no sense, not someone who found the question surprising because it did.

"What suitcase?"

Frank smiled. "The one you carried into your friend Majid's office. The one you left there when you took off on your boy's adventure chasing Detective Okoro."

"Your people saw that?" Rafe said, realizing.

"So did Okoro. He's a detective. He wonders about anybody carrying bags into the office of a money launderer."

"I thought you brushed him off."

"Well, not without a little conversation first," Frank said. "That would have been rude."

"Okoro's a crook," Rafe said. "Mister Hassan told me. Okoro tried to shake him down for a share of the profits from the Sahel Hydrocarbon disaster."

Now Sykes smiled, too. What was so damn funny? "So," she began, "Mister Hassan, who you told us wasn't part of that terrorist plot, told you that Detective Okoro came to him for a share of the profits from that terrorist plot. Did Detective Okoro have the wrong address?"

"I just told you. Mister Hassan *was* involved."

"We need a scorecard with you, buddy," Frank said.

"And now Mister Hassan wants to help us bring down the people responsible."

"You mean the people responsible other than him." Frank again.

"He didn't set the explosion. He didn't bet money on the outcome. He was a middleman. He had no idea at the time who his client represented. He didn't know what was about to happen. He just made an investment at a client's request. Which he does every day. It's his job."

Sykes swept an invisible speck of dust off her desk.

"And you know all that because he told you."

"Yes."

"But you didn't tell us before."

"He didn't tell me before. He thought he would be blamed. They threatened his family. But he's told me now. He doesn't want anyone else to be hurt. He feels terrible. He wants to make it all stop."

"In exchange for a deal?"

Rafe nodded. "No prosecution."

"So there's a limit on how terrible he feels."

Rafe could see a glimmer of satisfaction on her face, having proven, once again, that no one in the world was entirely honest or innocent or good.

"He's not the one demanding the deal," Rafe said. "I am."

"You haven't answered the question," Sykes said.

"What question?"

"What was in the suitcase?"

"Nothing," Rafe said. "Nothing relevant to any of this." Thinking, what else could he possibly say? Dirty underwear? Gym clothes? Things for a trip he was going to take after visiting Majid that day but then forget to take?

"You see my problem," Sykes said, not looking as if she had a problem. "Mister Hassan says he knows things that can help us. And his reference, the person vouching for him, refuses to answer a simple question about a suspicious activity that involves Mister Hassan."

"Talk to him yourself," Rafe said. "Ask him anything."

"But could we believe that he's telling us everything?" said Frank. And then, as if just then struck by the thought. "He's not an American citizen, is he?"

"No."

"Or a Swiss citizen?" Frank didn't wait for Rafe to say no again. "So there's no authority to object if he happened to end up in another country helping in the fight against terrorism, where he might be persuaded to tell everything he knows. With no deal required."

"Are we still doing that?" Rafe said, actually shocked. "Rendition?" Thinking of Majid in an Egyptian prison, of Majid in a Saudi dungeon.

Sykes said nothing. "International cooperation," Frank said. "Very helpful."

"We need him here," Rafe said, trying to sound firm without sounding desperate.

"Why?" asked Sykes.

"Because, if he's here, he can lead us to Homeboy. He can't do that if he's hanging by his thumbs in a cell in Cairo."

Sykes and Frank exchanged a look. Then she turned back to Rafe.

"Go on," she said.

GOOD BOYS

"Did you get my money?" The voice, low and husky, came via WhatsApp, encrypted, from Abuja, where its owner had a whitewashed six-bedroom villa with a screening room and pool. Not bad for an assistant inspector general of police with an annual salary of six million naira. If anyone asked, he would explain that he got it cheap ("The seller was desperate"). But no one ever asked.

Okoro was listening to the voice on his phone in the lobby of his one-star hotel, where the nightly rate was the equivalent of one hundred thousand naira. Two months there would take the assistant inspector general's entire annual salary. But the assistant inspector general always stayed in nicer places when he traveled.

"Not yet, sir," Okoro said.

"Why not?" demanded the voice from Abuja. "Wetin you dey do there? Learn to ski? Eat Swiss cheese?" The voice laughed. Not a friendly laugh.

"I found the investment firm they are using. I haven't found the man who controls the account."

"But the investment firm must know who that is."

"Yes, sir," said Okoro, lowering his voice as a middle-aged Chinese couple passed him carrying shopping bags from Fendi. Okoro had seen them before, arguing about something at the reception desk. The man was wearing an oversized watch on his wrist. He might as well have worn a sundial.

"Big firm? Small firm?" asked the voice from Abuja.

"Small. Basically one man."

"Good. So ask him to tell you."

"I have asked him, sir."

"Ask him harder. If you need them, there are a couple of good boys at the embassy who go fit help."

MIX-UP

It was a nondescript apartment on the third floor of a building on the far side of the train station, overlooking the pond in the Parc des Cropettes. There were photographs of mountains on the walls. There were no buildings opposite to see in the windows. The name on the buzzer downstairs was Fleurent. No one named Fleurent, or anything else, lived there.

Majid and Rafe sat on a brown leather couch. Sykes sat at a dining table, facing them, above them. There were bottles of water and iced tea on the table. So, Rafe noted, the CIA has a catering budget.

"His name is Stavro," Majid said.

Sykes looked interested, as if she didn't know that already. "Is he still in Zurich? Or back in Geneva?"

"I don't know," Majid said.

"And that's the last time you saw him? In Zurich?"

Majid nodded.

"What's supposed to happen next?"

"He wants me to short the stock of a cruise line. And meanwhile send off the profits from the first two shorts."

"Profits from the explosion in Africa and the poisoning in France that killed four children?"

"Yes."

"And the profits are to be sent where?"

"Two places. Ninety-five percent to a bank in Khartoum, five percent to an account in Malta."

"Five percent," Rafe said. "Sounds like Stavro's commission."

"No shit," Sykes said. Then, to Majid: "What have you done so far?"

"Nothing. He texted and I told him I'm still looking for shares to borrow. He wants the profits sent immediately. I told him that had to wait until Monday."

It was Sunday.

"Ninety-five percent for his principals," Sykes said. "What do you know about the people getting the ninety-five percent?"

"He said they're Arabs, Muslims. That's why they picked me."

"No other reason?"

"No," Majid said. "No other reason."

"Stavro must know who they are," Rafe said.

"We should definitely ask him," said Sykes. "The bank in Khartoum is unlikely to be helpful." She turned back to Majid. "If you told Stavro you had to meet him, would he do it?"

"I don't know. I told him that Rafe had asked about him. And the Nigerian. He's only communicating by text. I think he'd be suspicious."

Sykes nodded. "He needs motivation."

"Majid doesn't send the money," Rafe said. "That would motivate him."

"Too blatant," Sykes said. "And Stavro's bosses might think your friend here is keeping the money for himself."

"Even better," Rafe said. "Wouldn't that motivate *them?* They'd come after Majid. You could grab whoever comes and ask who sent them."

Majid looked at Rafe. *They'd come after Majid?*

Rafe saw the look. "We could guard him. Couldn't we?"

"Yes," said Sykes, her tone not completely reassuring. "But we'd be grabbing low-level thugs who wouldn't know anything. We want Stavro." She unscrewed the top of an iced tea bottle. "I think it would be better if Mister Hassan here made a mistake."

"A mistake?" asked Majid, relieved that the discussion had moved on from thugs coming after him.

"Instead of sending ninety-five percent to Khartoum, send five percent. A simple mix-up." Sykes sipped her iced tea.

"And the ninety-five percent?" Rafe asked. "We take it?"

Sykes shook her head. "The account is in Stavro's name, right? We can't take it without getting Swiss authorities involved. Accounts are sacred here."

"But we're not going to send it to Stavro," Rafe said.

"Of course not," Sykes said. "And, as charming as your friend Mister Hassan here is, I'd rather not leave that money under his control, considering he has just helped finance two terrorist attacks. We'll keep the money in Stavro's name but transfer it to another bank. But not the one in Malta. We want a bank where we have friends."

Rafe said, "There is one."

CORDELIA

Catherine's new boss's name was Armstrong, and his daughter's name was Cordelia. From Shakespeare, Catherine thought. She couldn't remember which play. Armstrong told Catherine that Cordelia was coming for a visit, and he hoped Catherine could have that promised chat with her about women in finance. Catherine said of course.

When she came into the office after a lunch with her father, Cordelia turned out to be petite and pretty, with soft features and a blue cashmere sweater that was tight and took a dive into cleavage that was impressive for someone her size. The men in the office took notice but quickly looked away when her father scanned the room. Cordelia didn't seem to mind the attention.

Catherine had some of her old accounts with Barnstable up on her screen when she saw Armstrong and Cordelia walking toward her. She blanked it.

"Catherine," Armstrong said. "Here she is. She's looking forward to talking to you."

"Nice to meet you," Catherine said.

Cordelia, who had been doing her own scan of the room, turned to Catherine and said, "Hi. Yeah. Thanks. I'm just looking for a woman's point of view about this. I'm thinking either banking or consulting."

"Good options," said Catherine. "I'll be happy to help."

Armstrong smiled. "I'll give you two my office. Take your time."

"Sure." Catherine stood up. "Maybe I could show her some account records so she can see the kind of work we do."

"No need," said Armstrong. "I think all she's looking for are broad strokes now."

"Is that right?" Catherine asked Cordelia.

"What the man says," she shrugged.

Catherine led the girl to Armstrong's office and closed the door behind them. There was a couch against one wall, but she took the seat behind Armstrong's desk and gestured for Cordelia to take the visitor's chair.

"So," Cordelia said, leaning forward, "what's it like to work for my father?"

"Actually," Catherine said, "if they were all like him, everything would be wonderful."

Cordelia nodded, pleased, while Catherine surveyed Armstrong's desk. There was a fountain pen in a stand. Photos of Cordelia and her mother and a dog. The usual markets ticker running on the computer. She looked for Post-it notes stuck on the monitor or the surface of the desk or the base of the desk lamp. Nothing.

"I think he's pretty cool," Cordelia said. "He's kind of pushing the idea of me in banking, but he says whatever will make me happy."

"That's what my father always said." Catherine stopped her survey of the desk, remembering. He had always said that.

"Was he in finance, too?"

"Not exactly."

Cordelia waited for Catherine to say more, but nothing more came.

"Well," Cordelia said, "I guess it could be interesting. My father definitely likes it. Do you?"

"I do," Catherine said.

"Not to mention lucrative," Cordelia said.

"Not to mention," Catherine said. "You know, there was a memo going around the other day about salary and bonus structures. It's supposed to be confidential, but I'm sure your father wouldn't mind."

"Not if we don't tell him," Cordelia said.

"I think I saw him put it in here." Catherine pulled open the top right desk drawer and also the built-in shelf above it. Taped to that was a white index card on which was neatly written in fountain pen ink, CoRdELiA44#! Catherine looked at it, pushed the shelf in, glanced in the open drawer, and closed that, too.

"I guess not," she said, "but yeah, in banking, you can do very well."

MESSAGES

The email from Catherine arrived at 3 a.m. Rafe opened it as soon as he woke up. The message read, "For the party we're planning!" Attached was a folder labelled "Sarah's Surprise Party." It contained lists of guests and party supplies and menu items ("Don't forget the salsa, if you can find any here!"). Every list had a blank page at the end, and some had blank pages in the middle (the guest list skipped a page between Suzanne Selzer and Kip Thomas). They were the kind of random formatting errors that can occur if one isn't careful. Rafe went to the first blank page and dragged and clicked his cursor to select the entire blank space. It turned blue. Then he opened the ribbon at the top of the screen and clicked to open the menu of font colors. He selected black, and the contents of the page, which had been there all along, white letters invisible on a white background, appeared like magic. There were numbers, and transaction dates and amounts, and the names of account holders. He repeated the process for all the blank pages and took special note of the names, which he proceeded to google, one by one.

*

Stavro texted Majid, asking if the short sale of the cruise line had been accomplished. Majid replied that he was still looking to borrow the shares. Stavro texted again the next day, and Majid replied the same thing.

Then Stavro started texting on a different subject, first angry, then frantic, then more frantic. *You made a mistake . . . Text me . . . What the hell did you do?. . . Get back to me now . . . Now!*

Majid did not reply.

DESIGNATED NATIONALS

"Can I ask you," Armstrong said, "where did you get this information? It's all confidential."

Rafe shook his head with a sad smile. "They don't even tell *me* about sources and methods," he said. "Informers? Whistleblowers? Wiretaps? It's need-to-know. But you're not denying that it's accurate, are you? That you do handle these accounts?"

"Honestly," Armstrong said, "I don't know. Some of these go back a few years. I'd have to check. I'm new in this branch."

Armstrong sat behind his desk at the Holborn Bank, the one with the fountain pen in a stand and Armstrong's computer system password written on the card taped to the pull-out drawer. Rafe was in the visitor's chair. Armstrong had handed back his Treasury ID after being suitably impressed, and Rafe had put it back in his jacket pocket. He could see the framed photos arrayed around Armstrong. One was of a young woman, most likely his daughter. Pretty girl.

"A lot of these people have been on the government's radar for a while," Rafe said. "Some have been on Treasury's SDN list for years. That's 'Specifically Designated Nationals'..."

"I know what it is," Armstrong said.

"Well, someone here didn't know. Or didn't care." Rafe knew it was in his favor that Armstrong was new in this office. Anything that happened before he got here couldn't be his fault. Simplest thing for him to do would be to clean house.

Rafe pointed to the list he'd laid on the desk when he arrived. "You've got two drug traffickers there, an arms dealer, at least one so-called charity linked to a terrorist organization. All of them with accounts here. You're not supposed to be dealing with them, facilitating them, conducting any transactions. The SDN list isn't a secret. It's *published* . . ."

"We're not a US bank," Armstrong said. Uh-oh, Rafe thought. Institutional loyalty? Armstrong did look like a company man. Time to bring out the guns.

"You have correspondent banks in the US. You settle trades in the US. Would you rather conduct your business—*all* your business—with banks in China? Russia? Iran? Holborn can be totally blocked from the center of the international banking system. Not very convenient for your customers. I'm sure they'd prefer to bank with institutions that *aren't* on the sanctions list."

Armstrong leaned back in his chair and gave up. "What do you want?" Rafe could hear his accent now. From somewhere down South, almost. "I can close these accounts right now."

"No," Rafe said.

"No?"

"Now that we've identified them, we want to watch them. We'd like you to keep us informed of their transactions. So we know what these people are up to."

"So I'd be working for the US government?"

"You'd be helping to fight crime and terrorism. I'm sure you don't have a problem with that."

"And what do I tell my headquarters?"

"As little as possible. We have no idea who sanctioned the opening of these accounts."

"I doubt anyone in London was aware," Armstrong said. "My predecessor here . . . he didn't have the best reputation." And added: "He's deceased. A sailing accident."

"Well, that's convenient then," Rafe said. "We can meet periodically. My agency has an expense account. Where do you like to eat?"

Armstrong smiled. “So we won’t be meeting in back alleys?”

“Unless you’d prefer,” Rafe said, “although I don’t think Geneva has back alleys.” And added: “There is one thing, though.”

Armstrong waited. Rafe leaned over and pointed to a name on the list. “We would like you to close *that* account. In the most emphatic way.”

JARDIN DES ALPES

Okoro walked down the Quai des Bergues with two other Nigerians—a husky Yoruba man who worked security at the mission in Geneva and another, thinner but taller, down from the embassy in Bern. They were both wearing suits. The taller man had a yellow tie with a matching pocket square.

"So who we go be?" asked the huskier man as they passed the Franck Namani boutique on the corner by the bridge over the Rhône. It had a fifteen-thousand-euro cashmere and mink sweater in the window. "Your bodyguards?"

"Business associates," Okoro said.

"You supposed to be police," said the taller man. "Police have business associates?"

The other two looked at him. "Look at you, you done become foreigner," the husky man said. "You forget that police is business?"

"This Switzerland," the tall man said, offended. "These people, do they know that?"

"I'll explain it to the man if I have to," Okoro said. "Nah me go do the talking, make I see if he wan help us." He was talking to fellow Nigerians now, mixing English with pidgin. Just like home.

He pointed across the street to Majid's building. "Over there. His office." A point brought home by Majid himself just then walking out the door. Okoro quickly turned around to face the river. "Nah him be dat."

The husky man looked at him, then looked at his watch. "Ten o'clock. Business hours. Where he dey go?"

They all watched as Majid walked east, in the direction of the Franck Namani boutique.

*

Stavro had called an hour before. He wanted to meet.

"I can catch the noon train to Zurich," Majid said.

"No," Stavro said. "Now. I'm in Geneva."

"Then come by. I'm in the office."

"Not your office. The Jardin des Alpes. By the café."

"Okay. I'll be there in an hour."

"Now! It's a five-minute walk. Don't fuck with me."

Majid held for a moment, trying to hit the right note. Not cocky. A touch of the respect that comes from fear. "I'll be there as soon as I can," he said.

Which had the advantage of being true.

*

It was warm for the season. The Bise had not returned, and the sun was bright. Tourists were taking photos of the monument at the entrance to the park. With multiple spires, it looked like the top ornament of a wedding cake, except where the plastic bride and groom should have been there was the tomb of an otherwise forgotten duke.

Majid paused there and looked beyond the monument to a shallow fountain and, beyond that, the faux-rustic café. At outdoor tables a waitress was serving sandwiches to an elderly couple wearing broad-brimmed hats. Near them a woman fully sheathed in black abaya and niqab was eating ice cream with her daughter, a little girl too young to be covered, who wore jeans and a pink T-shirt and spooned over-large helpings of ice cream toward her mouth, sending some spilling onto her shirt and pants. Her mother ate more delicately, lifting teaspoons of ice cream toward her face with her right hand while using the left to lift her veil just long enough to open a path to her mouth, and then letting it drop. A choreographed maneuver.

At a table beyond them, in the shade, sat Stavro. Majid took a quick look around, then moved in his direction.

*

The husky Yoruba had leapfrogged ahead of Majid while he walked; Okoro and the other had followed behind. Another tactical formation. When Majid entered the park, they regrouped by the mausoleum and watched him move toward the café.

"We go talk to him now?" said the husky man. "Maybe have a beer when we do it. I want shek Heineken."

"Maybe we carry am go into a corner," said the one in the yellow tie, gesturing to a small grove of trees at the edge of the park, by the Rue Adhémar-Fabri. "Make a talk with him there." He was a Muslim and didn't drink.

Okoro didn't answer. He was watching the man at the table Majid was approaching. The man was tall and of indeterminate ethnicity and he looked at Majid with a sullen glare. A client? Maybe. Perhaps a special client. A special client who preferred not to meet in Majid's office. Okoro watched as Majid reached the man's table and sat without shaking hands. Okoro spoke softly to his companions. "That man, too," he said. "Make we jist that man too."

*

Stavro spoke before Majid was fully in his seat. "What the fuck do you think you're doing?"

Majid sat. "What do you mean?"

Stavro had an empty whiskey glass in front of him. The waitress, seeing Majid arrive, moved toward them. Stavro brusquely waved her away, never taking his eyes off Majid.

"Where's the fucking money? I told you to send the fucking money."

"I did," said Majid. "I sent it. All of it."

*

Okoro briefed his companions. "You go to the left. You to the right. The man, Hassan, has met me. I will go to the table and ask to meet his friend."

"And if he no 'gree?" asked the husky man.

"Then you two will help me change his mind. If Hassan waka, let him. I know where to find him again. But the other man must not waka without talking to us."

The tall man nodded. He liked a clear task. "By hook or by crook?"

"Yes." Okoro started to walk toward the café.

After two steps, his path was blocked. A man squarely in his way. Not stepping aside. Not yielding.

"Detective Okoro," Frank said. "How nice to see you again. And who are your friends?"

*

"All of it? You sent all of it?" Stavro said. "Bullshit! You were supposed to send ninety-five percent to Khartoum. Khartoum got five percent. Five! The Malta account was supposed to get five percent. It got nothing. Were you fucking confused? Where is the fucking money?"

Majid said nothing. He signaled for the waitress Stavro had chased away. She came to the table and, while Stavro glared, he ordered a coffee. Stavro waited until she stepped back, then spoke in a fierce whisper. A whole other level of intensity.

"Do you care about your family? About your sister? Do you care about your own fucking life?"

Majid faltered. He took a breath. Was Stavro armed? Would he take out his phone and call people in Beirut? No, he would do nothing yet, not here, not now. Majid called on his anger to hold Stavro's gaze, to carry this through. "All the money was sent," he said. "Five percent to Khartoum, yes. But all the rest to you."

"To me?"

"Yes. Not to your account in Malta. I assume that *is* your account. It went to a bank in Geneva. The Holborn Bank. I took the liberty of opening an account there in your name. If you check, you'll find that nothing is missing. All the money was sent."

"What the fuck are you talking about? Who the fuck told you to do that?"

The waitress brought Majid his coffee. He stirred in sugar and took a sip and then looked at Stavro and told him. "Who told me to do it? You did."

*

The two men flanking Okoro froze. They looked at the man blocking their path. Waiting to see what this was.

"What brings you out to the park today?" Frank said. "The fine weather? It couldn't be our mutual interest in Mister Hassan, could it?" He nodded toward the table with Majid and Stavro.

"Actually," Okoro said, "I *was* thinking of going over there to say hello. And perhaps to meet his companion."

Frank smiled. A friend chatting with a friend on a sunny day in a pretty park. "You know what?" he said. "This really wouldn't be the best time for that."

The man was smaller than either of the men with Okoro. He was one and they were three. But that seemed not to concern him. At all.

"We could talk to him together," Okoro said. "I assume you're interested, too. Or are *you* just here to enjoy the weather?"

Frank looked at Okoro's companions for the first time. Then back to Okoro. "Your friends wouldn't be armed, would they?"

"Of course not," said Okoro. "Why would they be armed?"

"Good," said Frank. "Because mine are."

Okoro looked around the garden. At the elderly couple at the café table. The veiled Muslim woman with her daughter. The tourists still taking photos of the dead duke's mausoleum (was it really that photogenic?). By a parked tour bus on the Rue Adhémar-Fabri, he saw one of the "security guards" from the synagogue. Sitting in a taxi across the park, on the Rue des Alpes, his colleague. Behind Okoro on the quay, distant from everyone else, just looking on, he saw the incompetent American spy who had followed him to the synagogue.

Okoro smiled back at Frank. "In that case," he said. "We will just stand here and enjoy the sunshine."

*

It was beginning to dawn on Stavro that Majid's behavior was more than simple stupidity or stubborn resistance. He sat up in his chair, and he looked around.

"I told you to do that?" he said. "When did I tell you?"

"The last time we met. Don't you remember? That's what I told the bank in Khartoum when they called to inquire on behalf of their client."

Stavro took that in. A few tables away, the elderly woman in the broad-brimmed hat got up and started to walk toward the *toilette publique.*

"You told the bank in Khartoum?" Stavro said. "That I told you to send most of the money to me?" Processing now . . .

"I told them you'd been very specific. Five percent to them, ninety-five to you. They sounded surprised."

Stavro leaned forward. "You are making a big mistake." Majid said nothing. "I will talk to them and explain things. And then, I promise, you will be dealt with." He kept his voice low. The old woman was approaching, unsteady on her feet.

"I don't think you'll be able to talk to them," Majid said.

"I won't?"

"And they won't be able to talk to you."

Stavro stared. Majid was beginning to enjoy this. "Because you've disappeared," Majid said. "Presumably with your associates' money. It doesn't look good. I think they'll be upset."

"*I've* disappeared?" said Stavro. "You're dead." He stood up abruptly and reached into his pocket and pulled out his phone. Just then the woman in the broad-brimmed hat, passing their table, stumbled on an uneven paving stone. She reached out to steady herself and touched the back of Stavro's neck.

Two seconds later he was unconscious.

*

"Oh my," said Okoro. "It looks like Mister Hassan's friend is not well."

"Pity," said Frank. "Maybe it's something he ate."

*

The waitress saw Stavro fall back into his chair. Before she could do anything about it, Majid spoke up. "Mon ami est malade. J'appellerai une ambulance." He pulled out his phone and dialed.

An ambulance arrived remarkably fast. The Nigerians were still watching as attendants put Stavro on a gurney and into the ambulance and drove him away. By then Frank was gone. As were the elderly couple, and the tourists photographing the mausoleum, and the men from the synagogue. Okoro looked behind him to see if the incompetent spy was still there—he'd never gotten the man's name—but he was gone, too.

REGGAE

Majid was waiting at the bar when Rafe walked in. The nightclub was in the Paquis, not far from his apartment, but he had never been there. A reggae band was playing on a raised stage, and people, black and white, mostly young (with some surprising exceptions), were dancing. Majid looked animated, as if he was three drinks in, but the bottle in front of him said lemon Pellegrino.

"You come here often?" Rafe asked. Majid had picked the venue. It didn't seem like Majid's kind of place.

Majid was smiling. He wasn't used to feeling this way, riding this kind of wave, a wave that had peaked when he'd seen Stavro collapse back into his chair, unconscious. Defeated. *Some people think all Arabs are terrorists?* Well, some people are wrong, you fucking asswipe. You son of a dog. *Ya ibn al kalb.*

Majid noticed that Rafe was talking again. "I couldn't hear what you said in the park, but I gather you did a good job."

The band was singing. *The harder they come . . .*

"It didn't matter what I said. I just had to get him there."

"Yes. But even so." Rafe waved down the bartender and ordered a Woodford. The Double Oaked. "Maybe you have a knack for it."

"I took an improv class in Cambridge. Upstairs in Inman Square. People kept telling me I had to loosen up. I thought that would help."

"You did? Did it?"

"It taught me how to lie with conviction. Which turned out to be useful for recruiting clients." Majid had not stopped smiling. Rafe took another look at Majid's drink. The bottle did say Pellegrino. Had Majid poured something else into the glass?

"Where did they take him in the ambulance?" Majid asked.

Rafe shrugged. "Not for me to know. But safe to say it wasn't a hospital."

"Is he alive?"

"That was the point. Alive and talking."

"And if he doesn't? Talk."

"I suppose they drop him somewhere visible. Where his associates can find him."

Majid liked that. "Yes. The people who think he stole their money. They don't like that, do they?"

"No. And I don't think they register their displeasure by suing." Rafe's bourbon arrived and he took half of it in one swallow. He was feeling pretty good, too. "You got your robots on the camels," he said.

"Not soon enough." Majid's smile faded. "I never should have helped them in the first place."

"You didn't know it was *them*. It was just him."

Majid thought back to the beginning. If only he hadn't needed the money.

"He barely bothered to lie about the source of his funds. And I barely tried to check it out."

"Okay. But what did you think he was? Just a common money launderer, right?"

Majid shrugged.

"Like Pleski. Like us." Rafe lifted his glass. "To common money launderers. How we miss them." He drained his bourbon. Majid finished his fizzy lemon water and put down his glass. "If Stavro does talk, what happens to him?"

"I don't know. They give him a new name? Relocate him? Set him up with a shoe repair shop in Des Moines?"

"And who goes after his associates, the ones doing the killing? Not you."

"Of course not. I'm just a common money launderer." Rafe signaled for another drink.

"There's something else we need to talk about," Majid said.

*

Catherine stood inside the door to the club, reeling from the volume of the music. She saw Rafe with Majid at the bar, and she almost turned around and left. Instead, she squeezed farther in, past a man in a suit who was dancing with a woman in jeans and a belly shirt. She had decided to face other parts of her life. She might as well face this.

But what was this? Majid and Rafe were toasting and smiling, and Majid looked drunk.

Rafe saw her and looked surprised. Majid stood up to give her his stool. She hesitated, then sat.

"I didn't know we'd all be here," she said.

"Neither did I," said Rafe. He looked at Majid. "He invited you?"

Catherine nodded and looked warily from one man to the other. "Did something happen?" she asked. She read their expressions, "Something happened."

The men exchanged a look. "We were just in the Jardin des Alpes," Rafe said, as if that answered her question.

"Uh-huh. Doing what?"

"Business," said Majid.

"More Pleski business?"

"No," said Majid. "Other business."

Rafe said nothing.

"Okay." If they weren't going to tell her, she wasn't going to beg. New topic then. She turned to Rafe. "Was the information I sent you useful?"

"Yes."

"So what happens next?"

"Nothing that you'll be involved in. Nothing you want to be involved in."

Okay. She turned back to Majid. "That new account you sent me. What am I supposed to do with that?"

"Nothing. All you had to do was get it opened."

She looked from one to the other. "So I do nothing. And I know nothing."

"Exactly," Rafe said. Majid nodded.

"So why am I here?"

Rafe turned. "Yes, Majid. Why is Catherine here?"

Catherine and Rafe were on the stools. Majid stood above them, like a parent. "For clarity," he said. "I think it is time for clarity. We are not teenagers. We are not in a telenovela."

"Clarity?" Catherine sighed. *Oh shit.* "Can I please god have some vodka first?"

She could drink less tomorrow. She could drink less after this.

Rafe ordered her a vodka and soda.

Majid continued. "We can tell the truth. We can bear to hear the truth."

The bartender brought Catherine's drink. She took a large swallow.

"We all know the situation," Majid said. "I don't think it is tenable. I don't think it is fair to anyone."

The band was singing about somebody shooting a sheriff. Catherine was sorry she hadn't turned around and left the club. She didn't need this. She didn't want this.

"What do you suggest?" Rafe said.

"Catherine can tell us," Majid said.

"Tell us what?"

"You know what. She knows what."

They both looked at her. She looked at the dance floor. She took another swallow of her drink. "Wow," she said. "Reggae in Switzerland. Who knew?"

On the dance floor a couple was kissing passionately. A short man with a goatee and a woman with elaborate tattoos.

Majid was watching Catherine. "Maybe this was a bad idea," he said.

"You think?" said Catherine. "What am I supposed to do? Give one of you a rose?"

"He said no telenovela," Rafe pointed out.

Majid smiled weakly. "Or Rafe and I could have a duel."

Were they both comedians now? Catherine got up off her stool. "What the hell happened to you two today?"

Neither of the men answered.

"Maybe you should," she said. "Fight a duel. Let me know who wins."

They both said "Catherine . . ."

She left.

PLESKI

The Syrian always felt conspicuous on the Rue de Hesse—he hardly looked like a banker or a rich bank customer—so he never lingered. But today, after taking the bus into town, he did. He'd had an upsetting argument in the morning with his roommate who wanted to get rid of the cat. The roommate had lately become religious, attending mosque and wearing a *taqiyah*, a white skullcap, even when he wasn't praying. The cat, he said, had to go. But what about the Prophet? The Prophet's own cat Muezza? A false view, the roommate said. A corruption of the truth. The Syrian didn't know how long he could hold out against this.

Seeing the woman, even just lingering on her street, was a comfort to him. He knew he could never talk to her. He could not imagine ever touching her (although they had nearly brushed hands when he stole her purse). But she represented a better world, a peaceful, prosperous, beautiful world, and it was good to know there was such a world even if he could never be part of it.

And she had smiled at him.

A few days after that had happened, when he had seen her in the old town with the piggish man holding a heavy bag, he had spotted her again through the window of a restaurant on the Rue des Savoises. She was eating lunch with another man in a suit. He decided that all these men must have something to do with her business, nothing more. She was too good for it be something more. After her meal, he had followed her back to this street, where there were many attractive women dressed in fine clothes and many prosperous-looking men, piggish and otherwise. She walked into a bank building and did not come out. Her place of employment. Thereafter, when he was in the city, he would walk by the building, staying on the opposite sidewalk, and he saw her sometimes, generally around lunchtime, coming or going. He always took care to keep out of her sight. Even though, deep in his heart, he hoped that she would see him and, *inshallah*, even smile at him again.

Then, now, he saw the piggish man walk into her building.

*

Catherine was at her desk staring at a screen of LIBOR interest rate swaps. This was an area that had not interested her much in the past. But she had a client who had a large fixed-rate loan and was convinced that the LIBOR would be trending down. Holborn Bank's analysts felt otherwise, but the client had assured Catherine that he felt the downward movement in his gut. Most likely indigestion, she thought. But it was something for her to do, and the contents of the screen were something for her to know, as opposed to her business with Majid and Rafe, which they had made very clear required her to do nothing and to know nothing.

She noticed Armstrong leave his office and head to the elevator. Ever since she had counseled his daughter, he usually smiled or nodded to her as he passed, but today he did not. He took the elevator down.

Two minutes later her phone rang. It was Stanley Pleski. He was shouting. "I'm downstairs with your boss." She turned her headset volume down. "Where are you? I'm getting screwed down here! What the fuck is going on?"

"I don't know," she said.

And thought: Ah, thank you, guys.

*

The message had come from the bank, and Pleski thought he was there to meet Catherine. He assumed she was ready to talk about their new relationship. He was looking forward to working more closely with her. But when he gave his name to the receptionist, Catherine did not appear. Instead it was this geek Armstrong and two heavies in dark suits. Bank security. They ushered him into the fishbowl, where there were two suitcases sitting on the floor.

"Mister Pleski," Armstrong said, "I'll get right to it. We are closing your account."

*

Catherine almost didn't go downstairs, but then she wanted to see.

She didn't go into the fishbowl, just lingered outside and watched through the glass. Pleski was bright red and sweating. Armstrong was saying something when Pleski spotted her and interrupted him mid-sentence. He jabbed a fat finger toward Catherine.

*

"What did she tell you?" Pleski demanded. "Did this come from her?"

Armstrong looked genuinely puzzled. "From Ms. Cole? No. She had nothing to do with this. We only just now received some disturbing reports from American authorities."

"Who cares? So what? This isn't America!"

"No, it isn't. But this is our bank. And we have every right to choose our customers and close any account that doesn't meet our standards."

Pleski pointed again at Catherine. "She was very familiar with my account. She had no complaints."

"Of course not. She took you at face value, like any client. She didn't have access to the information that recently came to our attention. To *my* attention."

Pleski considered. Was this really not her doing? He thought about the people whose money he handled. They were into all kinds of shit. Even he had no idea what. Any of them could have attracted the attention of some cop or regulator, and a money trail could have led from any one of them to him.

Shit.

Armstrong was talking again. "As of this morning, your cash balance was just over four million dollars, as detailed on this statement." He was holding a sheet of paper. "We'll have to deal with the securities in the account later. But, for now, you'll find all the cash here."

Now? *What*? Here? *Where*?

The son of a bitch was pointing to the suitcases.

Pleski was incredulous. "You put four million dollars into two suitcases?"

"A courtesy," Armstrong said. "It turns out that forty thousand hundred-dollar bills weigh almost ninety pounds. Too much to carry in a single bag."

Pleski wanted to slug this prick in the face. "I don't want fucking cash. I'll give you another bank to wire it to."

"I'm sorry, sir, but that's a service we do for account holders only. And your account is closed."

"What am I supposed to do with ninety pounds of cash?"

Armstrong shrugged. Not his problem.

But it was Pleski's. He couldn't feed forty thousand bills into an ATM. Or walk into a bank looking like he'd just robbed a bank. Or cross a border without declaring it. Or declare it, and if anyone had ever snorted a single line of cocaine through one of those bills, there'd be narcotics dogs . . .

Armstrong nodded to the security guys, and each of them picked up one of the bags and they carried them out of the fishbowl and through the lobby to the front door of the bank.

"Jesus fuck," Pleski said. "Those suitcases don't even have wheels."

*

A chill had descended, and it had started to rain, and the Syrian was about to move on—lately he'd been working tourists in shops on the Rue de la

Confédération—when he saw two men carry suitcases out of the bank and put them on the sidewalk. They went back inside and the door opened again and the piggish man came out. He looked red and angry. He put his hands on the bags' handles and lifted them with an effort that made him turn redder. He put them down again and looked up and down the street. He raised his hand as a taxi approached but the taxi had a passenger and did not stop. Another taxi approached but it was hailed half a block away by another passenger who wanted out of the rain. The piggish man put his hands back on the bags, as if to make sure they were still there, as if he was guarding them. He pulled out a handkerchief and mopped water off his forehead and then lifted the bags again. Struggling with their weight, he moved slowly down the block toward the intersection with the Boulevard Georges-Favon, where there would be more taxis and also buses and a tram. Halfway there, he stopped to rest, and the woman appeared in the doorway of the bank. She didn't seem to mind the rain. She looked in the direction of the piggish man, who was mopping his forehead again, and she smiled. As she turned to go back inside, she glanced across the street and she saw the Syrian. She looked at him, and he looked at her. She didn't smile at him, but she pointed. She pointed to the piggish man and to the heavy bags he was carrying.

The woman went back inside. The Syrian crossed the street and fell in behind the piggish man, his eyes on the suitcases. The man was moving slowly, and the Syrian moved slowly behind him. Just then, on the opposite sidewalk, he saw his cat-hating roommate in the white *taqiyah* lingering near the door of another bank. What was he doing here? Had he followed him here to continue their argument? Now, of all times? Apparently not. He must have seen me, the Syrian thought. I'm right here. But, if his roommate did see him, he paid him no mind.

So the Syrian ignored him and moved a little closer to the piggish man and the bags he was protecting. The bags that had come from inside a bank. The bags the beautiful woman had pointed to.

The Syrian thinking, *inshallah*, this might turn out to be a very good day.

DEBRIEF

That morning Rafe had called Frank three times and every call had gone to voicemail. He didn't think it was unreasonable for him to be told what was happening with Stavro. Unless Stavro was being tortured, of course. He didn't need to know that. But hadn't he helped bring him down? Wasn't he a part of the team?

He had gone to his little office in the embassy, because the phones there were secure so it was possible that Frank would call him there. Sykes's office was down the hall, but he didn't even bother. He was sure she wouldn't give him the time of day. Literally.

In his office there was nothing to do except look at reports of possible money launderers afoot in Europe. Which seemed pretty pedestrian to him now. He picked up some papers and put them down again. He realized he would have to file a report on the outcome of the Pleski situation. Armstrong at the bank had told him it would be resolved soon, possibly today. Rafe's report to DC would have to be very carefully worded.

The phone on Rafe's desk rang. It was Frank. He sounded surprised, and a little disappointed, that Rafe picked up. As if he had done the decent thing by calling, and if Rafe hadn't answered, well, he'd tried. But Rafe had answered, so Frank gave it to him. In brief, anyway. Stavro was in good health except for a bad headache. He had caved fast. If there was one thing the guy knew, it was how to size up his options in any given situation, especially one in which Guantanamo was mentioned. The information he was prepared to provide would be useful. Action would be taken. Rafe did not need to know. Stavro was about to be dispatched to another location for more extensive debriefing. But first they had to deal with the money they'd sent in his name to the Holborn Bank. It was going to become the property of the United States government, but, for that to happen, Stavro had to sign it over. Swiss banking rules had to be followed. They could kidnap a man and threaten to send him to Guantanamo but they couldn't make a withdrawal from his bank account unless he signed the proper papers. So would Rafe please call his girlfriend at the bank and tell her to get them ready?

*

After he hung up on Rafe, Frank had made another call. A man answered and Frank said, "I've got someone I want you to eyeball." The man said something. Frank said, "That means have a look at him. Tell me if you've seen him before. Tell me anything you know about him. You know, the kind of stuff we've been paying you for."

RUE DE HESSE

The rain had stopped on the Rue de Hesse, but there were puddles by the curbs and the roadway was slick. Business hours were just over and bankers were heading home in the autumn dark as cleaners arrived for work. The stolid stone walls of the financial institutions looked on, indifferent. Their money was snug inside.

Rafe stood next to Catherine in the doorway of the Holborn Bank. Barely an hour had passed since she'd stood there watching Pleski stagger away, watching the thief trail after him.

"Busy day," she said. "First Pleski. Now this. Whatever this is."

"Did Pleski threaten you? Anything?"

Catherine shook her head. "Not a word. My ignorance was apparent and perfect."

So that had worked.

A Mercedes sedan turned in from the Boulevard Georges-Favon. It pulled up to the curb and stopped, its motor still running, its headlights on. Catherine asked, "Is that my client?"

"I think so," Rafe said. "Are the papers ready?"

"They just need his signature. And his money flies out. To an account in Maryland. Something called Consulting Services, Inc. He's hiring a consultant for six million dollars?"

"Not exactly," Rafe said.

The back door of the Mercedes opened, and Frank stepped out. He looked around, then nodded to another man in the back seat. Rafe had seen him before. He was the tourist from the synagogue. And later one of the backup people at the Jardin des Alpes. The third man in the back seat was Stavro, sitting in the middle. His hair was tousled and he looked tired and he had lost his suit jacket somewhere along the way. It had been thirty hours since he had been plunged into unconsciousness.

Frank walked to the doorway where Rafe was standing with Catherine. He said to Catherine, "Are the papers ready?"

Rafe answered. "Yes."

"They're in there," Catherine said. She pulled the door open and pointed through the reception area to the fishbowl.

"Lovely," Frank said. "You two been having a nice day?"

No one answered. Frank walked back to the car. Catherine turned to Rafe. "Who's he?"

"Frank."

"Well, that explains everything." She looked at him coolly. "I'm getting more ignorant by the minute, aren't I?"

Frank stopped by the door to the car and looked across the street again and waited as if he was expecting something to happen there. What happened was that a man in a white skullcap stepped out from a shadow and stood clear under a streetlight. He nodded at Frank, and Frank nodded at him.

Then Frank leaned into the car and pulled Stavro out.

"What's that about?" asked Catherine.

"I don't know," said Rafe, pointing to Stavro, "but that's your client." Rafe hadn't absolutely needed to be here for this, but he'd wanted to. And Frank and Sykes had thought his presence might be useful in case Catherine needed some hand-holding. Not that she was in any mood to hold Rafe's hand.

Stavro stood sullenly by the car's open back door until Frank took hold of his shoulder and turned him around so he was facing the man across the street in the white skullcap. Frank held Stavro in that position long enough for the man to get a good look at him. An exhibit. A show pony.

The man in the skullcap shook his head and stepped back into his shadow.

Frank shrugged, oh well, and turned Stavro around again, a pirouette, and the tourist got out of the back seat and joined them. He and Frank took Stavro by an arm apiece and started walking him toward the door of the bank. He moved grudgingly, but he moved.

Catherine was the first to see it happening. The man in the skullcap had reappeared and was coming across the street, fast. A taxi sped by and the man dodged around it.

"Who is he?" she said.

"No fucking idea," said Rafe.

Frank was close enough to hear them and turned to see what they were talking about. He saw the man coming toward them and held up a hand.

"Not now, Mohammed," he said. "We'll talk later."

The man kept coming. He was at the curb now.

This wasn't right. Rafe could see that, and so did the tourist. The man was on the sidewalk now, heading straight at Stavro. The tourist stepped between them and the man in the skullcap pulled out a knife and stabbed him in the throat.

Rafe and Catherine jumped back toward the door of the bank, but the door was shut and opened outward so they couldn't pull it open without moving toward the knife in the assailant's hand. His face was expressionless.

The tourist fell down, clutching his neck, his head pitching forward into a puddle by the curb.

Frank still had one hand on Stavro. With his other hand, he reached to his waistband and pulled out a pistol. But the man in the skullcap was right there. His knife was long and nasty, and he lunged with it at Stavro, who stepped back sharply, away from the knife, and bumped hard into Frank. Frank's gun hand had been swiveling to point at the man in the skullcap but Stavro's body knocked it sideways, so it ended up pointing at the parked Mercedes, and Frank fired a bullet into its right front fender. The driver, the banker from the synagogue, was out of the car, a gun in his hand, pointed at the man with the knife, but that meant pointing it at Stavro, too, and at Frank, and at Catherine and Rafe, so he did not fire but ran toward them, and Rafe and Catherine leaned back hard against the bank's closed door.

The banker had to run around the front of the Mercedes to get to them, which gave the man in the skullcap time to lunge again at Stavro, who jerked to his left as the knife came, which exposed Frank to the blade, which sank into his left side between two of his ribs. Frank fell to the sidewalk and the man in the skullcap pivoted with surprising speed and held out his knife as the banker ran straight into it. He fired his gun as he was falling and the bullet flew between Catherine and Rafe, inches from her head and his shoulder.

This had all taken eight seconds.

Catherine screamed and threw herself back against the door of the bank, and Rafe had figured out by now that there was no escape there, so he dove to the pavement. How he figured that out and why he dove where he dove he did not know. He wasn't thinking, he was just acting. Later he wondered if he actually did know, somewhere in his animal brain, that by diving just where he dove, he would land next to Frank's outstretched arm. Where Frank's gun was still in his hand. Rafe looked up and saw Stavro jammed back against the door now with Catherine. And the man in the skullcap upon them, his knife hand moving. Rafe lifted the gun out of Frank's hand and pointed it at the man in the skullcap and pulled the trigger. The bullet went dead center into the man's back, and he pitched forward, falling onto Catherine, who screamed again and tried to wriggle away. Rafe climbed to his feet as she freed herself and the man fell flat on the ground and Rafe pointed the gun and shot him two more times and ran to Catherine, uncertain if he had shot her, too. "Are you okay?" he said. She was hunched down, leaning against the door, and she looked at him without speaking. He asked again, "Are you okay?" She nodded, still silent, and Rafe looked down at the man in the skullcap, who was lying still, his face planted on the steps to the door of the bank. Rafe leaned over and pulled the knife from his hand and tossed it into the street. He kept the gun pointed at the man, who still didn't move. Then he looked around for Stavro.

And saw him running away fast, turning a corner, disappearing from sight.

DEAD-EYE

They met the next morning in Frank's hospital room. The banker was elsewhere in the same building. The tourist was dead.

Sykes was standing next to the bed when Rafe walked in. Frank had a tube up his nose and an IV needle inserted between two knuckles. He turned with a slight grimace and said, "Dead-Eye Dick. Where did you learn to shoot?"

"I didn't," Rafe said. "Just pointed and pulled the trigger. Who was that guy?" That guy being the man in the white skullcap whom Rafe had shot three times.

Frank and Sykes exchanged a look. Then Sykes answered. "A terrorist. Working for the same people Stavro was working for. They were either angry that he had stolen their money or they figured out he was talking to us and wanted to make that stop."

"Uh-huh." Rafe came all the way into the room. He was looking at Frank. "You called him Mohammed. You knew him."

Frank shrugged, which made him grimace again. "I get around."

"The hokey-pokey guy," Rafe said. "He was your source at the mosque."

"Playing a double game," Sykes said. "That's how it goes sometimes."

"We invited him—*you* invited him—to be at the bank?"

"We wanted to see if he recognized Stavro, if he knew anything about him," Frank said.

"So your plan was not to give him a chance to kill Stavro?"

"Correct. Getting myself stabbed wasn't part of the plan either. Error of judgment. That's how it goes sometimes."

"That's how it goes? *People died!* You almost died. He could have killed Catherine."

"But he didn't. Thanks to you. Her knight in shining armor. You have a nice night with her afterward? Was she grateful?"

Rafe didn't know. She had gone home, alone. He saw no need to mention that.

"By the way," Sykes said, "we do like to talk to these people. You didn't have to kill him three times."

"Sorry," said Rafe. "I was kind of caught up in the moment."

Which, he realized, was exactly true.

"What happened to Stavro?"

"We're looking for him," said Frank. "So are the Swiss. Apparently, he broke some banking regulations."

The door opened and a young doctor came in. She had a medical chart open on a tablet and said, "I need a minute alone with my patient."

Rafe and Sykes headed to the door. "Dead-Eye," Frank called after them. Rafe turned. "Did I forget to say thank you?"

In the corridor, a young patient was moving slowly with a walker. Two nurses hurried past Rafe and Sykes.

"We could get you trained," she said, "so if this ever happens again you would actually know what you were doing."

"What else is there to know? I mean, besides point and pull the trigger?"

Sykes thought for a moment. "Actually, I guess that is the gist of it."

"Also," Rafe said, "it helps not to get stabbed first."

"We'll add that to the training manual. Anyway, odds are you won't be doing this kind of thing again."

Rafe nodded.

"You'll be going back to the boring stuff. Money laundering."

Rafe nodded.

"How are you coming with that Pleski situation?"

Now Rafe thought for a moment. "It turns out," he said, "that's off the table. The bank closed Pleski's account. He's out of business."

"He is?"

Rafe nodded.

"Nothing to be done there?"

"Nope."

"Just like that? In the middle of your case? The bank shut him down?" Sykes looked at him appraisingly. "How come?"

"Beats me," Rafe shrugged. "I guess the bank got suspicious. He was kind of blatant."

Sykes was still looking at him.

"That's how it goes sometimes," he said.

AU REVOIR

Majid, Rafe, and Catherine met at the hotel bar where the Harvard Business School held its receptions. It was late afternoon and rain clouds were massing again in the mountains to the north and people were drinking, except for Majid, of course. Catherine wasn't drinking either. Rafe nursed a bourbon, warily. Catherine had invited both men to join her. Safety in numbers?

"I'm leaving Switzerland," she said. "Tomorrow."

Rafe looked at Majid. Apparently this was news to him, too.

"I'm going back to New York. Remember Nancy Cardoza from Cambridge? She's at Morgan Stanley. She has a job for me."

"Morgan Stanley?" said Majid.

"Solid," said Rafe.

"Yeah," Catherine said. "Plus she pretty much promised it wouldn't involve suitcases full of cash or gunfire or lunatics with knives."

Both men nodded.

"And," Catherine said, "I can be near my father." As far as she could tell, he still had his girlfriend, Karen. Maybe she could become friends with Karen. They could have family dinners. Well, pseudo family dinners.

"Tomorrow?" said Majid.

Catherine nodded. "I need a break. A clean break. This has all been a little . . . too much."

Nobody could argue with that.

"I may be in New York, too," Majid said. "I'm closing the fund. It seems like time to wrap it up." The dead partner on the office floor, the trades for terrorists . . . new clients weren't flocking in.

"Also New York?" Rafe said. "There's a coincidence."

"That's where the business is. I have connections there from Cambridge, too."

Catherine turned to Rafe. "Are you staying here? With your nonexistent hedge fund? Or whatever it is you're actually doing?"

He started to say something. She held up a hand. "Don't. Just don't."

She stood up. "So, I wanted to tell you both."

She picked up her bag and walked toward the door.

Majid got up and walked after her.

*

Rafe considered getting up and following, too, then decided against it. Two men chasing her—that had been part of the problem. Not to mention that he'd nearly gotten her stabbed and shot. He would give her some space. He would call her later. If he got to New York.

He lifted his glass and discovered it was empty. He signaled the waiter for another drink. And looked up when he heard the waiter bringing it, but it wasn't the waiter. It was Okoro, looking pleased with himself. He sat in the chair Majid had just left and said, "That is a very fine-looking woman."

"She's not available," Rafe said. "Quite a coincidence running into you again."

"Not a coincidence," Okoro said. "You're never hard to find. I told you. Bad tradecraft."

"You here to give me a lesson?"

"No," said Okoro. "There's something I want to show you."

SIMPLE

To get to the Nigerian mission, you turned left just before the sculpture of the gigantic chair with its leg blown off. Another left and then into a cul-de-sac, where the Nigerian complex, a glass and concrete high-rise, loomed over Turkey's and Benin's. Okoro, driving, showed a credential to a guard and was waved into the building's courtyard. The guards did not ask who Rafe was, nor seemed to care.

"We have more security than this," Rafe said.

"We have more that you don't see," said Okoro.

"But you have status here. You sail right in."

"Of course. I am an officer with the Nigeria Police Force, here on official business."

Rafe thought briefly before he spoke again, then decided why the hell not?

"And by official business you mean trying to get a share of terrorist profits for your boss back home?"

Okoro drove around the side of the building. He parked where they had a view of a loading dock and turned off the ignition. "You heard that from Mister Hassan," he said.

"And he heard it from you. You didn't keep your mission here a secret from him."

"Unless I did," Okoro said. "Which would he be more likely to believe? That I was an honest policeman or a dishonest one? Whose questions would he be more likely to answer? Remember, he had something to conceal from an honest one."

"But you knew what had happened. You knew about the money. About the investment. How did you know?"

"I was sent here by a dishonest policeman who thought I was one of his. Now he'll have some surprises in store. In fact"—Okoro looked at his watch—"one just about now, as he is getting arrested."

Rafe was processing that—it was a lot to process—as a gray panel van backed up to the loading dock. The driver got out and rolled up the van's back door.

"Did you ever hear of the Dikko affair?" Okoro asked.

"No."

"It was famous in its day. Nineteen-eighty-four. There was a Nigerian exile in London whom the Nigerian government wanted back. But he wouldn't go, and the British government wouldn't hand him over."

The door of the loading dock was rolled up by someone inside whom Rafe couldn't see.

"So he was snatched," Okoro said, "and put in a diplomatic pouch to be shipped to Lagos."

"Put in a pouch?" Rafe said. "Was he a dwarf?"

"A diplomatic pouch can be any size. It just has to be properly labeled."

A forklift rolled up to the loading dock door from inside the mission. Suspended on its forks was a large wooden crate, a meter wide and a meter deep and two meters long. It looked to be very sturdily made. Stenciled on its side were the words "DIPLOMATIC BAG - Federal Republic of Nigeria." The forklift driver lowered it slowly into the back of the panel van. The movement was surprisingly gentle.

Rafe watched all that happen. "Any size?" he said.

Okoro nodded.

And Rafe knew. "Jesus! He's in there."

"Jesus is?" Okoro smiled.

"Stavro is." He turned to Okoro. "How? Were you at the bank?"

Okoro shrugged. "I've told you, you're easy to follow. I thought you might be going somewhere interesting."

"I didn't see you."

"You never see me. Anyway, you were too busy shooting people."

The driver of the van climbed into its cargo hold and strapped the crate down.

"When he ran, you got him?"

Okoro shrugged modestly.

"Why do you want him so bad? The money is gone."

"I never wanted the money. I wanted him."

"Evil," Rafe said, remembering. "God put you on earth to bring evil to justice. That's what you told me. That struck me as so . . . simple."

"Is that a bad thing?"

Rafe thought: is that a bad thing? Firing Frank's gun had been simple, it had happened without thought, and that had not been a bad thing either.

"The man is an accomplice to murder in Nigeria," Okoro said. "He can lead us to cthers involved. If Nigerians were involved, we want to know. I don't think that would be a priority for the Americans."

The driver of the van climbed out of the cargo bay and circled back to the cab.

"What if I tell my people? Or the Swiss?"

"A diplomatic pouch cannot be touched. It would cause an international incident."

The driver got into his seat and started the engine.

Okoro turned to Rafe. "You're not going to pull out a gun and start shooting, are you?"

"No," Rafe said. "I think my shooting days are over."

"Really? You were good. The professionals went down, and you got the job done. I was impressed."

The van started to move. It passed them as it drove to the exit of the parking lot.

"Maybe you should reconsider," Okoro said.

The van turned right and disappeared into traffic, and Rafe, thinking about yesterday and about his brother and Afghanistan and about what he wanted to do with the rest of his life, said, "I don't know. Maybe I will."

ACKNOWLEDGMENTS

I am indebted to Amanda (Binky) Urban, who sold this book, and to Lilly Golden, who bought it and gently suggested that I cut out the bad parts.

My wife, Liza Levine, suspected (I think) that I spent the entire pandemic typing "All work and no play makes Ed a dull boy" and was relieved that I wasn't.

Phil Benedict and Judy Segal and several of their friends introduced me to Geneva. (That's Phil and Judy with the groceries in the elevator.) Tenley Le Sann took me to the restaurant that serves shrimp in white chocolate curry sauce.

Several members of the financial world in New York and Geneva explained to me how things work and are not responsible for the liberties I took with the facts.

Steve Smith checked me on diving and Kip Curren on sailing.

Ahmadu Garba provided help on Nigerian Pidgin and other things Nigerian.

Finally, special thanks to Olly Owen of the University of Oxford, who provided introductions to Emma Nnadozie, crime editor of the Vanguard newspaper, as well as Emmanuel Ojukwu and several other members, past and present, of the Nigeria Police Force, who generously met with me in Lagos. It was one of the latter who told me, as we sat in a police officers' mess, "I am Catholic, and Episcopal, and Jewish. I was created by God and deposited in Nigeria for a purpose."